Trouble with Girls

TROUBLE

WITH GIRLS

Marshall Boswell

Marshall Boswell

4/5/03

To Nancy —
with warmth, gratitude,
and all the best wishes.

A SHANNON RAVENEL BOOK

Algonquin Books
of Chapel Hill
2003

ℝ
A SHANNON RAVENEL BOOK

Published by
Algonquin Books of Chapel Hill
Post Office Box 2225
Chapel Hill, North Carolina 27515-2225

a division of
Workman Publishing
708 Broadway
New York, New York 10003

Grateful acknowledgment is made to magazines and other publications where several of the stories were originally published, some in a slightly different form: "Stir Crazy" (as "Bottoms Up") and "Venus/Mars" (as "Hidden Agendas") appeared in *Playboy*, "Bloody Knuckles" in *Yalabousha Review*, "Between Things" (as "In Between Things") in *The Missouri Review* and *New Stories from the South: The Year's Best, 2000*, and "Born Again" (as "How to Prosper during the Coming Bad Years") in *The Sun*.

This is a work of fiction. While, as in all fiction, the literary perceptions and insights are based on experience, all names, characters, places, and incidents are either products of the author's imagination or are used fictitiously. No reference to any real person is intended or should be inferred.

Library of Congress Cataloging-in-Publication Data
Boswell, Marshall, 1965–
      Trouble with girls / by Marshall Boswell.—1st ed.
         p. cm.
      "A Shannon Ravenel book."
      ISBN 1-56512-344-1
      1. Young men—Fiction. 2. Southern States—Fiction. I. Title.
PS3602.O85 T7 2003
813'.54—dc21   2002038611

10 9 8 7 6 5 4 3 2 1
First Edition

For Rebecca

We dream much of paradise, or rather of successive paradises,
but each of them is, long before we die, a paradise lost,
in which we should feel ourself lost too.

—Marcel Proust

Contents

Trouble with Girls

1. READY POSITION

You are twelve—thirteen, whatever—essentially nondescript: a confusion of hormones and dread. You are in right field.

Right field: that exile of the inept, that purgatory of the poltroon. How embarrassing, how ignominious it is to be a right fielder. And second to last in the batting order, too, right behind Marty Feezer, who whiles away the tense gradual bench-shift to the batter's box reading dog-eared *Spy vs. Spy* paperbacks, about which activity no one, not even the coach, seems to have a problem. Oh are you embarrassed, oh are you racked with shame. You're not supposed to be here, alone in right field. You're a big kid, second tallest boy in your class, funny and clownish and popular, you suppose, within the narrow confines of your own set. King of the Dweebs. You're also blond, suburban, blue-eyed, and—even you realize it—overwhelmingly privileged. You have no reason to complain. Yet you would trade it all, this entire treasure chest of blessings, for a weathered pouch of athletic grace. Engage in a test of wills and you collapse into self-consciousness. To this day you cannot play tennis without fearing vaguely that the fluid in your ears will tip like water in a bucket and send you and your racket sprawling across the court. You are also ruinously myopic, with thick wire-frame glasses and, now that you are twelve and a responsible young man, new soft contact lenses. All of which explains why you have no hand-eye coordination. If the exercise involves only your body and empty space, you can be as graceful as Roger Banister slicing the tape at Oxford. Introduce into that space an orb of any sort and you enter a ponderous gravitational drift, your limbs careening every which way.

Your baseball coach that season had two steadfast rules: stand in a "ready position" at all times and never go swimming on game days. Firmly convinced that prolonged exposure to chlorine impaired vision, he didn't want his players fielding fly balls wrapped in auras and radiating fuzzy halos. Whereas you broke the latter rule constantly and without guilt—you wore goggles, anyway, which somehow corrected your underwater vision—you followed the first rule with blind obedience. You loathed the stigma attached to the outfield. You hoped that by ostentatiously following the coach's advice you might score a spot at first base or shortstop. But no matter how ready you looked (at all times), you would

*ex
except when
you caught
it*

remain in this inane position—bent over, legs shoulder width apart, hands on your knees—for seven solid Little League innings and never once touch a baseball. The ready position wasn't exactly kneeling, not quite, but it was close. The point is, you thought about God constantly that summer—God and sex, to be more precise, though not always simultaneously—and as such you felt His presence most keenly during baseball games, with your left hand sweating inside your mitt and your rear end facing the woods, which stretched out beyond the home-run fence.

In the chiaroscuro of your memory, you are simultaneously you and not you out there in the grass: *you* because you remember the moment in a vague, sensory sort of way, which is to say the person who took in the evening air that night feels like you; *not you* because the cells change every seven years. Since then, you've grown a whole new skin.

a little basic

SO THERE YOU ARE, in right field, in the ready position. It is nighttime in the suburbs, solemnly and politely quiet. You are alone and bored under the outfield lights, fighting the gnats. A boy is at bat, but he is very far away. You can barely detect the infield chatter—*Hey batterbatter-batter suuwiiingg!*—while the progress of the game comes to you like the plot of a movie you've been watching all night with the sound down. *later...* You don't even know the count. Behind you in the woods, some younger kids on motocross (MX) bicycles have constructed a ramp out of a fallen log and a discarded piece of the home-run fence. The board bears the friendly orange Burger King logo, but the kids— a ratty bunch of smart-alecky suburbanites in football jerseys and iridescent running shorts and knee socks—ride right over it, a resistant marketing demographic even then. *LOL* You can hear them better than you can hear the game in which you are allegedly involved.

Beside you in centerfield, Marty Feezer has taken off his mitt and placed it open-palmed on his face. He stretches his arms out wide as if the mitt has fallen to him from some great height: an ungainly bird swan-diving to its death, right on Marty Feezer's face. You outfielders are a secret society. You share in each other's fear and humiliation as you stand alone in the high outfield grass, sit at the end of the dugout bench, catch fly balls all day in practice. Marty Feezer's glove falls off his face. With a nimble kick of his foot he catches it before it drops into the murky grass. Behind you a kid wipes out on his MX bike.

There is nothing to do in the outfield is what you're getting at. It is July. The year is 1978. Marty Feezer is a hopeless dweeb who doesn't care much about baseball or *anything* as far as you can tell. Although at the time you say to yourself that you admire Marty's blithe insouciance, you now realize you could not possibly have thought any such thing, since you've only known the meaning of the word *insouciance* for three or four years, if that.

The kids behind you are rearranging their ramp. You can

smell damp grass and the sweet sugary tang of Bazooka bubble gum. You feel against your skin the thick weight of summer air. You are all by yourself in right field.

So what you do is that stupid-kid thing where you say to yourself, *What if I'm not me?* It's one of those experiments you try on yourself, like when you walk several miles home and just when you see your house emerge in the distance you say, *What if I were back at the beginning of the whole journey?* just to see if maybe, just maybe, it will work, and you're even kind of afraid it *will* work, that you'll be right back where you started from, with the whole walk ahead of you again, and it's kind of exciting, this tempting Time or Fate or Existence or God or whatever, but nothing ever happens. You're still there on your street with your house well within sight. It is a leap of faith to believe the journey will start all over again; after a while, you just get tired of experimenting with yourself and start actually talking to girls.

So anyway, you're bored out of your skull there in right field and just to do something you sort of test your existence by asking yourself, *What if you're really not you?* and for a suspended second there it really works. In a delicate, uncanny sort of way, you don't feel like you. You have, no shit, this *out-of-body experience*—an extremely tiny one, the merest edge of a second, tops—where you feel like you're simply some kid you only know *pretty well*. Even the flesh against the chafing Little League uniform doesn't quite seem like yours. Under the vast openness overhead—the Not

and yet, here you are writing about it years later, I'm guessing...

You—you feel like you are not you. Somehow in your mind this moment becomes proof of God's existence, or proof of life after death, or maybe just the fleeting possibility of transcendence (which is not to say you needed proof then: it's only now you see this incident as a fragile, if also fraudulent, instance of "proof," whereas then it was just part and parcel of something you never doubted), and at this exhilarating moment you pop a boner. It's one of those sexless in-class erections, nothing more, really, than dumb hormonal energy in search of an outlet. The body, that elusive entropic system, sometimes mixes its signals. St. Augustine cites the unwilled boner as proof of Original Sin, and he may have a point. On the other hand, since it (the erection) arose out of an abrupt affirmation of immortality and the divine, perhaps it was also evidence of life everlasting, since sex is the body's way of affirming its right and need to continue living. (Or maybe it was just a boner.)

And all at once you hear the solid ping! of a baseball hitting an aluminum bat. The bleachers swell with communal awe as you look up to see arching your way against the flat-blue evening sky that Little League rarity: a perfect pop fly. Although you are, for all intents and purposes, utterly alone here in right field, you fear your erection will be detected. As a Believer, you mix sex with shame in a benign Protestant sort of way. You are afraid to stand up and move toward the ball, which has already begun its downward descent. So you stay just where you are, immobile and terrified, in the ready position. Hunched over with a rigid prick, you feel God's presence as well as His judgment as you reach up into the immense air and open your glove. You enter a pocket of timelessness amid the rise and fall of human events. You close your eyes, though not necessarily out of religious faith. As your coach keeps telling you, your hand-eye problem stems from the fact that *you don't keep your eye on the ball*. As a transparent paisley swims across the inside of your closed eyelid, you hear and feel the ball smack perfectly into the pocket of your mitt. Inside your baseball pants your penis softly melts.

When you open your eyes again you look in astonishment at the nest of your mitt. A scuffed white object lies nestled there. More round than oblong, like a tiny globe, and for the most part smooth except for a winding seam that has no beginning and no end—an infinity symbol unwound—the thing seems to radiate in your glove. It throbs there, quiet and indifferent, emitting warmth and mystery and something else, and then quickly cools and clarifies into an obdurate fact. It becomes, miraculously, the third out.

THE CATCH ENDED THE INNING. The infielders trotted nonchalantly to the dugout, Marty Feezer scooped up his outfield mitt, the crowd broke for snow cones. And now, as you crouch here on the outskirts of this experience, in the ready position, you discover something even more important, even more miraculous. You discover you knew the count all along: sixth inning, two outs, man on second, three balls and a strike. The batter swung with three balls, one strike, and even a right fielder knows you don't swing with three balls and a strike. It's so *obvious*. What's less obvious—and here's the real mystery—is what you do after the bat goes crack. Run to the ball or let the ball come to you? There's a riddle for you, and now here's the solution: it doesn't matter, son, so long as you're *ready*.

2. BLOODY KNUCKLES

We were all connoisseurs of pain in those days. The boys, at any rate. Right now I am unable recall a single game we played that did not somehow involve violence. Modes varied, of course, and my older brother, Scott, mastered them all.

There was, for instance, the frog, a swift, sinister punch aimed at the thigh or biceps. In other parts of the country this punch was known as the Charley Horse or the Knuckle Buster, while one kid from my fifth-grade class—he was from California—called it, rather exotically I thought, a Monster Mash. But we just called it a frog, in lowercase letters. Not a proper noun at all.

To execute a Texas Titty Twister all you had to do was pinch your victim's nipples between your thumb and forefinger and twist outward, right hand clockwise, left hand counterclockwise. Other favorites along this line included the Noogy, the Fart Blossom, and the Monkey's Uncle. The Chinese Corker was essentially a variation on the frog, the crucial difference being a cocked middle finger. A thwack on an erection constituted a Pecker Wood, a vile form of torture popular at Boy Scout outings and, in my case, Grandma's house, where Scott and I shared a sofa bed. Take a kid's forearm in your two hands and twist the skin—again, right hand clockwise, left hand counterclockwise—and you've got an Indian Rope Burn.

As I said, Scott mastered them all, a virtuoso of violence without peer. He was, after his own fashion, an artist of sorts, and pain was his medium. He was a Beethoven of bruises, a da Vinci of discomfort. For him, agony was both an essence and a palpable reality. One of his favorite forms of torture was positively Platonic: after getting his saliva good and viscous with a glass of milk or a bowl of ice cream or (just imagine it) a hefty plug of Red Man chewing tobacco, he would pin you to the floor and let descend, ever so slowly, this adhesive rope of spit which, if you were lucky and you did not move, he would slurp back up just before it broke and dropped along your chin. No pain was involved, you understand: just bald torture reduced to its quivering essence.

But it was Scott's resourcefulness that finally set him apart from the others in my neighborhood. A simple thump of the finger, for instance, achieved a kind of Zen-like majesty in Scott's capable hands. With well-deserved pride, he would lick his middle finger, cock it back like an archer lining up an arrow, and then, with an adroit and muscular flick of his wrist, thump your cheek, head, or hand. It hurt so bad your ears rang. All the kids in my neighborhood tried to master it, and soon a game called Thumps emerged, a simple act of endurance similar to Bloody Knuckles, a game in which you and your opponent would take turns scraping a comb across the back of each other's hands. In both games the object is not to flinch; the first one who does loses. To my horror, Thumps almost eclipsed Smear the Queer in neighborhood popularity.

Perhaps I am exaggerating Scott's part in all of this. Maybe he didn't really invent Thumps. It just seemed at the time like he did. At that stage of my life, it seemed like he was responsible for just about everything.

HENCE, THE CRUELEST THING he ever did to me—the single most audacious and revolting atrocity I ever suffered at his hands—fills me now, in hindsight, with a kind of misty-eyed admiration. Perhaps it is just a function of memory, the way all our acts, no matter how embarrassing, acquire a halo of goodness in recollection. I suppose that is what we mean when we speak of the good old days: the past is that part of ourselves that has entered the Eternal, where nothing ever changes, where everything is remote and innocent. And anyway, recollected pain is hardly pain at all, being, as it is, painless. Rather, it is something else, though what that something is eludes me right now.

The year was 1976, that bloated Bicentennial summer of my childhood, and my family and I were trekking cross-country, westward ho. The fall before my father had left home for a while and when he returned that spring, he and my mom were tentative around each other, like two wary cats forced to share a home, so I suppose that trip was their way of getting reacquainted again. I can recall with photographic precision not only the tension that radiated from the front seat but also all the hotels we inhabited, including their swimming pools. (I was crazy about pool slides that summer—pool slides, roller coasters, and dolphins, in that order; also Jules Verne, Paul McCartney and Wings, and erections—my own, exclusively). If I make an effort I can also recall gaudy souvenir shops, mounds of turquoise "Indian jewelry," a bubbly Elton John/Kiki Dee single, and the Democratic National Convention, which my father insisted on watching every night, sprawled like a beached whale on the hotel bed in nothing but a pair of open-fly boxers and a Hanes tank top.

I think we got as far as Arizona and then turned around. I saw the Grand Canyon.

On the whole that trip marked the fullest flowering of Scott's brutality. Things got so bad that at one point—somewhere in Texas, I suppose—my father pulled our red Delta 88 to the side of the road and moved Scott up front, leaving me in the backseat with my mother. For the last 130 miles Dad had been threatening to "pull over" and the man was true to his word. To my eternal gratitude.

Scott was fourteen that summer. He sported thick teardrop wire rims, long blond hair parted down the middle in the feathered style of that era, denim flares, and pinhole jerseys. He wore a choker and braces, of the clear plastic variety also in vogue. He was probably about five six, five seven, something like that, but he seemed enormous.

The seventies were in full swing, in other words, and my brother was perfectly attuned to the times, thoroughly assimilated to all the latest trends, insofar as a fourteen-year-old can assimilate to the prevailing culture. On the other hand, despite my protests, my hair stayed short; I wore ill-fitting tennis shorts and knee-high tube socks. Something felt vaguely wrong with my appearance, something slightly out of kilter and uncool, yet even as I scratched my sock-chafed shins I was unable to put my finger on the problem.

We were right outside Flagstaff at a Best Western hotel boasting a Grand Canyon motif I loved. I was a kid and had no taste. Although it was the height of the Arizona tourist season, this particular hotel, chosen by my father, was a good hour or so from the canyon itself and was therefore full of vacancies. To all outward appearances we were the only family around. I think perhaps my parents were fighting and this was Dad's revenge.

IT IS EVENING and Scott and I have the hotel pool all to ourselves.

The poolside lights in my foggy perception are wreathed

in rainbows. My skin is slick as a mink's, glossed antiseptically in chlorine. Since I'm not wearing my contacts the cast-iron deck furniture is completely invisible, the whole poolside decor dissolved into deceptively airy blurs of black and blue.

My older brother, wielding a tightly rolled wet towel, is chasing me.

This has been going on for about ten minutes. So far he has thwacked me twice, on the back of my left thigh both times. But somehow I end up on one side of the pool and he ends up on the other, thus effecting a stalemate. Between us the water sends forth a vast turquoise glow, the same color as my father's new Navajo bracelet. My nose burns with chlorine as I gasp for air.

Scott says, "Come on, pussy."

I put my hands on my knees and steady my breathing. "Suck my thing, you butthole."

"I'm serious, don't be such a fag." *Fag* and *pussy* are essentially interchangeable epithets in Scott's limited repertoire, both conveying the same withering charge. Scott has made it clear to me, repeatedly, that I am in danger of becoming both, though I have no clear idea what either actually is. "Get your own towel."

"Dream on, dick breath, dream on."

"Get a *towel,* Parker. Don't make me have to kick your ass."

An interesting dilemma: either I get a towel and lay myself open to repeated thwacks on my thigh, or I refuse and get beaten up. Sometimes Scott explains his beatings as an attempt to make me a man; unlike chicken, little boys apparently toughen if you pound them senseless. Other times he says he is just trying to provoke a "reaction"—that's all. When he punches me, he explains, he's just trying to see what I'll do. Of course as soon as I *do* anything—like fight back, for instance—I am quickly reminded (in words first) that I can *never* hope to kick his ass, and then I am swiftly subjugated, having made the grave mistake of piquing his anger *(Hey, dickhead, you bloodied my lip; you're gonna pay for that, you little prick)*. He must somehow assume I haven't caught on yet—or maybe he genuinely forgets why he was tormenting me in the first place.

"I'm going in," I tell him, though I don't really mean it.

"Okay," he says, reconsidering, "here's what we'll do. You do this one thing I ask and we'll call it a truce. One thing, a dare kind of, and it's over. No one wins."

Technically, of course, this isn't a truce at all. What I mean is, *I* have to do something—me, the losing team—before all things are equal. But it's as close to a truce as you'll get with Scott.

"What is it?" I ask. I am not uninterested. "Will it hurt?"

But he has dropped his towel and is already climbing onto the deck furniture. I can barely see him from across the pool.

"Get over here," he says, his back turned to me. "I said it was a truce. I won't touch you."

I am crazy with anticipation; my own impending fate

fascinates me. What does he have in mind? I dive sleek and supple into the pool and let my momentum shoot me in one elegant underwater arc to the other side. I am still young enough to enjoy pretending to be, say, a dolphin.

Scott has unhooked from the corner of the supply shack a purple fluorescent bug zapper. It is plugged into an orange extension cord that sits coiled like a cobra at the base of the pool fence, the male end suckling at the teat of the silver outlet located just outside the supply shack's locked front door. He walks toward me, the orange extension cord uncoiling as he proceeds, and extends the throbbing device out like a peace offering. In the lamp's eerie glow his teeth look as translucent as fingernails.

"A friend of mine did this once," he tells me, then places the lamp on the ground. My body tenses with fear. "It's incredibly cool."

"You better put that back where you found it." Highest on my list of fears is *getting caught*—doing anything. I have yet to develop a hierarchy of evil. "We're dead if someone catches us."

"Who's gonna catch us? We're the only retards out here." He stands back and regards his work. The lamp is propped against a deck chair, glowing, humming.

"What happens," he explains, "is the whole light turns white if you pee on it." He just looks at me, as if I know what he's talking about. Which, in truth, I *do*. As if to reassure me, he adds, "Brett did this once at his pool."

"I'm not peeing on the thing." Inside my wet trunks my little nubbin shrivels to the size of a chickpea.

"This is all you gotta do, Parker, I promise. Nothing happens, except the light turns white. That's all. It's no big deal. And anyway, if you do this we've got a truce, just like I said."

"Have *you* ever done it?"

"Tons. I already told you, Brett and I do this at his pool all the time."

That isn't exactly what he told me, but I buy it. The idea of the truce appeals to me. Also, I don't know much about electrical currents or fluorocarbons: as I said, the thing that concerns me most is getting caught. I am suddenly seized by a vision of the Best Western staff storming out here with handcuffs and searchlights, and there I am standing shame-faced with my pecker in my hand. The quicker the better.

"Okay," I tell him, "but only if *you* do it next."

"I promise," he assures me, straight-faced. "You bet."

I yank the string on my trunks and whip it out. The bright side to all of this is that I really do have to take a leak—wet trunks and all— so the whole thing looks like it will be over in a jiff. As a dribble leaks out and I start to take aim, I feel a moth brush past my cheek, see it swoop down in front of me, hear it snarl against the lamp, which, as Scott suggested, sustains a tiny white scar where the moth met its doom. My stream gains momentum and I find my target.

Oh, I saw white, all right.

• • •

THE THING IS, what did I ever do to *him?* What exactly was the guy's beef with me?

Well, for starters, I showed up. After all, he was three and a half when I was born, old enough to have certain ideas about himself and his place in the divine order of things. Scott had every reason on earth to believe that he was, in some measure or other, the center of the world. Young parents with their first child, in clamorous company with a whole bevy of other young couples, all with first children of their own: that was his world. Everywhere he turned he encountered friendly adult faces lowered to his scope of vision and contorted for his amusement. Every accomplishment of his was greeted by ebullient applause, by calls to Grandma and Grandpa, by a shower of hugs and kisses. There was, truly, no one else in town.

Children, as everyone knows, are solipsistic little monsters. Before the onslaught of self-consciousness there is simply an inner certainty of need. The pronoun *I* refers to something vague and elusive that, for the first two or three years of our lives, might as well be the entire known universe. A six-year-old will howl in rage at having to share a Tonka truck; a three-year-old will strike out and bite with all the territorial fervor of a wild dog. The first and most difficult fact of life is the realization that the world must be shared.

So I showed up and displaced my brother. I invaded the center he once inhabited and he struck out in protest. I made him recognize himself *as* a self and he hated me for it.

I guess I can understand that.

I THOUGHT ABOUT my brother obsessively. To me his inescapable presence seemed, with all the vague uncanny certainty of a dream, always there, always somehow nearby. When he was in the house I hid from him, locked my door and listened for his footsteps to come thundering down the hallway. When he wasn't in the house I anticipated his arrival with teeth-numbing dread. When I was out playing with my friends I fretted about going home. Every time I took a leak at school there were kids playing Thumps: he was omnipresent.

Upstairs, my bedroom door was the first one on the right. It opened to a spacious room for a twelve-year-old—at least it seemed spacious at the time—and felt to me, upon entering, like the inner sanctum of a vast labyrinth. I could lock my door, but only for form's sake. A coat hanger inserted into the hole in the doorknob successfully sprang the so-called lock, and besides, there was something of an injunction in our house against bolting anything other than the bathroom door. With the exception of my poor mother we were a family of boys, open-door pee-ers all of us.

Even my bedroom wasn't safe from Scott is what I'm trying to say. I could lock my door, sure, and even cower in my own walk-in closet, but in the end he always prevailed. Ten seconds with a bent coat hanger and he was in, armed with a new "reason" to inflict punishment. *Lookit, you pussy, what the hell is this with locking me out?*

He would pound up the stairs while I, sprawled on my bed reading an immaculate paperback copy of an H.G. Wells science-fiction novel, would grow rigid, drop my book, and stare at my door. Scott never knocked. He just jiggled the knob, then pounded. In these situations I would usually stay quiet, hoping to trick him into thinking the room was empty —a touching bit of reckless optimism, now that I think about it—but the pounding would continue.

"Hey, butt pirate, open up!"

This particular ritual had as its most horrific aspect the following: not content with a concise broadcast of his desires, Scott would steadily drum on the door until I let him in, which meant that even as I was turning the lock mechanism the whole door, knob and all, would be quaking in my grasp.

The door flies open, my brother fills the frame.

"What's up?" he says, helping himself inside. For good measure he tries to frog me in the arm. I deflect the punch but still catch it on my wrist. Which isn't to say I don't feel some pain.

Scott picks up my book, cracks it to the page I'm reading, and tosses the text aside, thereby pissing me off on two accounts: first, he has lost my place; second, he has cut a permanent crease down the book's spine. Next he turns down my stereo, lifts the needle and palms the playing surface of my record, a gesture that is especially infuriating in view of the fanatical care with which he handles his own records. He drops the LP back in the still spinning turntable, entirely missing the spindle. The record wobbles once and then careens to the floor, nicking the stylus en route. My mild fastidiousness, my tendency toward solitude and self-absorbed brooding, my love of order—for some reason, these things infuriate him. He regards these aspects of my personality as somehow womanly, as "faggy," and has thus taken it upon himself to beat them out of me. If you just pound hard enough, he apparently assumes, you'll find a man underneath.

"What are you doing with these?" he snaps, holding up a pair of white tube socks adorned with fading Puma insignias. "You got these from my closet, didn't you? When were you in my room?"

"Eat me with a spoon," I tell him. My record—Kiss *Destroyer*—now sports a chalked slash on side 2. "Mom put them in there, don't blame me."

But he has forgotten about the socks. Now he is busy with my computerized football game, which beeps and tweetles idiotically.

"Hey, I'm going to the weight room to work out," he says, working his jaw, scoring a TD (the game squiggles out a computerized rendition of the "1812 Overture," first measure). "Go with me."

I sleeve the record, my hands shaking with excitement. Mark Luthardt and I lift weights at his house on weeknights after *The Six Million Dollar Man* (Mondays), *Happy Days* and *Shields and Yarnell* (Tuesdays) and *James at 16* (Thursdays). We do dumbbell curls, the bench press, squats, all of which Scott showed us last Christmas when Mark got his totally boss set of Universal home weights, each plate molded in dull silver plastic. Each night after lifting I lie in bed, my arms sore (or so I like to imagine), and run through several enticing revenge scenarios concerning muscular me and my repentant older brother, and yet the irony of his asking me to go along with him on this gloomy February afternoon to pump some iron totally escapes me. I guess I'm too thrilled at the prospect really to notice.

"Who's going?" I ask warily.

"Just you and me. Hurry up, I'm leaving in a few minutes."

I squirm into gym clothes (a jockstrap is not yet part of my arsenal) and try to look nonchalant.

THE WOODS WE TRUDGE through are as stark as a black-and-white photograph. Above my head the February sun hides behind a gauze of gray. Beneath my feet twigs crackle and pop. Stopping about three paces ahead, Scott withdraws from his tube sock a can of Copenhagen snuff, thumps the can against his wrist to pack it tight, and helps himself to a hefty plug. Silently, he passes me the can. Having no previous experience with this delicate art, I pause a moment before extending my hand, then decide it's now or never. In my palm the can feels as big as a hockey puck and lighter than a cupcake. Following his lead, I thump the can against my own wrist, screw off the lid, and pinch a mound between my thumb and forefinger. After a deep breath, I force the foul-smelling stuff into my bottom lip. It tastes like a spoonful of dead ants. My mouth waters and my eyes flood, but still I persevere, still I concentrate, for everything he's telling me is crucially important, involving as it does such matters as high-school football, marijuana availability, and the sexual peculiarities of several prominent teenage girls, two of whom (Paige Brown and Camille Latour) had in previous years actually baby-sat for me. By now the plug of Copenhagen has disintegrated into a sludge of poisonous mud, some of which has slid to the back of my tongue.

"How's your dip?" he asks.

A string of syrupy saliva escapes from my mouth. "'S gleat."

We tread across the empty school parking lot as Scott fishes out his dip in one swift motion, using only the tip of his tongue. I take this as my cue to follow suit, but all I manage to do is cover the roof of my mouth with the vile stuff, which pretty much does it. With no advance warning, I vomit all over the backs of Scott's brand-new Adidas Country.

"Whoa, sport." He moves beside me, oblivious of his shoes, and drops a reassuring hand on my back. "Stay bent over, just like you're doing. Get a little air, then breathe deep. That's it. Another breath. Take it easy." My vision begins to clear, the pavement quits buckling beneath my feet. "What'd you do?" he laughs, and pats me on the back. "Dumb fuck."

When we get to the weight room he keeps it up, this unexpected air of brotherly affection. Part of it is genuine, the rest is for show. The sole audience is Scott's soon-to-be defensive-line coach, this daunting mountain of a man named Virgil Stallingsworth, who sizes me up and concludes without hesitation that I will be bigger than Scott. Natch. Stallingsworth is a creature of indomitable confidence and energy, with biceps the size of footballs and a neck so massive his whistle, which he wears even in the off-season, bounces against the solid shelf of his chest, the little ball within rattling like a marble inside a paint can. His mustache looks like a small gerbil, while his thighs fill to capacity the polyester pant legs of his gray coach's shorts.

This weight room is a no-nonsense kind of place, with steel rafters along the ceiling and cold concrete floors underneath. The benches sit on thick rubber pads and cast their silent reflections in a series of vast wall-length mirrors. The free weights, fashioned into black cast-iron disks, have been primly arranged on triangular display racks, each upright peg like an enormous roll of Certs photographed in the negative. A draft tickles my shins. Inspirational maxims, painted in bold Wolverine red, decorate the upper walls, each maxim fashioned in severe block letters: NOTHING WORTHWHILE COMES EASY. WINNING IS THE ONLY THING. 110 PERCENT! I read these admonitions as Scott and Stallingsworth run me through what they both insist is a "standard" workout, both of them barking encouragement throughout, Scott's voice a withering parody of his coach's baritone thunder.

In a couple of years I will become a frequent crawler of this very room. My hands will develop at the base of my fingers raw calluses. The pungent rich swirl of freshly cut August grass will become forever associated for me with pre-season two-a-days. I will be assigned a locker on which I will scrawl in black Marks-A-Lot my last name and jersey number. These memories and sensations, coupled with a matrix of worry and dread, will to all accounts be mine, and yet, on this February afternoon, I know vaguely (it's just a flutter of recognition) that I am simply inheriting something, that this exercise room and everything that goes with it will never truly be mine. I will always be "Little Hayes," Scott's less gifted younger brother. Another thing: Stallingsworth will be my coach and in the same breath not be my coach. How excruciating it will be, during my unspectacular stint as a Middlesburg High School Wolverine, to endure daily athletic embarrassment under the shared umbrella of my last name, which, it sometimes feels to me, I inherited from Scott rather than my father.

I should have played a different sport. I was not suited for a game like football, being as I was a recipient, rather than a bestower, of blows. I should have run track, tried my hand at wrestling, stuck with swim team. I should have mastered a sport that would have better exploited my penchant for solitude, one that would have pitted me against nothing more tractable than my own endurance and courage, something elegantly and irreducibly mine so that later on I might bask in the luxury of recollecting my emotions in tranquillity.

What do I remember most about that afternoon? I

remember Scott saying "fuck" a lot. I remember Stallingsworth scratching his balls. And I distinctly remember the
acid discharge of fear I felt when Scott declared that I could
bench press considerably more than my initial, and not very
conservative, estimate.

This is the kind of thing he always does. *Be like me, do
what I do.* At the moment he wants me to approach his
strength, so as to shorten the distance between us. I have my
misgivings.

"Just let me add a five-kilo plate on the end," he insists, already slapping on the extra weight. "What'd you think,
coach?"

"Fucking-A," Stallingsworth agrees, spitting into a nearby
trash can. "He can do it."

Since I know nothing about kilograms, it is not altogether
clear to me how much extra weight he is adding. Then again,
the actual increase isn't really what's at issue.

I settle myself on the bench press, grasp the barbell, brace
my feet, which barely reach the floor. The bar is thicker than
the one at Luthardt's house. I can't really get a good hold.
Also, my thumb knuckle rubs against the finely waffled surface. In my arms tingles a premonition of failure. Scott
looms above me, gripping the center of the barbell, his face
flat and foreshortened.

"Ready?" he asks.

I nod.

Arching my back I heave at the weight which, to my astonishment, lifts effortlessly, as if I had just hoisted a slab of Styrofoam rock. Confidence races through my arms. For a moment I am convinced—absolutely, genuinely convinced—that I can throw the thing right through the ceiling.

"Let's fucking do it," I say, figuring I've earned the right.

Scott lets go. All at once the enormous, invisible finger of God reaches down from the heavens and pushes the barbell into my chest. Wham! The impact is so solid my feet kick out, striking Stallingsworth in his massive shins. I fear my heart is going to squirm up my throat and out my mouth.

Scott shouts, "Push it, goddamn it!"

"C'mon, biggin," Stallingsworth encourages, "squeeze it out."

"You can do it, Parker! Push it, push it, push it!"

But the weight won't budge. My face feels like it's going to explode. To my sudden shame, I have to fart.

"C'mon, man, don't give up!" Scott yells, taking the barbell in his index fingers. The load lightens.

"That's it, now, that's it, you got it." (Stallingsworth)

Scott adds another finger and the load gets lighter. The barbell rises an inch.

"Almost there, Parker, just a little more, man, you almost got it."

At long last my elbows lock, to which Stallingsworth winks, "Atta boy." But I am too terrified to move. The barbell does not seem heavy anymore—the whole concept of weight has been disrupted in my mind—and I don't know where my hold on the barbell ends and Scott's begins. Scott guides the barbell to its resting perch and I let go, my arms dropping to my sides like spaghetti noodles.

And as I lie there on the bench trying to wrestle with the agonizing sensation of failure coursing through my muscles, I catch a glimpse of Virgil Stallingsworth scratching his balls with all the blithe feral impunity of a dog sniffing its own crotch. When he catches me looking at him he peels off a fat, fatherly smile and says, "You'll get there, little buddy. You stick with this brother of yours and you'll turn out just fine."

Above me Scott nods. "That's right, coach. We'll make a man of him yet."

And the idea does comfort me, in a vague, conflicted sort of way. It lets me know that in this, as in so many other things in my life, I don't really have much of a choice.

3. BORN AGAIN

In the summer of 1979 I fell ruinously in love with a coltish, athletically robust Greek girl of fifteen named Nicole Liarkos. When I think of her now (which isn't very often), I always imagine her poolside, her velvety cinnamon-colored flesh punctuated by the triple triangles of her buttercup-yellow bikini and her left arm blocking the sun from her eyes. We met in July of that year, on a church retreat to Panama City, Florida, and as fate would have it I fell for her the exact same week Bob Dylan accepted Jesus Christ as his personal Lord and Savior. I was thirteen years old. I knew next to nothing about sex, death, or God and absolutely everything about progressive rock. I was a happy boy, the last happy boy on earth. Before going on that trip I never imagined I could love anything as fervently as I did my record albums, my science-fiction novels, my paper route.

Thanks to the latter—which I inherited from a boyhood friend who, like so much else that year, would leave me for good at the end of the summer—I had enough disposable income to buy all the records I wanted, to which end I had amassed nearly a hundred in all, the whole collection prominently displayed in my locked bedroom in alphabetical order, Aerosmith through ZZ Top, the As out front and the Zs bowing under the burden of their beloved brethren. That July, Bob Dylan would change everything.

The boyhood friend was Mark Luthardt. Though more or less the same age as Nicole, he was nevertheless my emotional coeval. Perhaps he was even a year or two behind, hard to say. He lived across the street. I've already said we lifted weights—or tried to, anyway; we also took care of each other's dogs, split lawn duties, and shared the paper route. He was an angelically gentle boy, with perfectly straight brown hair cut into a Dutch-boy bowl, a narrow Scandinavian jaw (on which facial hair had already started to sprout), and crooked wire-frame glasses, the left temple screw replaced by a tiny safety pin and both side arms worn, in the name of a tighter, safer fit, outside his hair, thereby producing a humorous burlesque of sideburns.

Every morning during our final summer together, I trotted across the street to Mark's house and sat, bored to oblivion, in his kitchen while he pored over the silver-and-gold price index in the morning paper, his pathetic glasses perched on his forehead and his nose pressed against the microscopic print. By fourteen he'd amassed over ten thousand dollars in South African gold Krugerrands. I was the one person in the world to whom he had chosen to reveal the full extent of his wealth. Just before he left that August, Mark had declared himself a full-fledged libertarian, a complete set of heavily annotated Ayn Rand novels carefully sealed in their very own Mayflower box and insured against damages and his weather-worn briefcase packed to the clasp with multiple copies of Howard J. Ruff's *How to Prosper during the Coming Bad Years*—sort of a cross between *The 7 Habits of Highly Effective People* and *The Late Great Planet Earth* —a book that he had begun handing out to people who weren't aware of the financial apocalypse just around the corner.

Mark had the paper route first—an afternoon route, as it happens, and one of the last of its kind before cable television obliterated evening newspapers—and since he was my best friend (that is, my only friend), I started helping him out, gratis. When we weren't out delivering our papers we were riding our bikes downtown to hobby shops, bookstores, record emporiums, and anywhere else we could think of to spend our hard-earned income.

Little in my subsequent life has compared to the bliss of walking out of a Peaches record store on a hot summer day —my thighs wobbly with fatigue, a twenty-mile trek home still ahead of me—and withdrawing from its thin brown paper bag a new Be Bop Deluxe or Bruce Springsteen album.

With Mark looking on and sharing my contagious excitement, I would stroke the cellophane wrapper, admire the jacket art, read the song titles, and put off for just a little while longer the moment of truth, which in the world of vinyl records began long before you actually put the record on your turntable. First you had to assess the packaging. Was this a gatefold cover? Was there a lyric sheet? Were there specially designed labels on the record itself, and did the packaging include a poster, decals, order forms for T-shirts, and Velcro wallets? Next came the thrilling slide of the thumbnail down the cover's left side, a delicate moment that, to the attentive record lover, released like a genie in a bottle the faint but unforgettable smell of virgin vinyl. Finally, there was that unrepeatable first look at the smooth unblemished inner sleeve (lyrics!), at the shiny disc within (specialty labels!), at the perfectly cut grooves glistening in the sun, in which lurked a very real genie indeed.

Mark granted me my music, as I granted him his financial obsessions. Though I admired Mark's genius, I also understood that I was almost totally alone in recognizing it. Mark had no other friends, either. Somehow he had managed the transition from middle school to high school without changing a single thing about his wardrobe (loose-fitting sans-a-belt slacks, T-shirt or untucked Oxford button-down, black soccer sneakers), his grooming habits (wet comb, shave), or his daily schedule. I knew that in high school there were people called seniors who drove automobiles and smoked marijuana, and I knew there were fragrant girls with big billowing haircuts who, when talking to you, cradled their spiral notebooks against their "bosoms," a word I could barely utter without feeling aroused. Mark was unmoved by all this. He still came home every afternoon from school, helped me fold my papers, did his half of the route, and spent the remainder of the evening shooting baskets with me or reading his coin magazines while I listened to my albums. Mark never once referred to a single classmate in casual conversation with me. I was it for him: I was his Chosen One.

All of which might explain why Mark was so hostile to my decision—forced on me by my mother—to spend a week in Panama City with my church youth group.

"The whole thing sounds totally gay to me," he complained, folding a newspaper and shaking his head in disappointment, glasses wobbling down his nose. "I can't believe you can't worm out of it."

Actually, I could have, but for some reason I chose not to. Before that summer I had only gone to a few of the Sunday night meetings and hadn't enjoyed myself at all—pizza, singing, group activity, a Talk—so in our arguments about the trip Mark was quick to remind me of how much I hated the whole concept of Methodist Youth Fellowship (MYF for short). "They're going to *brainwash* you," he'd say, waving his fingers over my head, adding in an ominous voice, "Repent. Date nice girls. Drink more Kool-Aid." He also cited the fact that my going away would occupy a full *week* of summer—and not just any summer but (averting his gaze) "our very last summer before I move away." Pause. "For-ever." And he grumbled about having to do the paper route alone.

All of this was no doubt true: I granted him the whole list, no caveats. Yet I still decided to go. For a year my mother had been pestering me to get more involved with the youth group, to ask home some "nice boys" from school, to get a girlfriend—in short, to do all the things I was resolutely not doing so long as I spent my time with Mark Luthardt. And I resisted her every step of the way, partly because, like Luthardt, I harbored a boiling contempt for most of my peers, most of whom cared only about being *popular,* and partly because I felt she was trying to come between me and Mark. I didn't want to become part of a group, let alone en-gage in group activities. I had Mark and my albums and my paper route: that was enough. I resisted her in direct defiance of her fallow bourgeois hopes for me, and I resisted her out of solidarity with Mark. And then, one day, I stopped resisting.

THE BUS LEFT the church parking lot late Sunday evening; by driving straight through the night the trip's directors ensured that we would arrive at our cottages, re-freshed and ready, early Monday morning, thereby maxi-mizing our allotted time on the beach. I saw an additional and purely personal advantage to this arrangement: it would allow me to put off for a good twelve hours—the length of

the drive from Memphis to Florida—any face-to-face inter-
action with my bus mates. I planned to hunker down in the
back and sleep off the entire drive, and that is precisely what
I tried to do—for about three hours. Then I gave up. I had
to: the bus was in pandemonium. The cabin lights stayed
on, the aisles clamored with shrieking teenagers, and fifteen
different cassette decks fought for airspace. The other problem was that all these smiling, helpful, hopeful kids kept
plopping down beside me and introducing themselves. Hi,
I'm Jenna-Jeff-Holly-Hal-Matt-Michelle-Doug-Donna-Patti-
Pat. Whatcha listening to, whatcha doing, welcome praise
Jesus. There was no place to go, no way to escape their
kindness.

Then came the first of the trip's veritable miracles. At
around 2 A.M., while feigning sleep beneath my down sleeping bag, I felt a gentle tap on my shoulder. Sitting primly beside me and extending her hand in greeting was a smiling
high school girl in an aqua-blue surf shirt and khaki shorts,
her perfectly straight teeth brilliant in the murky bus light
and her cheeks punctured by two pretty little dimples. "I'm
Nicole," she said, and tilted her head.

"Parker Hayes," I replied, gently squeezing her hand. She
was the most spectacular creature I had ever seen. As I would
later learn, she had been spending her summer mornings
working as an assistant coach for her country club's swim
team, so she was already radiantly tan, a fact that only en-
hanced her intrinsic air of calcium-enriched good health.

Her dark brown hair, with its sun-bleached streaks of amber, was fashioned into an ingenious shag, with stylish feathered bangs out front, a perfect sort of haircut to frame and highlight the perky particulars of her face—the aristocratically high cheekbones, the dark arched eyebrows, those dimples. The one odd note was her lips, which were less pink than a pale tan. In 1979, however, this oddity had the advantage of making her look like she was born wearing lip gloss.

She waited for me to say something else. When I failed to do so, she said, "I've never seen you at MYF, so I thought you'd be a good person to meet. You're my third."

"Your third what?"

"Third new person. Of course it's easier for me, since I've only gone about six times. My mom wanted me to come on this trip, which is fine. How about you? Is this your first time with the group?"

"No," I told her, my voice quivering, "I've been a couple of times."

"Right. So you shouldn't have any trouble getting five people. You can count me as one if you'd like."

I shook my head in bewilderment. "Five people?"

She studied me for a moment. Her eyes were a cool ice green, with a thin black border around the irises. "You know, the Meet 'n' Greet thing?" She waited for this to register, then added, "On the itinerary sheet? The one we had to sign?"

Actually, I had signed a stapled document before boarding the bus. I just hadn't read it. Since my mom was the one writing the checks and buying the supplies, and since the whole trip was her idiotic idea to begin with, I let her handle the fine print.

"You can look at mine," she said, and scooted forward in the seat, her knee brushing my thigh. From her back pocket she withdrew a stapled document folded lengthwise. I took the pages in my hand: they were still warm. "Page 4," she explained.

And there it was, just below the supply list:

Group Activity #1: Meet 'n' Greet!

On the bus ride down, introduce yourself to at least FIVE (5) new people you don't already know. Ask 'em where they go to school, what their hobbies are, and where they are in their walk with Christ! We'll all compare notes on Monday night, and the one with the most names and info MIGHT JUST WIN A PRIZE!

No wonder all these people had been so eager to introduce themselves to me.

"I guess I missed that," I told her.

"It's kind of geeky, huh?" She took the sheets back, folded them once, and slid them back into her pocket. "But I'm almost done, so it's not so bad. Like I said, you can count me as one."

Which was how I met Laine Blevins, the one figure from

the trip whose friendship and influence would outlive the summer. Thin and soft-featured, with longish brown hair so straight you could still see the lines left by the teeth of his comb, Laine had entered his early adolescence in full command of a style best described as Seventies Mellow. Whatever, man, it's cool. Although the coming decade would expel Laine right out of the mainstream and into his school's parking lot, where the other stoners huddled together over the open doors of jacked-up Trans Ams and rusty Pintos, that summer he was still very much a part of the zeitgeist, albeit a zeitgeist that was on the cusp of a radical shift—from mellow to uptight in one presidential election.

"What's up," Laine murmured in halfhearted response to my halfhearted introduction. After giving me a limp handshake, he ran his hand through his bangs (perfunctory middle part), the hair falling back into place as smoothly as a shuffled deck of cards. A pair of expensive Bose headphones embraced his narrow neck, the coiling cord affixed to an exact replica of my own Panasonic portable eight-track player.

"Nice equipment," I commented, gesturing toward the headphones, to which Laine returned a faint and dreamy smile, the Seventies Mellow gesture of thanks. Then I asked the decisive question: "What're you listening to?"

Laine looked me over. Since I'd come to him, I was very likely just another MYF geek; on the other hand, I'd had the good taste to acknowledge his headphones; at the same time,

I might just be buttering him up for a Bible assault. "Floyd," he finally said.

"Pre– or post–*Dark Side?*"

"Pre."

"Syd Barrett or Roger Waters?"

"Post-Syd, definitely, but still pretty cool."

"I hear you," I said, and despite myself, I smiled. As did Laine. Verily, there was a God.

I was officially done with Meet 'n' Greet. For the rest of that bus ride, from Mississippi through Alabama and all the way to the northwestern tip of Florida, Laine and I talked music. I also learned that he, too, had been inveigled to come on this trip by his mother—just like me and Nicole Liarkos, whose whereabouts on the bus I did not for a single minute cease monitoring (three seats back, two seats ahead, lateral movement to front of bus, here she comes again). In short, life was good. In the space of one hour I had made a brand-new friend and contracted a voluptuous virus called Nicole Liarkos. For the first time in several years, I completely forgot about Mark Luthardt.

NICOLE LIARKOS WAS TOTALLY out of my league. I ascertained this little fact early Monday afternoon, sometime after our first group meeting, held in the cafeteria postlunch (grilled cheese sandwiches, grape Kool-Aid). I was in back, smirking with Laine. Sitting Indian style on a table just in front of us was a tall, lean blond boy in blue swim trunks who, between sing-a-long numbers, kept extending his long leg to the table in front of him and inserting his big toe into the belt loop of Nicole's cutoff jeans. Without turning around she would slap his hand away and resume singing. Laine would then turn to me and shake his head in disapproval. *Pansy*, he seemed to be saying. Playing grab-ass with a bunch of girls. I nodded back, secretly envying the blond boy. I never played grab-ass with girls. I never even played patty-cake with girls.

Group meetings were run by Josh McVray, the trip's head counselor and MYF director, a stupefyingly intense twenty-four-year-old divinity student, amateur marathon runner, and all-around motivational life force who, I later learned, had talked my mother into talking *me* into going on this trip. He weighed about 145 pounds, all of it dense muscle. He had a shaggy beard and thinning brown hair, which he wore straight, so that it simply fell behind his ears and down his long neck. When he talked, which was very often, and particularly when he grew ardent about his subject, which was every time he talked, he would stare at his auditors with great intensity and *without blinking*. A tiny but tenacious drop of saliva would also palpitate in the corner of his mouth, producing a slight lisp.

"So here we are," Josh was saying from the front of the room, saliva spraying his beard, his acoustic guitar hanging like a vendor's tray along his chest, "in Panama City, Florida, a paradise if I've ever seen one. Sunshine, palm trees, the ocean. And no school, no studies—who doesn't think that's paradise?" Gentle laughter. "But before we all race out to the beach I want us all to turn our thoughts, just for a moment, to our Lord and Savior, Emmanuel. In the fall we'll all go back to school and worship at the altar of fact and reason, but for now I want us to try something different. This week I want you to change your thinking just a little bit. While we're all here in paradise, on vacation from school, I want us all to turn off that reasoning part of our brains and turn on"—dramatic pause—"*unreason*. That's right. You heard me. Now what do I mean by unreason? Well, God says in I Corinthians—"

"You're Parker, aren't you?" It was the blond boy. Without my noticing it he had somehow transported himself from his table to mine, and now he was sitting just above my shoulder, his thin arms crossed along his folded knees. "I'm Caleb," he whispered. "I meant to introduce myself on the bus but I was, you know, sorta busy." He ran the moist tip of his tongue along his top lip. "Anyway, I was talking with Shelley over there and she says she *really* wants to meet you. Catholic girl, if you know what I mean."

I looked where he was inclining his head. Two tables down the Shelley in question was looking back at me, smiling without a hint of self-consciousness, despite her headgear and braces, while oblivious beside her sat Nicole Liarkos, in cutoffs and a T-shirt that bore the wet imprint of her bikini bra. I did nothing. Not one thing. Girls didn't normally look at me, not even girls in headgear. Although I thought about girls incessantly—in the abstract, anyway—I rarely talked about them with Mark Luthardt who, to my knowledge, recognized only two female human beings in the world, his sister and his mother, both of whom he dismissed as minor irritants. Josh continued to talk ardently about unreason, in response to which Laine coughed the word *bullshit* into his fist. Caleb toed me again in the rib cage. After a tense moment of indecision, I waved at Shelley.

Caleb took over from there. "Forget about Nicole," he assured me out in the ocean later that same afternoon. "I already got the scoop from Shelley, who goes to her school. Basically, Nicole only dates older guys, seniors and shit, so she's a lost cause. Sorry, man. You'll get *nowhere*. Trust me, I've tried. On a trip like this, Parker, what you're looking for is *willingness*." He made a squirt gun of his cupped hands and nailed me in the cheek. "That's the primary issue here: all other things are secondary. You've only got one week after all." He squirted me again. "And for willingness above and beyond the call of duty, I give you Shelley Broward."

For Caleb, Methodist Youth Fellowship was first and foremost about nookie. His particular genius lay in the fact that he flirted with every girl on the trip, including the homeliest of the homely. By being so indiscriminate and generous in his affections, he came off to the desirable girls as a dangerous rake and to the counselors as a thoughtful paragon of Christian goodwill. Meanwhile, he was scoring like an NBA All-Star.

"So you're saying you've been with Shelley?" I tried squirting him back but couldn't figure out how to cup my hands correctly.

"That's right, little man. Been and gone. On the bus ride down, to be exact, just outside Southhaven. While you and Laine were jerking off to Pink Floyd, Shelley and I were playing Hide the Finger under a sleeping bag."

My heart dropped: Southhaven was about twenty minutes south of the church. "You're lying."

"Fine, don't believe me. Go see for yourself." With that he took me by the shoulders and playfully pushed me into a crashing wave.

About ten minutes later Shelley, pluckily unimpeded by the waves, forced her way toward us and, giving me a hearty masculine handshake, introduced herself. Caleb fell back in the water and whooped for joy. Shelley was exactly my age, give or take a month, and exactly my size, with better muscular definition than I would have for several years, from her finely articulated biceps to her prominent wrist veins. That afternoon, for convenience sake, she wore pigtails which, coupled with the braces and the bikini, made her look like a pornographic parody of Heidi. Running her tongue along the inside of her cheek, she poked me in the chest, then jerked her head at Caleb. "What's he been telling you about me?"

"That you're a ridiculous flirt," Caleb cried, and within moments the two of them were engaged in an exuberant game of Mercy. They grunted and grinned and tumbled as one into the water, where they disappeared for a disconcertingly long time.

An island of bubbles appeared where they went down. Without warning they both exploded into air, choking and laughing, Shelley's striped bikini panties slightly askew along her hip. "Defeated again," Caleb sighed, and fell back again into a wave, his arms held above his head in triumph. Readjusting her suit, she then turned to me, her braces glinting in the sunlight, and raised her hands. "Now your turn."

"I'm wearing contacts," I meekly objected, which was true enough.

"I'll be gentle," she assured me, and locked her fingers with mine. We commenced our struggle. Within moments I realized Shelley Broward meant business; this was no mere flirtation, she was out to win. And she almost succeeded. Biting her bottom lip, she squeezed my fingers in hers and steered me back into a wave. So unexpected was this show of force that I still had my eyes open when I went under. Blindly I fought, my legs entangled with hers and my arms pinned to my side.

Somehow I managed to right myself, whereupon Shelley, with an impish smile, relaxed her grip, and amid this sudden lapse of friction I fell right on top of her. Underwater she went limp in my hands. Though I had the good sense to close my eyes this time, I recognized her thigh when it brushed my knee and the tip of her breast when it touched my arm. All at once I recalled Caleb's story about the bus ride down *(just outside Southaven, Hide the Finger),* and just as instantly realized I was in way over my head. I had no idea what to do next. I barely even knew this girl and here she was, nearly naked and wrestling with me underwater. Everything had happened too fast; instead of a gradual transition we had made an abrupt leap. With God watching all the while. In a panic I let go and leapt to the surface, gulping for air.

"You win," she announced a moment or two later, but I didn't answer. I was blinking and rubbing my eyes and still hoping against hope that my right contact lens had not actually dissolved in the ocean. If it did, then I would have to wear my glasses for the rest of the trip; I was clearheaded enough to understand that this was a tragic development. How could I swim in the ocean? How would glasses affect my chances with Nicole? Maybe the lens had slid up my eyelid; perhaps all was not lost. Shelley touched me on the shoulder. "Hey, you all right?" I brushed her away as fear filled my lungs: God was punishing me for my sins. I blinked and blinked and in a moment of despair uttered the following silent prayer: *Forgive me, Father, I was only fooling around.* And at that exact moment, the missing contact lens slid back into place.

Shelley was backing away from me in the water, a confused look on her face. A boomerang of pelicans drifted lazily overhead. Tentatively, she asked, "Did I do something wrong?"

"No, of course not," I assured her, and lowered myself in the surf so that only my head was visible. She wavered in my watery vision. "I just had a little trouble seeing, that's all. Problem with my contact lens, nothing big. But everything's clear now. Everything's fine."

I ENDED UP SHARING a bunk with Laine, and at night we would stay up late, passing his headphones back and forth like a peace pipe. Caleb was also in our room; somehow he had a full bunk to himself, an injustice made all the more galling by the fact that he rarely slept in it. After lights out, as Laine and I debated the Beatles versus the Stones or Seger versus Springsteen, Caleb would construct a dummy of his sleeping self from our accumulated laundry and climb out the window.

"That guy's an asshole," Laine observed one night from the bottom bunk. "I don't know how you stand him."

"Oh, he's all right," I objected, and let the subject drop, though in fact I kind of agreed with Laine. Caleb was self-absorbed, narcissistic, and thoroughly corrupt. His jokes—all of which, in one way or another, touched on the (to him) hilarious subject of homosexuality—were almost unfailingly at my expense. Worst of all, he was a boastful, swaggering slob, proudly displaying for our admiration such unpleasantries as the skid marks in his cotton briefs and the underarm stains on his T-shirts. For all of that, I clung to him, and for one very simple reason: he was my ticket to Nicole.

With Laine, I was in a purely male space, a boyish land of record albums and shared esoterica and displaced affection.

It was Mark Luthardt all over again: not altogether a bad thing. The problem was, there was no room in this friendship for girls. Caleb, on the other hand, had no room for anything else. At group meetings he always plopped himself down among the girls; on the beach he lounged among the bikinis like a suntanned sultan. Without Caleb to hide behind, I don't know if I ever would have approached Nicole; with Caleb, I found the courage, or at least a good enough pretext, to settle down beside her at group meetings, to fetch her Frescas from the soda machine, and to sit with her on the bus whenever we went out as a group.

I did all these things and more. One afternoon, while sunbathing poolside, I explained to her the plot of *Tommy*. A day later she reached behind her, unhooked the clasp of her yellow bikini bra, and quietly asked if I would apply some Coppertone to her shoulder blades, which were bisected by a narrow strip of shy skin that blushed beneath my gaze. She accepted my presence without complaint, but also without much enthusiasm. Since no one else was pursuing her—which is to say, since no one else was foolish enough to pursue her—she had no reason to reject my advances, such as they were. I wasn't hurting anything; I could be endured.

Oh, but *I* was hurting. I was in exquisite, delicious pain. Sitting beside her on the bus I would experience paralysis of the tongue, while out on the beach, as she made a delectable sky offering of her skin, I would run sand through my fingers and sulk at the hopelessness of my plight. All the other kids knew I was in love with her and pitied me. Of all people it was finally Shelley Broward who stopped me outside the dining hall and, squinting against the sun, asked, "How you doing? You gonna be okay?" Meanwhile, no one seemed to fault Nicole for her relative disinterest in me: just the opposite, in fact. By suffering my presence so selflessly, she was, in their view (and mine as well), practicing Christian kindness.

Still and all, I was not the only amorous hopeful striking out with Nicole. Despite the trip's narrow focus on frolicsome good fun—the pointless days at the beach, the afternoons at Putt-Putt golf, the group activities and the harmless pranks (stolen underwear, shaving-cream fights)—there remained a serious component to it all, a complex message of salvation and sin that Josh disclosed to us gradually, day after day, like a substitute teacher slowly regaining control of a rambunctious classroom. He began with his lesson on unreason and continued to develop his theme with each passing meal and progressively cozy group meeting. Even Laine, the biggest skeptic of us all, stopped sneering at group meetings, and by midweek it was safe to say that nearly every member of the group was growing more serious in their Commitment to Christ. Everyone, that is, except Nicole. Josh, too, she spurned. The serious message of the trip, which everyone else was now openly discussing, slid off her like oil on ice water. She listened during group, sang all the folk songs, participated in group activities, and each morning she was back on her lounger, working on her tan and placidly thumbing through her fashion magazines.

EVERYTHING TOOK A DECISIVE turn on Friday afternoon. After lunch (hot dogs, Kool-Aid), Josh stood up at
the front of the hall and, holding his acoustic guitar, lowered
his head as if in meditation. He stayed this way—motionless,
deep in thought—for at least three or four minutes, during
which time the room slowly quieted down. Soon the only
person still moving was Nicole who, sitting indifferently beside me, was adjusting the strap on her baseball cap. Everyone watched as she settled the cap on her head, pulled her
hair through the rear mouse hole, and leaned back on her elbows: a supine Diana in damp T-shirt and khaki shorts.

"Something incredible has occurred," Josh began, lifting
his head slowly and scanning the room. "There are people,
good devout people, who will tell you that God is no longer
at work in the world, but I'm here to tell you they are wrong.
I'm here to give you clear evidence of a miracle." He paused.
"Does everybody know who Bob Dylan is? The famous rock
musician?" Stunned, I turned to Laine, who was looking
with rapt intensity at the front of the room. Dylan and the
Doors were two of his fiercest obsessions. "Well, about
twenty minutes ago I learned that Bob Dylan, the most in-
fluential rock musician of the last twenty years, has accepted
Jesus Christ as his personal Savior. Think about that for a
moment, people. *Bob Dylan*. Has found the Lord." He waited
for this news to settle in; receiving no response, he led everyone in a round of applause. We all joined in, though no one
was really sure what we were applauding. For the last week
none of us had so much as looked at a newspaper. By now,

however, the news of Bob Dylan's conversion to Christianity had ascended into the airless afterlife of public opinion. For most of the world it was a fascinating tidbit; for Josh McVray, a child of the sixties and a fervent evangelical, it was an Event, a genuine turning point in his life, on par with the Nixon resignation and the death of Jim Morrison.

"All week I've been listening to your rock music," he continued. "The tape players and the radios have been going nonstop for five days now. And I understand why this is so. I was once just like you. I once owned *hundreds* of albums. I went to *a ton* of rock concerts. I got so I couldn't wake up in the morning without first putting on a record, and by college I couldn't fall asleep unless I had music going. Then one day I realized something that changed my life forever." With impeccable stagecraft, he unstrapped his guitar and set it aside; he now stood naked before us, without a prop. "My love of music was getting in the way of my walk with Christ. I was enslaved to my records. My head was filled with secular music when it *should* have been filled with my love of God. How much of that music glorified God? How much of it glorified Satan? You know what music I'm talking about. You know the groups I mean. So what did I do?" He looked around, making eye contact with nearly every person in the room, including me. A chilling moment. I, too, fell asleep to music; I, too, could not begin my day without first putting on a record. My head was stuffed with song lyrics, album covers, liner notes. I was enslaved to vinyl records. Beside me

Nicole applied nail polish to her left big toe. "I'll tell you what I did. I burned all my albums, every last one of them. Hundreds and hundreds of albums, all up in smoke. And why? Why on earth did I do this? Because I knew, in my heart of hearts, that it was the right thing to do. What does not bring me closer to God takes me away from Him. It's that simple, guys. And now, this miracle. Now we learn that Bob Dylan has accepted the Lord. His days of secular music are over. Do you people realize how important this is to the community of God? Do you understand the significance of what has just happened?"

I understood. Suddenly I remembered a kid in my sixth-grade class who, upon returning home from a Baptist youth group retreat, set fire to all his Aerosmith albums. I remembered his curious explanation for this rash act—something about secular versus sacred music—and I vividly recalled thinking how easy it would have been simply to have given *me* the fucking albums. Afterward this same boy began listening exclusively to Christian rock, and since I was the most re-spected music critic in our class he loaned me a few of the al-bums, to gauge my opinion. Though I gave the records only a cursory listen, I remained unimpressed: the songs certainly *sounded* like rock music, and the lyrics were cunningly devised to seem, at first blush, like standard love songs, revealing them-selves only on closer inspection to be *love songs for Christ,* but all in all this was tepid, unconvincing music, somewhat like a television producer's faulty but well meaning idea of rock and roll (think the Partridge Family, think the Monkees). Now I understood what this boy had been trying to tell me.

Later that evening I asked Laine, "What did you think of group meeting today?" We were standing in line for a ride at the Miracle Mile, a local Panama City amusement park. It was our last night in Florida. In honor of this fact, Josh, in lieu of the standard postdinner Talk, informed us that he had a wonderful surprise in store and herded us all onto the bus. Miracle Mile was the surprise.

"You mean the Dylan thing?"

"More or less." We shuffled forward. Though I wasn't exactly pleased by the fact, Nicole and Shelley and Caleb were in the haunted house just around the corner. Everyone agreed that it looked like a gyp, but Caleb took the ironic line and declared it great. Laine and I opted for the Rockin' Toboggan, an unspectacular high-speed merry-go-round set to deafening rock music. "I mean, it got me thinking, you know? That's me, if you think about it. I'm just like that. I mean, I'm not saying I agree with everything he said, but it just, I don't know. It got me thinking."

"It was pretty heavy, all right." Laine tore off a tuft of cotton candy, offered me some, then craned his neck. "That's weird about Dylan, though."

"Yeah, isn't it? But it's also good, don't you think?" I realized I was treading on dangerous turf here. Was he with me in my walk, or was he holding something back? I wasn't sure which I wanted; I was waiting for Laine to tell me where I was heading.

"Depends on his next album," he replied, then wadded up the now bare cardboard cone, positioned himself at an imaginary free-throw line, and sunk the wad in a wire wastebasket some fifteen feet away. Several people in line applauded. "You done talking about this?"

My heart dropped. "Sure, whatever. Sorry."

"I didn't mean it like that. I mean, if you're not done, that's cool. We can keep talking about it. But if you're done, I need to ask you something."

"What about?"

"You and Shelley. I guess I'm asking if there's anything going on between you guys."

"Where'd you get that idea?" I thought everyone was charting my doomed pursuit of Nicole.

"Just checking. What I'm saying is, you won't get uptight if I try my luck?"

"Of course not," I laughed. "Be my guest."

"Cos I don't want something like that coming between us."

And from that moment on, Laine was my new ticket to Nicole. After the Rockin' Toboggan we met up with the girls again, and within the half hour Laine was sharing one Ferris wheel seat with Shelley while I shared another with Nicole. Contrary to what Laine had feared, something *had* in fact come between us, and it was the one thing that would never come between Mark and me.

"I hate these things," Nicole remarked, looking down at the gently drifting crowd rushing toward us. She was dressed in white jeans, a pink Izod golf shirt, and a baseball cap. Her painted toes poked from the burgundy straps of her brand-new Pappagallo sandals.

"What do you hate about them?"

"This. The way they stop." We began moving again, our little cart tilting back and forth. We passed the carny in charge, then the rumbling engine, then began our ascent back up to the top. "I just wish it would go around and around."

"But they have to let other people on."

"Not necessarily. They don't stop roller coasters."

I wasn't prepared to argue this point. As we moved inexorably toward the moon, I began to pray that we would stop at the top, whereupon I suddenly realized that this was the whole point of Ferris wheels to begin with: to get stuck on top with your girl. And lo and behold, that is what happened next.

"Oh God," she cried, and squeezed my hand hard enough to grind my knuckles together. "I'm terrified of heights."

I tried to think of a snappy reply but came up blank. The fact is, I *never* knew what to say to Nicole. I had no idea what interested her, no clue what she liked or disliked. After a full week of tireless devotion, I had not bothered to learn the slightest thing about the way her mind worked. She had neither helped nor hindered me in this process; I simply had not known what the hell I was doing. I knew nothing about girls, that was the problem. Desperate to make this moment on top of the Ferris wheel mean something to both of us, I asked, "What did you think of the Bob Dylan story?"

Gently, she withdrew her hand. Peering over the railing,

her eyes somehow illuminated by the bright moon overhead, she replied, "What songs does he sing?"

"Who? Bob Dylan?"

"Yeah. Like what songs of his would I know? On the radio, I mean."

"Gosh, Nicole, I guess I . . . This is *Bob Dylan* we're talking about. You know who Bob Dylan is, don't you?"

"I think so."

"'Like a Rolling Stone'?"

"Oh sure, I know the Rolling Stones."

"No, that's the title of a *song* by Bob Dylan. Totally different sort of thing."

"Hey look, there's Caleb." She pointed down at the pavement: sure enough there he was, leaning against a rail and talking to a group of teenage girls, all of them plucking and chewing on billowing puffs of cotton candy. The Ferris wheel began moving again, at which point Nicole did an unexpected, if also perhaps unintentional, thing: she pressed her thigh against mine. When I looked down I saw that her hand was resting palm up along this very same thigh. It was mine for the taking, this hand. I simply needed to reach for it, and that would be that. Instead I asked, "Can I kiss you?"

The great wheel surged, thrusting us out into the sky and then tugging us to the pavement, where Caleb was still regaling his girls. Nicole's hand stayed right where it was. With a great crunch the wheel came to another stop, this time for us, and just as the cigarette-smoking carny unlocked our safety rail she said, "Maybe."

AT MIDNIGHT THAT SAME EVENING I was standing, blindfolded, in a line that was slowly moving off the bus and across what I took to be the cottage compound. Nicole was in front of me, Shelley in back, and behind her stood Laine. After donning our blindfolds we had all been commanded by Josh to hold hands, so now we walked in staggered single file, giggling and whispering, tickling and copping feels, and forming, to use his term, a "human chain of Christian fellowship." Josh tried to quiet us as he led us into an air-conditioned room, which I understood to be the dining hall, and once we were all assembled he asked us all to sit down on the floor and remove our blindfolds.

We had been arranged into a circle. The lights in the dining hall were out, so it was hard to see who was sitting beside whom. Still, I knew that Nicole was beside me since I had been holding her hand all this time. A couple of coughs escaped into the darkness. After a moment or two a black ghost crawled into the middle of our ring and lit a candle. Eerily, Josh's bearded face appeared out of the gloom, the candle's flickering light casting macabre shadows across his severe facial features. A hush enveloped the room.

In a near whisper he began: "We've been having a wonderful time this weekend, but now we need to turn our thoughts to Jesus."

Nicole Liarkos was clear across the room from me: she was sitting Indian style next to Shelley Broward, who was in full orthodontic headgear, and she was trying unsuccessfully to stifle back a giggle. Was she laughing at the clever way she'd ditched me? When had we been separated? My heart pounded with dread; truly, miracles were afoot.

"Tonight," Josh was saying, "I want to share with you one word. It is the word of our Lord, Jesus Christ." He got comfortable in the middle of our circle, brought his knees to his chest, and continued. "The word I want to share with you guys is *Joy*—the Joy you can receive when you accept Jesus as your personal Lord and Savior. Now what is the meaning of *Joy?* I'll tell you. Joy is three things." He brought his clenched fist to his face and began counting off with his fingers: "Joy is Jesus first, others second, and yourself last. Jesus, others, and yourself. That is what true Joy is.

"Tomorrow we're going to leave this wonderful place. We'll get on that bus and return to our everyday lives. But how many of us are going to go right back to the same old way of living? How many of us are going to act like this week didn't happen? How many of us are going to put our needs in front of those of our loved ones? How many of us are going to forget all about Jesus?"

With the back of his wrist he wiped a dollop of saliva off his beard and paused long enough to let his words sink in. Was Nicole Liarkos listening to this? Did she feel Jesus in that room? Did I? I squinted to catch her expression but she had her head down. I think she was adjusting her sandal straps. Beside her Shelley yawned.

"I think we can all feel Jesus in this room right now," Josh continued. "I can feel him, you can feel him, we can all feel him. Yet how many of us are going to put Jesus first, others second, and ourselves last?"

Several people murmured their assent. Josh nodded, collected his thoughts, and resumed.

"In John 3:16, Jesus tells us that because God so loved the world he gave his only begotten son, Jesus, so that whosoever believes in him shall never perish, but shall have eternal life. He also tells us that there is no way to the Father but through him. There is no middle ground. Either you're with Jesus or you're against him. So now I want to ask each and every one of you some simple questions: Are you prepared to accept Jesus Christ as your personal Lord and Savior? Are you ready to give your life over to him, placing all things in his hands? Are you prepared to choose Eternal Life over Eternal Damnation in the Fires of Hell?"

From out of the darkness, a tiny female voice said, "I'm prepared."

"That's wonderful, Tammy," Josh whispered, and I saw in the murky candlelight his mouth spread into a sinister Cheshire grin. "That's just great. Praise the Lord. Who else?"

No one said a word. Unable to sit still any longer, I stretched out my leg and began to steady my breathing. I felt a slight quiver in my throat, as if there were something down there prompting me to speak.

"Okay," Josh finally said, "some of us are shy. I can understand that. But there's really nothing to be shy about. This is a wonderful thing we're all about to do. If you're ready to accept the Lord, all you have to do is say so. And once you do accept Him, all you have to do is tell five people. That's all: five people. And from that moment on, from that *second* on, you will have Eternal Life. So if you're ready to let Jesus into your life, simply repeat after me: 'I accept.'"

I held my breath. As I sat there in the mounting silence, I thought bitterly about Mark Luthardt, who was abandoning me at the end of the summer. I thought about his adherence to the principles espoused by Ayn Rand and the way these principles stood in direct opposition to the requirements for Christian immortality. According to Mark, three things stood in the way of true egoism, the chief virtue of capitalism: the worship of unreason, the demand for self-sacrifice, and the elevation of society over the individual. These were the virtues that lay at the root of Nazi Germany, he once explained to me, and they were now poised to destroy the very core of America itself. But perhaps Ayn Rand was wrong. Even worse, perhaps Mark Luthardt was wrong. I thought about all the various coincidences on the trip—my meeting Laine, my returned contact lens, my inability to account for Nicole's sudden appearance across the room—and how these things *possibly* pointed to some guiding hand. And I thought about Nicole, who was apparently equating me with the evangelical component of the trip and giving us both a pass. Finally, I thought about the evangelical component of the trip, of which I had suddenly grown very possessive, the same way I sometimes felt about underrated rock bands. I was helpless to explain how I had arrived at this moment, in this circle, with Josh sitting before his candle and so on, but I knew I was there, and I knew, or at least I felt, that it all added up to something.

"I accept," Josh repeated, prompting us along.

Someone said something—a female voice, I couldn't tell whose. The word *I* broke the silence and I felt a renewed surge of conviction. There in the dark, my stomach fluttering, I opened my mouth and the words poured out.

WHEN I GOT BACK HOME I was sullen, secretive, terminally lovesick. Aside from Josh, I had told no one else that I had accepted Jesus Christ as my personal Lord and Savior, so I knew I still had to make my admission of faith to four more people, the burden of which task weighed on me like a cross. I had also made a promise to myself, in the white heat of my new convictions, to burn all my albums as soon as I returned home, a duty I was dreading more than anything else in my life up till then. "That's how you know it's the right thing to do," Josh assured me on the bus, when I told him about my misgivings. "It's time to break free of your enslavement to the secular world and follow Christ. Have faith. Use unreason."

My albums were the first things I saw when I walked into my room and dropped my sleeping bag on the floor. They leapt into the light like beloved friends applauding my return. My beautiful albums! How much time and energy I had spent collecting them all. How rich in memory and association they were. Each one evoked a specific, poignant recollection: I could recite the exact circumstances surrounding the purchase of all ninety-seven separate records, the whole collection forming a private transcription of my long, rich, and now doomed friendship with Mark Luthardt. I began flipping through them, my hands trembling. I suddenly resolved only to burn the ones that seemed especially sinister and secular. I pulled out all the Kiss records, since there was a rumor that the group's name was an acronym for *kids in service to Satan*. I withdrew every record that contained a song with the word *hell* in the title. After about an hour I had some twenty records ready for the match. I gathered them up, tiptoed downstairs to the kitchen, located a box of matches, and walked out into the humid summer night. Tiptoeing across my backyard I entered a cluster of trees that surrounded our property and settled the records on the dirt and struck a match.

I REALLY DID MEAN to burn them all. And to this day I firmly believe I *would* have burned them all had they been in my immediate possession the night of the candlelight vigil. But in the end I only burned the Kiss albums. I had outgrown Kiss, after all. I may have been willing to accept Jesus Christ as my personal Lord and Savior, but there was no way

I could accept a lifetime of listening exclusively to Christian rock.

The next day I went to see Mark Luthardt. I had been dreading this encounter almost as much as the album burning. In a dim way I felt that I had betrayed him that final night; in fact, the whole trip felt like a betrayal of our friendship. He was hunched over the kitchen table reading the stock quotes; the moment he saw me he sat up, repositioned his glasses, and smiled. "You're back. Nice tan."

I did a quick Charles Atlas pose then dropped into my normal chair against the wall. The intercom radio was tuned, as always, to Rock 103. Kansas was playing. We neither hugged nor shook hands; public displays of affection were not part of our intimate vocabulary. He set aside the newspaper and regarded me for a moment. "So, how was it?"

"Not bad," I said.

Apparently satisfied with this answer, Mark immediately began telling me about someone named Lyndon B. LaRouche, a libertarian politician who had recently gone public with some *very* disturbing accusations about the United States government. Mark told me all about LaRouche's newsletter, the *Executive Intelligence Review,* to which he had recently subscribed, and about LaRouche's shocking revelations about the World Trade Organization—really a front for a New World Order government—and the queen of England— actually a CIA operative engaged in the Columbian drug trade. As he relayed all these extraordinary revelations, I sat there trying to decide what to tell him about the trip. Should I tell him that I had found a new way to make friends? That I was sick with love for a girl who would never love me back? That I didn't really give a shit about Lyndon B. LaRouche, whoever he was? That I had outgrown our friendship? Because it was true. More than anything else, that trip to Florida irrevocably changed my attitude about Mark Luthardt. It had torn me from his gravitational pull and given my reluctant heart a chance to leap prematurely into the afterlife, which for me would always be, from that moment on, my life post–Mark Luthardt. Fate, like a skillful pediatrician, had distracted me while inserting her needle, and I realized I was already starting to heal from the wound of his leaving.

When Mark stopped talking about Lyndon B. La Rouche, I cleared my throat and said, "I've accepted Jesus Christ as my personal Lord and Savior." I started to tell him about Bob Dylan and about secular versus sacred music and about how I had promised to tell five people my good news, but instead I waited for Mark's reaction. That would decide how I would proceed.

Luthardt looked at me for an incredulous moment. "What the fuck did you just say?"

"Nothing," I muttered. "Forget it, I was just kidding."

And that was that. Mark and I finished out the summer under a cloud of discomfort, this eleventh-hour awkwardness the only painful side effect of the cure Fate had devised for us. We continued to do all the things we'd always done and said our shy good-byes in August. That September I went back to school a changed person, though changed in what specific way I couldn't decide. I hovered around MYF for another year or so then dropped out when I got to high school. All told, I'd say my conversion to Christianity lasted about as long as Bob Dylan's.

Nicole Liarkos never again returned to MYF. Sometime after my graduation from college I finally got over her. Sort of.

I went to visit Mark a couple of times during high school, and I was pleased to see that he had scored the biggest room in his new house all to himself. As the years rolled on, this cavernous bedroom became a bunker of sorts, the broad hardwood floor supporting massive stacks of Lyndon B. LaRouche's *Executive Intelligence Review* newsletter, which Mark had started stockpiling in anticipation of the impending New World Order. The last time I visited him was just before my freshman year in college, in the summer of 1984, Orwell's year. He continued to drift further and further into the frightening fringes of the far right, reaching a crisis point midway through the Iran-contra hearings of 1987, during which time he experienced a minor breakdown. When he returned from the hospital a month or two later, he formally accepted Jesus Christ as his personal Lord and Savior.

4. NEW WAVE

Sometime around the tenth month of Ronald Reagan's first term in office, and one month prior to becoming a licensed driver, Parker Hayes inaugurated a campaign against everything decent, wholesome, and suburban. This upheaval occurred late in his sophomore year in high school, the same year he tried out for the varsity football team and had his head shaved bald by the starting seniors. He began by hurtling an everlasting "nay" to conformity. His loafers he banished to the back of his closet. His Lacoste golf shirts he sent to Goodwill. Likewise all his lime-green madras and khaki dress slacks. Only the button-down Oxfords remained, largely because his mother caught him, one quiet school night in September, tearing off the sleeves of his newest Polo pinstripe. She seized the ruined shirt and called for his father. There followed not only the threat of grounding but also a lengthy talk about respect for property and the importance of personal hygiene and the poignant and almost existential transience of first impressions, all of which convinced him to hang on to, if not always to wear, the Oxford shirts. But he took this minor setback in stride. As he had learned in history class, successful subversion was, by definition, subtle: to make an angel eat your deviled food, you must first sugar it down. He resolved to wear the enemy's uniform only when behind enemy lines. Otherwise, he would leave the sheep of Middlesburg High School to their own pathetic grazing.

The chief catalysts for all this were a recent expatriate from San Pedro, California, named Mike Alvezados and a new girl from Dayton, Ohio, Tonya Treakle. They brought the gospel of punk to Middlesburg. Or if not punk, then at least new wave. Pioneers the both of them, they bestowed on Parker a set of thrilling and at the same time puzzling possibilities that, a decade or so later, he would still be sifting through. They loomed over him, first as heroes and later as sources of longing and regret; then they shrank and, like him, eventually grew up—where was anyone's guess. They grew up, in various and sundry forms, without him.

Mike descended on Middlesburg amid the heavy heat of late July. The event transpired in a vacuum: no record of his arrival exists. Parker first heard about him late that August, one week before the new school year and two weeks into football two-a-days. The first official report came from

Alison Hartsfield, who had heard something from Charlie McDougal, who had heard something from Jennifer Sweeney, who, generally speaking, could be trusted.

"He lives in your neighborhood," Alison explained to Parker over the phone. "At least that's what Charlie said."

Alison had been in Parker's homeroom the previous year. She was a small, thin, redheaded girl with a light, freckled complexion and hair so thin that when she walked it gently sustained itself on a plane of air. Her chin tapered daintily to a narrow point; her lips were like pale pink strokes of a pastel crayon.

"But did Charlie actually meet him?" Parker was sitting on the laundry room floor, his back against a rumbling washing machine and the twenty-five-foot cord from the kitchen phone threaded between his toes. His body ached all over.

"I don't think so. I think it was Jenny who met him. Anyway, whatever. All I know is he has spiked hair, a safety pin through his nose, and a skateboard. And that's it. That's all I know. I'm just telling you what Charlie told me. And I quote."

An expatriate of New York City, Alison had glamorously divorced parents, the mother an academic and the father an essayist for *The New Yorker*. One weekend a month she visited her father in New York, the details of each trip she would relay to him the following Monday morning in homeroom. Often she brought back cassette tapes of exciting new English rock groups. While their homeroom teacher caught her last postcoffee smoke in the teacher's lounge, Alison would pass him her Walkman and, smiling with embarrassment, place the feather-light headphones over his ears: dissonant, oversaturated guitars would fill his head, the sound reproduction so rich, so full-bodied and three-dimensional that the hair on the back of his neck would stand on end. No one else in Middlesburg even knew this stuff was going on. A paradigm shift in youth culture was taking place overseas, and no one had heard the news yet.

"Okay," Parker reasoned, granting Alison her admittedly hearsay knowledge, "but if he lives in my neighborhood, why haven't I seen him yet?"

"Hey, kid, *I* live in your neighborhood and you haven't seen me all summer."

This was true, it suddenly dawned on him. They were classmates, was how he saw it. Although they regularly called one another about school assignments, phone conversations that sometimes stretched on for an hour or more, Parker had never once thought to seek her physical company outside of class. As for the summer, he had spent most of that either cutting neighborhood lawns or working out in the Middlesburg High School weight room.

"Yeah, well, I've been pretty busy."

"I know, I know: football. You stud you. Which, by the way, brings me to the real reason I called, in case you were wondering, which I doubt you were."

"I thought you called about the punk rock guy." He

wasn't sure how to interpret the "stud" reference. To girls like Alison, the very concept of high-school football was a big, unfunny joke. She rarely, if ever, went to the games; she claimed not to know the first thing about the sport; and the senior members of the football team were sources of wry amusement and little more. The fact that Parker played on the team seemed to disappoint her somehow. Yet did her disappointment in him stem from the simple fact that he went out for the team or from the fact that he went out but did not start? Offhand remarks like the one about his being a stud brought to light these intricate distinctions.

"Yes, but there's an even more urgent matter we need to discuss. You see, there's this little um, tidbit, let's say, currently spinning like mad through the Middlesburg rumor mill. It involves the sophomores on the football team, and since you fall into that category I thought you could maybe give me some firsthand confirmation."

"That depends on the tidbit." Guiltily, he rubbed the peach fuzz on his scalp and held his breath.

"Okay, fine. The tidbit is that every last one of you had your heads shaved bald by the seniors."

"Really?" He stood up in the laundry room and began moving toward the kitchen door. In one week they would meet again in homeroom, she full to bursting with news of her summer in New York and he as bald as Uncle Fester. Yet he was reluctant to admit to his part in the head shaving. He could think of no way to explain why, under no more threat than a supposed thrashing that any senior would have been instantly thrown off the football team for administering, he had lowered his head in obedience, the horse shears snarling in his ears, the seniors all about him shouting and swinging from overhead pipes and pounding the cast-iron lockers like inmates in a prison riot. He couldn't even explain it to himself. Why he had submitted. Why such cowardice had felt, momentarily, like bravery. Why he wanted to play on this team in the first place. "Bald might be putting it a little strong."

"Okay: shaved *very* close."

"Oh, well now you're just splitting hairs."

She was silent for a moment. He expected her to laugh. Instead she said, simply and quietly, "You didn't." It wasn't really a question.

"Didn't what?" He was already in the kitchen, his shaved head rolling against the wall beside the phone cradle. His arm ached with a desire to hang up. Click. End of conversation.

"Oh, Parker, no. I don't believe—"

"You'll find out in a week!" he blurted, his voice an airy bubble. "Listen, seriously, I gotta go, my mom—"

But she hung up before he could finish.

As it happened, Mike Alvezados both lived up to and failed to fulfill his billing. Parker got his first glimpse of the guy on the second day of classes, in the halls of A-Building between fifth and sixth periods: Alvezados was standing im-

pressively against a bank of lockers, his legs out wide, his
hands clasped together at the crotch, and his head lowered
so as to allow the assembled group of cheerleaders and female socialites to touch and feel his hair. He did have, as
Alison had promised, a spiked haircut, yet it was a far cry
from the wet-finger-in-the-light-socket shocker Parker had
been picturing. Alvezados's hair was perfectly coifed and delicately moussed, sitting atop his head as primly as a hum-
mingbird nest. And though safety pins were an integral part
of Mike's basic day-to-day wardrobe, these pins pierced not
his nose but rather the Polo icon on all of his button-down
pinstripe shirts, which he wore untucked. Mike also wore
faded Levi's 501 button-fly jeans—the first such pair Parker
had ever seen: his own jeans still sported zippers—and
checkerboard sneakers that looked more like bedroom slip-
pers than athletic wear, jaunty, flat-footed shoes that gave
Alvezados a lithe, low-heeled grace. One more incongruous
thing: Mike Alvezados was almost preternaturally good-
looking, with perfect teeth and Robert Redford jowls. Far
from looking disaffected and *nihilistic* (a new word Parker
had picked up from Greil Marcus in *Rolling Stone*), Mike
Alvezados looked regally and untouchably *cool*.

Parker encountered Tonya Treakle later that same day in
chemistry class.

"Your head is shaved" was the first thing she said to him.
Not a conventionally pretty girl—not at least by Middlesburg standards, which Parker had already rejected—Tonya

was nevertheless striking in her own way, with short, boyish brown hair, green-gumdrop eyes, and pouty lips that, even compressed, betrayed a slight, if also very cute, overbite. Like the dancing girl in *Flashdance,* which had been all the rage last year, she wore leggings and, around her forehead, a tightly wound turquoise bandanna. Though Parker couldn't exactly pinpoint why, he suspected she was growing out her hair. The rest of her outfit consisted of blue jeans (new) and an elaborate Edwardian shirt with billowy sleeves and a ruffled wreath around the neck. Her small body lay buried beneath the shirt, evading his appraisal.

"That's true," Parker whispered back, for class had begun, with lugubrious Mr. Behn in his soiled white laboratory jacket swaying from foot to foot in front of the classroom, his gaze directed at the ceiling, his lecture directed at everyone and no one.

"But why?"

"Why what?"

"Why is your head shaved?"

A tricky question. If Parker told her he had had his head shaved by the seniors on the football team, he became a blind camp follower who, at the very least, played football. If he told her he had chosen to shave his head, he'd be a liar. By now she would have registered that twenty-two other male students from the sophomore class had the same haircut.

When it became clear to her that he wasn't going to answer, she gently touched his arm and whispered, "I only asked because I was thinking of doing the same thing my-self." Nothing in her tone suggested she was kidding.

"BUT YOUR *curls*," Alison cried. "They robbed you of your curls!" Delicately, she stroked his scalp and gener-ated a pretty convincing look of dismay. "One minute they're there, next minute, *poof.*"

"Alison, stop it, I—"

"And lookee here, a little scar, right above your ear. And a lump, up here at the top. Did you know you have a lump on your head? I'm a bit rusty on my phrenology, but offhand I'd say you're marked for a life of criminal wrongdoing, perhaps a bloody career as a violent, unregenerate sociopath, maybe a Republican, I don't know."

"The teacher's looking, Alison, seriously, just—"

"Oh, and, gosh, what's that, are you *peeling?* Is that flaky skin I'm seeing?"

"Yes, now stop, I had to cut my lawn yesterday—"

"And no hair to protect your poor little head."

"Enough," he hissed, batting her hand away. "I get your drift."

"Touchy, touchy." At the front of the class blue-haired Mrs. Archer scratched ungrammatical sentences on the board, the chalk tapping away with the regularity of an old clock. All around the room classmates passed notes and coughed obscenities into their fists.

Alison picked up a ballpoint pen and began copying Mrs.

Archer's sentences into her spiral notebook. "So," she said, without looking up, "have you seen him yet?"

"Who?"

"The Sid Vicious of Middlesburg."

Parker smiled, and picked up his pen. "Yes, though he didn't seem too vicious to me."

"I thought he was yummy."

His pen jerked across his page, leaving a little slash in the paper. *"Yummy?"*

"He's *gorgeous,"* she purred, still scribbling away. "Everyone thinks so. All the girls are just tingling all over. It's kind of sickening, actually."

"Did you really just say *yummy?"*

"In my tummy." Then she rubbed the flat, anatomical organ in question.

His cheeks tingled. "That *is* sickening."

"Parker Hayes!" Mrs. Archer called from the front of the room. Parker looked up, still blushing, as every face in the classroom turned his way. Snickers, giggles. The only face not directed at him was Alison's. She, and only she, was conscientiously copying sentences from the board.

"Yes ma'am?"

"Have you corrected sentence 4?" Mrs. Archer hooked a gnarled hand on her broad hip. She scowled at him over her black reading glasses.

"Um, no ma'am, I was just—"

Beside him Alison's hand shot up.

"Yes, Ms. Hartsfield?"

"The participle's dangling, ma'am. You've got a dangling participle there, right after 'boy.' "

"That is correct," Mrs. Archer said, and tapped the board emphatically with her chalk. "Do you see it, Mr. Hayes? Do you see what Ms. Hartsfield's talking about?"

"He'll see it, Mrs. Archer," Alison said, lowering her hand. "I'll make sure he sees it."

FOR THE NEXT TWO WEEKS, Parker shamelessly pursued both Tonya Treakle and Mike Alvezados.

Surprisingly, Tonya was the easier catch of the two. Since she sat beside him in chemistry, he could pursue her covertly. After all, she was right there, every day. Even better, he was forced to confine his pursuit to the passing of surreptitious notes, his preferred means of intergender exchange, anyway. Parker and Tonya revealed their feelings through an elaborate code comprising obscure rock bands. *What do you think of the So-and-Sos?* Parker would write, and slide the note across the table, past the rusted sink and the two-pronged gas valve that separated them. *They were good before they sold out,* she'd reply, and slide the wafer of notepaper back his way. His heart would thunder inside his chest as he read these discriminating judgments. *Yes,* he would agree, *but their last album had its moments,* and back it would go. The simple phrase *They've got a great album of b-sides* would open up before him a vast expanse of ripe potential, while the line *I heard they broke up* never ceased to make his heart skip a beat. Her list of last year's five best albums by English rock bands contradicted his by only two entries.

"I like your hair," she told him one day before class started. When she spoke she stared directly at him, her smooth face utterly free of guile, like a child watching a magic show. "It makes your head look small."

"Well," he decided to admit, "it wasn't really my choice."

"So what?" She touched his scalp. "Nothing's our choice."

He resisted the temptation to rear back from her touch. It was hard to look at her, so intense was her gaze. "You believe that?"

"No," she shrugged. "I don't believe anything."

She never dressed the same way twice. Some days she showed up in standard preppy regalia—wool skirt, white stockings, loafers. Other days she wore jeans and a black T-shirt commemorating some concert or other that Parker, invariably, would have given his left arm to have attended. She was equally at home in black leggings and ripped jeans, camouflage army fatigues and floral peasant dresses.

No one else in the class, let alone in the school, seemed to have noticed her. Alison, who had chemistry third period to his fourth, never uttered a single word about Tonya Treakle. Neither did anyone else. She was invisible to the greater population of Middlesburg High School, a ghostly figment of Parker's confused desire. This suited him just fine. Like those rock bands he and Tonya wrote about in chemistry class, she was his own little secret, a private discovery that mainstream popularity would ruin.

Mike Alvezados was another matter. Apparently he had already been pegged as Noncollege Material, so he and Parker didn't share any classes. They did have the same lunch period, though. Parker made this discovery on day 5. He was standing in line with his tray, gazing with diminishing appetite at a tub of hamburger patties floating in an oil-slicked pond of water, when he felt a bump on his shoulder.

"Someone told me you saw the Clash last year."

And there he was! Mike Alvezados, in the flesh! Same untucked Polo, same carefully affixed safety pin, same pincushion of hair. Parker cleared his throat and blinked. "Where'd you hear that?"

"I don't know. From someone."

"Have you seen them?"

"Yeah," Alvezados said, pushing his tray along the chrome runner with his fingertips, "way long time ago, before they sucked."

Parker laughed in disbelief. "The Clash don't suck."

"They do now."

"You're serious?"

"Way serious," he said, bumping Parker's tray. Unlike Tonya Treakle, Mike Alvezados stared at some vague spot over your shoulder when he spoke to you.

"Well," Parker continued, "they didn't suck when I saw them. Far from it. Best concert I've ever seen, bar none. It was like"—he hesitated here, trying to remember a line he'd read recently in *Trouser Press* magazine—"like kissing a locomotive head-on."

Mike nodded and withdrew from the counter his plastic plate of wet hamburger and pasty fries. Parker now found himself standing at the cash register bearing an empty tray. "That's why they're called the Clash," Alvezados replied.

Parker's heart plummeted: that was the next line in the *Trouser Press* article. The worst of it was, the concert *did* suck. The Clash were sloppy and uninspired, the sound was muddy and smothered in echo, and Parker had spent most of the evening trying to stand his ground against an army of angry bald-headed slam dancers who had picked him out as the night's designated suburban weenie. "So they say," Parker concluded, and without another word he withdrew his empty tray and slid it ceremoniously under his arm.

PARKER WAS NOT ONLY mesmerized by Mike Alvezados; he also saw in Mike a way out of a pressing dilemma. The year before—his freshman year—Parker had inaugurated a campaign to become popular. Numerous factors contributed to its failure. First and foremost was the unpleasant fact that he had come to Middlesburg High not from the sibling middle school but from Pine View Elementary (K–8), which fact necessarily diminished his standing amid the Middlesburg demimonde. To an outsider, Middlesburg must have seemed like one big suburb. To the locals, subtle yet crucial distinctions characterized each discrete subdivision. Rolling Hills was "tonier" than Rolling Valley, while Pine View, though respectable to be sure, didn't quite have the "history" of, say, Fox Trot Estates. The kids who went to Middlesburg Middle School lived in older, historic subdivisions—specifically all those sections of town built before the McDonald's and the Kroger—while the kids from Pine View Elementary, kids like Parker, all hailed from the outlying suburb of the same name, the same suburb that housed both the McDonald's and the Kroger.

Then there was Parker's devotion to his studies, which he couldn't bring himself to shake. Not to mention his inability to ingratiate himself with the three most glamorous males of the freshman class, Bruce Boxton, Adam "Alice" Cooper, and Mark "the Mooch" Munser, charmless jocks all three and the arbiters of all that was desirable to Middlesburg freshman girls. By way of a sense of humor they made lame jokes about penis size, and instead of conversing, they insulted one another. They were basically interchangeable— jeans, button-downs, feathered bangs, with a lumbering gorilla roll to their walk that Parker, a good ten pounds lighter than "Alice" Cooper, the lightest of the three, couldn't quite master. Each day after lunch Mooch and Co. would convene in A-Lobby and lean against the trophy case in their freshman football jackets, insulting girls and drawing abuse, sometimes physical in nature, from the seniors. Parker couldn't even *buy* abuse. The seniors had all played football with

Parker's older brother, Scott, and thus respected Parker by proxy. And Mooch and Co. took their cues from the seniors. As for girls who paraded through A-Lobby, the only response he got from them was stern disapproval. Finally, his repertoire of penis jokes was, even he had to admit, inadequate. So he turned his envy into contempt and left A-Lobby for good.

He needed to establish himself as something other than Scott's little brother. He not only loathed Scott's legacy—star jock—but also knew, deep down, he'd never live up to it. Barring the star jock identity, however, he had nothing, so he carried within himself a wounded conviction that he was misunderstood by everyone. Certainly he did not understand himself. He could never decide which he hated more, surrendering his perceived uniqueness to the anonymous flow or being shut out of the anonymous flow. It seemed an insoluble dilemma.

Then Mike Alvezados showed up, whereupon Parker realized that he could both remain in the flow and keep outside it, all at the same time. He simply needed to become a punk rock jock, the only such person in all of Middlesburg High.

Which is not to suggest that Parker was some sort of punk-rock-come-lately. He had been hipped on punk as early as 1979, around which time Scott started bringing home cheap-looking records by groups like the Jags and the Sinceros and the Vapors. All these groups had names that began with "*the.*" The *the* was crucial. It made all the difference in the world. Parker would sneak into his brother's room and listen to these exciting, adrenaline-packed records, the same way, only two or three years before, he had secretly listened to all of Scott's progressive rock LPs, most of which came housed in elaborate trifold record sleeves with acrylic paintings of floating mushrooms and armadillo tanks. These groups composed album-length pieces scored for rock trio, designated drum solos "percussion movements," and wrote lyrics inspired by J. R. R. Tolkien and Robert A. Heinlein, both of whom Parker had begun reading. Around 1979, however, Parker learned—or perhaps Scott had told him— that such music was not only passé but, worst of all, *pretentious*. When he looked up *pretentious* in the dictionary, he couldn't decide which of the two definitions applied to progressive rock. The first definition read, "Claiming or demanding a position of distinction or merit, esp. when unjustified." The second, less oblique, definition read, "Making an extravagant outward show; ostentatious." All of this was presumably bad. The more Parker listened to the Buzzcocks and Jules and the Polar Bears and the Dickies, however, the better he understood why pretentiousness was bad. Overnight he came up with a whole new criterion for musical quality. Whereas in sixth grade he had stood in the Pine View Elementary School bathroom explaining to his classmates that Emerson, Lake & Palmer, who were classically trained, were far superior to Kiss, who couldn't play or sing and therefore sucked, in 1979 he found himself articulating why the Ramones, who couldn't play or sing, were far superior to Genesis and Rush, who were classically trained and therefore sucked. Sometimes the distinction was too fine even for him to explain. Sometimes, truth be told, he did not altogether understand it himself. But he knew what he knew.

So he was already familiar with the records. He knew them by heart. It was not until Mike Alvezados, however, that Parker realized he could take the next step and actually *be* a punk. In Middlesburg of all things. The thought had never occurred to him. Not once. Punks lived in London or New York or L.A. They made punk rock records. And if it had never occurred to Parker in the sixth grade to go to school wearing a sparkling black bodysuit with silver shoulder panels, why would he ever consider going to high school wearing a polka-dot shirt and a laminated checkerboard tie?

Mike Alvezados changed all that. He made Parker understand that punk was an attitude, an identity. The whole punk rock ethos, Mike explained, hinged on nonconformity at all costs. Conformity was nonpunk; nonconformity was punk. All punks agreed on this basic principle. They were unanimous in their hatred of conformity. They were an army, tall and strong, unified by nonconformity.

"Like the Top Forty," Mike theorized one Saturday afternoon early that school year, while performing roundhouses on his skateboard. "That's *way* conformist. I want the Top

Forty destroyed, done away with. Period. And these lame-ass preppies in their Top-Siders and khaki pants—I say kill them all. I'd rather die than dress like that, you know what I mean? I would rather *die!*"

Parker's blood boiled at the possibilities. This was, after all, 1981, the same year in which America's most popular teen icon was Alex Keaton, the archconservative adolescent overachiever who, each week on *Family Ties,* lambasted his parents' hippie pieties. This was a year in which the most popular rock group among high school students was REO Speedwagon. Nothing had happened yet, not MTV, not Iran-contra, not even *Rambo.* The entire country—the entire *world,* it seemed—was asleep. No one wanted anything to happen. Conformity was a sitting duck. A shaved head was already half the battle.

"So," ALISON SAID to him one day in English, "word's out that you've become bosom buddies with Sexy Sid."

Mrs. Archer, forlorn at the front of the room, was dispirit-edly outlining the basic structure of the *Beowulf* verse form. Adam "Alice" Cooper, sprawled mouth open to Parker's left, swung his hanging arms back and forth so that his knuckles scraped the floor. In the back of the room a bubble-gum bubble loudly popped.

"So it's Sexy Sid now? Quite the vamp we've become."

"Yes, well. There's lots about me you don't know." Alison abruptly shot her hand up in the air. "Mrs. Archer," she called out, "could you explain the split in the middle of each line again? I got lost there for a moment."

"Certainly, Ms. Hartsfield," Mrs. Archer beamed. "I understand your confusion. Nowadays we have such a different view of poetry, don't we?"

"Yes ma'am," Alison smiled, and took her hand down. Once Mrs. Archer was safely under way again, she whispered, "I can't believe you haven't introduced me yet."

"To who? Mike Alvezados?"

"Duh," Alison replied.

"But I didn't know—"

"Of course you didn't, Parker. What with me being so *secretive* about it." Up shot her hand again. "Mrs. Archer, what happens when they translate it into modern English?"

"Well, Alison, that's an excellent question. Now, if you look here, at your textbook . . ."

"Okay," Parker whispered after a moment, "I get your drift."

"You do."

"Next chance I get, I'll mention you."

"No. Not that. Don't just 'mention' me. That'll seem too obvious, like you're pimping or something. I'll come up to you at lunch when you're talking to him. Tomorrow. I'll come up to you tomorrow. Just be ready."

"You've planned this, haven't you?"

"Be prepared, kid. Boy Scout motto."

Parker allowed himself a brief smile, though, in truth, he

didn't think much would come of a meeting between Alison Hartsfield and Mike Alvezados. They just didn't match up. Despite Mike's staunch nonconformity, he had eyes only for the school beauties—the cheerleaders, the doctors' daughters, the sorority presidents. And they, like English aristocrats on safari, had eyes for him. Mike Alvezados was in a position to bag big game, that much was clear. Parker just couldn't see him squandering such a golden opportunity for the sake of a quaint butterfly like Alison Hartsfield, rare specimen though she was. After all, as even Mike Alvezados might admit, nonconformity had its limits.

AND THEN SOMETHING HAPPENED. One Friday night about two months into the new school year, with no warning, Tonya Treakle dropped by his house. Parker was at the fieldhouse at the time, climbing with numb indifference into his game uniform, a ridiculous carapace of fiberglass and foam rubber that, thanks to his third-string status, would remain essentially unsoiled for the duration of his sophomore season. So he didn't hear about Tonya's visit until he got home later that night, well after eleven.

"Who is this 'friend' of yours?" his mother asked the moment he walked into the kitchen. As usual, the Wolverines had won, a conclusion that was foregone as early as the second quarter. Parker had spent most of the game gnawing on his mouthpiece in a blind double panic: first, he worried that, with such a sizable lead, he would actually have to play a few downs; second, he feared that, as usual, he would get left behind as his teammates roared away from the fieldhouse en route to the postgame party circuit. Given as he was to solitude and studying, he had few genuine friends on the football team; even worse, he was still several months away from receiving his driver's license. Things did and did not turn out. Although he didn't have to play, he nevertheless ended up driving around the parking lot of the local McDonald's with an acne-ridden third-string safety named Stuart Bledsoe, whose chief concern was offering rides to stranded freshman girls.

"I have no idea what you're talking about," Parker told his mother, which was true enough.

"This is all part of that music you listen to, isn't it?"

"*Who*, mother? *Who* are you talking about?"

"Tamara, Tricia, something like that. I can't remember. I opened the door and took one look at that child and my mind just went blank. Then I thought, 'Her poor parents.'"

"It was a *girl?*"

"She told me her name but I can't place it. Lord have mercy. Leonard," she called into the living room, "your son is home."

How Tonya had found his house was the first mystery. Perhaps she had consulted the phone book. Or maybe she had just asked around. The second mystery involved her coming by on a Friday night. Obviously she hadn't caught onto Middlesburg social patterns yet—everyone at school went to the football games—but did she genuinely not know that Parker was on the team?

"Good game," his father declared from the doorway. He shuffled by in his socks, his comb-over in a sad state of collapse. "For a minute there, I thought you'd get some playing time."

Ignoring him—standard behavior that year; Parker's shame at failing to earn a starting position on the football team made him shy around his father—Parker turned back to his mother. "It's *Tonya*, Mom. Her name is Tonya Treakle and she's in my chemistry class. She just moved here from Dayton."

"Really?" His father smiled as he took this in. "Who woulda thought? *Dayton*."

"I just never saw anything like it," his mother was saying with genuine wonder in her voice. "She had on this, I don't know, how would you describe it, Len?"

"I would describe it as a red minidress with holes in it," he said, and walked back into the living room wielding a big spoon and an open carton of orange sherbet.

"And these fishnet stockings," Parker's mother continued, "with heels like you've never seen before in your *life*. And she had on these elbow gloves with the fingertips missing and her hair was standing straight up like a"—she cast about for a suitable metaphor—"well, I don't know, like a bad haircut is what *I* think—*Leonard* come back here!"

"I can hear you fine from here, Brenda."

She scowled into the empty doorframe and turned back to

Parker wearing a look of benign, parental concern. "Now listen to me, honey. I'm sure this is all just some, I don't know, some sort of *phase* I guess is what they call it nowadays, but sweetie, you really have to be careful who you're seen with. You may not want to believe this but the company you keep is a reflection of—"

"I'm going to bed." Parker seized his duffel bag and brushed past her.

"You come back here, young man," his mother called, though by now Parker was nearly to the other side of the living room, his father's eyes following him like the scope on a sniper's rifle.

"Parker!" His father's stocking feet gave off a sad, attic smell. The carton of sherbet rested precariously on the dome of his stomach. "Don't you turn your back on your mother when she's talking to you."

Parker dropped his duffel bag and held up his hands. "What? What do you want from me? I didn't *do* anything? I wasn't even *here,* for Chrissakes!"

"Honey," his mother said quietly from the kitchen door. After a brief pause—long enough for Parker to cross his arms and tap his foot once, for effect—she appealed to Parker's father. "Explain it to him, Len."

His father's eyes remained fixed on the television, where a *Mannix* rerun clamored away. When the last car bounced to its fiery demise, he chuckled and said, "The kooky kid was wearing a dog collar, son. A goddamn *dog collar.*" Then he shook his head and rammed his spoon into the sherbet.

His mother nodded in agreement and folded her arms. "You see? Do you understand what we're trying to tell you, honey?"

Still on the other side of the room, Parker picked up his duffel bag and glanced quickly at both his parents. "Not even remotely."

SHE LIVED WITH HER FATHER and an eighteen-year-old brother named Greg, neither of whom Parker ever met. Mr. Treakle was a chemical engineer with particular expertise in the field of agricultural insecticides. Greg was primarily an absentee. No one kept tabs on his comings and goings, his move to Middlesburg being little more than a formality, as he spent most of his time back in Dayton, shacking up with friends and sustaining himself on a hefty all-cash salary whose source was never divulged. Mrs. Treakle, meanwhile, was languishing at the Payne Whitney mental hospital in New York.

"What else do you want to know?" Tonya asked him in a flat noncommittal tone from the driver's seat of her father's Chrysler LeBaron. "There's plenty more if you want to hear it. I could write a book about us. It'd be an instant bestseller. I could tell you about my mom and her Valium habit and my father's affairs and my brother's outside business interests, and you know what? Some of it would be true. Most of it, even. Or maybe none of it. What do you think? You think I'm telling the truth?"

They were driving around together, just the two of them,

on an orange Saturday in October, the day after Tonya's unforgettable appearance on the Hayes's front porch. She had
called ahead this time, which allowed Parker to plan ahead.
To avoid any more difficulty with his parents, he suggested
she pick him up at the top of his street, to which plan she
agreed, wheeling up at exactly twelve-thirty sharp, her hair
freshly washed and blow-dried, her outfit a kind of warped
appropriation of Middle-Aged Husband at the Bar-B-Que:
Mickey Mouse T-shirt, baggy gold madras shorts, black
socks, and a brand-new pair of white deck sneakers.

"I guess so," he replied. "Why? Aren't you?"

"Maybe I am, maybe I'm not. The thing is—oh look—"
She pointed out the window to a Salvation Army store and
proclaimed, "Jackpot." She brought the car to a stop in the
left-hand turn lane and glanced at him, at his clothes and his
Nikes and his haircut (in that order). "It's time you learned
how to dress. Just sit back and let me do my stuff."

With gratitude, he obeyed. From an enormous Mayflower
box of mateless shoes she put together a pair of size 9½
Converse All-Stars, one black and one red. She picked out a
pair of striped polyester flares and some nearly new black
parachute pants patchworked with zippers and buckles and
hooks. Rummaging through the shirts they found an old
blue bowling jersey with CHIEFTANS stenciled on the back in
sweeping major league baseball script. It was Parker, however, who spotted the day's winner: a vintage olive-drab
army parka with all its pockets and zippers perfectly intact,

a bonafide English mod icon exactly like the one worn by the
male model on the front cover of the Who's *Quadrophenia*
album, an older, prepunk record lately given new life by the
mod revival that was sweeping England that year *(England!
England! England!)*.

Afterward Tonya drove him back to her house, which
was empty. They walked past the front foyer (cold speckled
marble) and the hallway (bare walls, track lighting) and
directly to Tonya's bedroom. She settled down on the bed,
an ashtray resting at the apex of her crossed shins, and
watched as he emerged with sardonic self-conscious pomp
from her adjoining bathroom in all his new finery. She applauded or booed each new appearance, Parker bowing or
shrugging in kind. After about twenty minutes of this sort of
thing he finally stepped from the bathroom in the appalling
flares. Instantly Tonya squirmed to her knees and waved him
over.

"Turn around," she murmured, a cigarette clamped between her lips, her eyes squinting against the smoke. After a
tense moment, he felt her fingers slide into his back pocket.
He jumped away as if electrocuted.

"Whoa, cowboy," she chuckled as he whirled around.
"I'm just checking the fit."

His cheeks flushed. He didn't know how to answer, how
to cover his embarrassment. He finally said, "These are so
stupid." Outside the sun streamed through the drawn blinds
in mild rebuke: the day was slipping by without him. As a

little boy he had loved Saturdays, with their steady march of morning cartoons, their formless days at the creek, their long solitary evenings in front of the television or in bed with a book and the stereo headphones. Lately, however, the wide-open aimlessness of Saturday afternoons had begun filling him with dread. Saturdays now seemed like a waste. In the middle of a random Saturday—like this Saturday, for instance—he was apt to feel he should be elsewhere, doing something clean and suburban. The cigarette smoke made his stomach turn, while Tonya's strange stranglehold on the day made him edgy. He had never before been in an empty house with a girl his own age. "I mean," he added, steadying his voice, "no one would ever wear these right now, period."

"I know, I know, that's why they're so great." She resumed her cross-legged position on the bed and fixed her gaze on him. "God, you've never really done *any*thing, have you?"

"What do you mean?"

"You know. Anything."

He walked back into her bathroom and closed the door, his hands trembling on the knob.

"I mean, your *house*," she called from the bedroom. "It was totally like, I don't know, *Leave It to Beaver* or something, Ma and Pa Kettle and all. You should have seen your parents when they opened the door, really just your mom, she was the one who answered it—anyway, she was like, I don't know, she looked at me and her eyes went—"

"Yeah," he said, stepping back into the bedroom in his normal clothes, "she told me about it."

"Seriously, you'd think I had come to murder her baby. Her face I mean, the way her face looked. You could tell she'd never seen anything like me before, not here at least, not in this crummy place. I mean what a fucking hole, I totally can't believe I live here, you know? Middlesburg, Tennessee." She scrunched her nose, took a drag on her cigarette and tried again, this time in an exaggerated Southern drawl: "Yessir, Billy Bob, I live in Muddlesburg, Tennessee, U.S. of A."

"It sucks all right," Parker agreed, warily sitting down beside her on the bed, his stomach aswarm with butterflies. His poor innocent parents: he felt he should defend them.

"You want to know a secret?" she suddenly asked.

"Sure."

"I can't have children."

Parker blinked twice and swallowed. "Really?"

"Really. It's my great tragedy, or at least it is for my mother, she made a big deal about it when we came back from the doctor—here, put this record on, side 1. No, wait, just press the reject button, right there, see it? It does it automatically. There you go. But honestly I didn't care one way or another because—and here's the thing—I think, or at least I'm pretty sure, I'm a lesbian."

The needle skipped across the first track and stopped dead at an explosion of drums and guitars.

"Hey," she cried, crawling on all fours across the bed to stare down at him as he sat crouched before the stereo. The neck of her giant Mickey Mouse shirt yawned open to reveal what Parker had suspected all afternoon: she wasn't wearing a bra. "That's an import, you know."

"Sorry." Nervously, he scrambled to his feet.

She rocked back into a sitting position, caught the ashtray as it slid into her crossed shins, and took up the cigarette, all in one swift motion. "But like I say, I don't really know yet. It's one of those things it's always hard to say for sure, you know, particularly with the move and the uh—"

"Look, I really think I should be getting home, I never told my parents where—"

"It's only four o'clock," she said, checking her watch. Then she presented him the exact same smile an adult gives a child who has just confessed to wetting his bed. "I'm totally freaking you out."

"No no, I mean, I just, you know, I didn't—"

"I'm only *kid*ding, Parker."

At the edge of this embarrassing impasse the record played on in tightfisted machine-gun accompaniment. Why was he getting all of this wrong? Why didn't he know how to respond? Why couldn't he *get the joke?* When he looked at her again he was relieved to see that she seemed as confused as he was.

"I don't want you to leave yet," she said simply, her voice registering a tone he just now realized he had not heard her use all day: sincerity.

"I know, I know, it's not like I *want* to leave or anything. I mean, I'm not running out on you. I just think—"

"No," she said, "I'm scaring you off."

"You're not. Honest." He sat down beside her again and thought hard. But his mind yielded nothing appropriate. "It really doesn't freak me out if you're a lesbian," he finally said, his tongue lolling over that last word.

Silence. The next song kicked in on the record and Tonya scooped up her cigarettes and stood up and said, "Wrong answer, bucko. Now get your shit and let's take off."

ALTHOUGH MIKE ALVEZADOS, like a good many Middlesburg females, eventually learned to eschew the school's processed lunch offerings, he did not eschew lunch period itself. Lunch period opened him up, made him garrulous and ready for contact. Soon he began to rely on Parker's lunchtime company. With his shaved head and his new Tonya-approved wardrobe—the weather had turned just cold enough to warrant unveiling the new mod army parka—Parker was now cutting a rather punkish figure. He made a suitable complement to Mike Alvezados's particular brand of upscale new wave: Mike's checkerboard Vans to Parker's mismatched Converse All-Stars, Mike's safety-pinned Polos to Parker's downscale bowling jersey. True, Parker had heard more than one snide reference to Mike Alvezados's influence on his, Parker's, sudden change in appearance, but Parker shook off these small-minded criticisms, secure as he was in their inaccuracy. Mike had had nothing to do with influencing Parker's new look. That honor belonged to Tonya Treakle, who never showed up for lunch, anyway. Not once had Parker even run into Tonya outside of chemistry class. She was to him like a teacher is to a pupil, wholly confined to the classroom in which he encountered her, so he was free to move through the clamorous lunchtime crowd of Middlesburg High with proud impunity, his feet in their canvas sneakers bouncing happily along the speckled cream tile, his olive-drab army parka—on the back of which he had recently spray-painted, in white, THE JAM—swinging behind him like a superhero's cape.

Everyone knew Mike. Everyone was fascinated with him. And his claims to nonconformity notwithstanding, he knew everyone, too. Though a good four inches shorter than Parker, even counting the spiked haircut, Mike still led the way on these lunchtime social calls, which took him and Parker from one end of the giant cafeteria to the other, Mike passing out good-humored abuse ("Look at that shirt, Cooper. You look like a church youth counselor") and Parker adding supportive laughter. When the girls reached up to touch Mike's hair, he reared back as stiff as a Disney World animatron. When they reached up to touch Parker's hair, they usually did so in order to remove a piece of lint that had got caught in his peach fuzz. No matter. Parker felt part of something for the first time in his experience at Middlesburg. He and Mike were now their own subculture. The year was turning out better than Parker could have hoped.

"You two are such social butterflies," Alison declared one day, not without some distaste.

For Alison, too, had become something of a lunchtime fixture, about which Parker had mixed feelings. Alison's normal crowd consisted of homely, strange girls who took art classes and edited with great care and mincing authority the school's creative-writing "magazine," a mimeographed pamphlet called *Crossroads*. Alison's crowd sat hunched in the corner of the cafeteria nibbling like timid squirrels on triangular cucumber sandwiches. Alison's crowd made allowances for such sad disfigurations as harelips, eyeglasses, and orthodontic headgear. Yet ever since that day several weeks ago, when Alison, right on cue, sidled up to Parker and asked him about an English assignment and Parker, also on cue, turned and introduced her to Mike Alvezados, who responded with a preoccupied, noncommittal nod, Alison had made it a daily habit to disengage herself from her normal crowd and follow the two boys on at least one or two of their daily cafeteria rounds. Mike rarely acknowledged her sudden presence beside them and never commented on it afterward. Still, he seemed not to mind her all that much, and after this pattern had played itself out for a few days he even began asking her questions, usually about girls Alison deeply loathed.

"We're no such thing," Parker told her. "We're just walking around to avoid eating the slop they serve us."

"You used to eat this slop without complaining," she said.

"I used to do a lot of things without complaining."

"Alison, hey." Mike was standing off to the side in his usual position: legs spread apart like a soldier at-ease, right hand on left wrist, Vans rocking back and forth on the lime green tile. "That girl over there, in the red sweater, who's she sleeping with?"

Mike had long ago explained that, in his old school in San Pedro, California, "sleeping with" was standard argot for "going with." This was only one of a number of Pedro-isms he had brought with him to Middlesburg. To wipe out on a skateboard was to "Wilson-It," this in honor of Corey Wilson, a famous, and now paralyzed, California skateboarder from several years back whose final wipeout had transformed his name into a verb. By way of a deft functional shift, the noun *way* became an all-purpose intensifier suitable for any occasion ("She's way hot," "That test was way hard," "I'm way, way wasted"). *Skank* referred to what one "got" when one secured sexual intercourse with a "bim" (i.e., girl). Not that Parker explained any of this to Alison.

"You can't mean Debbie Denton," Alison sneered, but of course that was exactly who Mike meant. "That girl has the brains of a gnat."

"Exactly," Mike smiled. "Who's she sleeping with?"

"Depends on what day of the week, Mike."

"Hey," Parker interrupted, "did you guys hear about the theme for the homecoming dance?"

"I heard," Alison said.

Mike said nothing, so intent was he on Debbie Denton,

who, at the moment, was winding a pink strand of chewing gum around her manicured finger.

"New wave!" Parker proclaimed, though already he felt the news was falling flat. "That's the theme, if you can believe that. New wave. Like it's just a, you know, some sort of movie or something."

"The Breaks are playing," Alison added helpfully, now playing along. Both of them, Parker realized, were appealing to Mike Alvezados, who still had not acknowledged a word of their conversation. "I heard they're pretty good."

"Shitty cover band," Mike finally said, and turned around. "A total joke. I saw them last week at the Satellite. It's like Top Forty new wave. All of them are middle-aged geeks with bad haircuts. One has a mustache. We heckled them way bad, threw ice at the drummer, spit on the stage. Pathetic."

"You went to the Satellite?" Parker's heart lurched within him. The Satellite was the city's only official new wave club, a twenty-one-and-over joint downtown to which Parker had never even dreamed of going.

"Yeah, sure." Mike stood up on his tiptoes and scanned the room for other people to talk to.

"How'd you get in?" Alison wanted to know.

"Through the door, doofus."

Parker shoved his hands into the pockets of his army parka. He did not want to be seen allying here with Alison, yet he, too, wanted to know how Mike had gotten into the Satellite. He wanted to know how Mike, also fifteen years old, had secured a ride downtown, and he wanted to know who Mike had gone to the Satellite with. Instead he asked, "That must have been a pretty slow night at the Satellite if those losers were playing."

"It was all right," Mike shrugged. "They were just the opener. We stayed around till closing."

Again that *we*. People brushed by them en route to the cafeteria line, while overhead the first warning bell rang. Class in five minutes. Parker looked at Alison, who looked at Mike, who looked across the cafeteria at Debbie Denton sashaying out the main entrance and up the steps to A-Lobby.

"Who'd you go with?" Parker asked.

"Some chick, Tonya something, you don't know her." Without another word he clucked his tongue and scampered away, out the cafeteria entrance and up those stairs, in pursuit of Debbie Denton and her gnat-sized brain.

"Well," Alison finally sighed. Neither of them had moved. Any minute now the second bell was going to ring, which meant they were both going to be late for English. After a moment, she resumed. "I know the girl he's talking about. Tonya Treakle. She's in my econ class. A complete slut. I can totally picture her taking him to the Satellite. She sits in class every day writing stupid little love notes and passing them back and forth to these idiotic jocks in the back of the room, all of whom think she's this neurotic basket case or something, which is probably true enough, though I wouldn't put it past any of them to bed her down just for the fun of it. Oh, and it doesn't hurt matters that she never wears a bra. If you ask me, that girl—"

Fortunately, second bell cut her off.

FOUR O'CLOCK, HOMECOMING DAY. Parker, locked in his bedroom, was shoving his evening's outfit into a duffel bag and bopping his head in time to Elvis Costello and the Attractions. For his appearance at the New Wave Homecoming Dance, he had selected his thrift-store parachute pants, a brand-new red dress shirt with a beautifully narrow collar, and a thin, checkerboard necktie he had picked up last weekend at the city's premier shopping mall. As he zipped up the bag he heard a knock at the door.

"It's your father, Parker. Open up."

With a sigh, he dropped the bag and turned down the stereo. His father always came home early on Friday afternoons to hang around the football field with the other fathers and watch the Wolverines prepare for that evening's game. Parker knew these Friday afternoons meant a great deal to him. They were, in fact, the main reason Parker stayed on the team. Still, it pained him to see his father on the sidelines in his red Wolverine windbreaker, bumming smokes from the other dads and jawing about the college prospects of the team's stellar offensive backfield. It pained him because he imagined how desperately his father wanted his own son to be among those for whom "college prospects" and "football" were synonymous.

Parker unlocked the door and returned to his bed. "It's open."

His father was already outfitted in his sweater and jeans, all in preparation for his big night at the stadium. Parker clutched his duffel bag and stared out the window.

Dad joined him on the bed. "Nervous?"

"About what? We'll win, if that's what you're worried about."

"What's the coach been saying? Anything to look for tonight?"

"What are you asking me, Dad?" Now Parker faced him head-on. "Are you worried what the coach is saying about the game or about my performance?"

His father shrugged. "Both, I guess."

"About the game, he's saying we better win or else. About my prospects, he's saying nothing."

"Relax, son. I'm not here to interrogate you." He looked around the room. Recently Parker had taken down all his old model airplanes, many of which had hung from the ceiling on thin white thread. Now the walls were covered with posters. Over the bed hung a new poster of the Pretenders, an English group with a sexy female lead singer. On the back of the door he had taped up an enormous, four-foot poster featuring a foggy, black-and-white photo of a bass player seconds away from smashing his instrument onto the floor of a crowded stage. He felt his father's disappointment as the old guy took in this new decor. "Actually"—vaguely waving his arm—"I want to talk to you about all this."

"They're posters."

"I know what they are, son. Don't get smug." He paused. "Fact is, I don't give a damn how you decorate your room. You sleep here, not me. If you really wanna know, I don't have much of a problem with anything you do. You've never disappointed me, as far as I can remember. Not once."

Parker looked at him. In the last couple of years his father's face had begun slowly to sag beneath the skin, gravity tugging down on his handsome features and softening his appearance, yet for all of that his father was still a commanding presence, a figure of great charm and bluster. "I'm going to be late," Parker said. "I could use a ride, if you don't mind."

"No sweat." His father stood up and walked to Parker's dresser, where Parker still displayed all his old trophies from his days on the country club swim team. Swimming: that was his real sport. Fingering the trophies, his father continued: "It's your mother, son. She's worried about your clothes."

Parker got ready to protest but his father stopped him with a raised hand. "I know, I know. It's silly. Hey, I'm just the messenger." He chuckled. The ghost of Parker's mother entered the room, a concerned look on her face. "She's worried you've got yourself caught up in some newfangled crowd, some group of juvenile delinquents is how she put it." Now Parker permitted himself a laugh. "I keep telling her it's just the music. That's all it is. You've always loved music, I remind her, ever since you were a little boy. Maybe we should have signed you up for piano lessons, I don't know. It's just that, after Scott made such a stink about practicing . . . Well." He returned to the bed and patted Parker's knee. "Why don't you explain it to me. What's the big deal about this music, this new wave or whatever you call it?"

Parker tried to laugh again, but the effort fell flat. What did his father want him to say? How could he explain it? "It's just music, Dad. Every kid gets into music."

"I know that. Hey, when I was your age I was crazy about Dixieland jazz. My dad hated it, thought it was black music, which in a way it was. That's why I liked it so much."

"Exactly. That's all it is. Music to drive your parents crazy."

"But why the clothes, Parker? Why dress like a poor kid from a trailer camp? What's wrong with all the nice things we bought you? I never see any of those kids on the team wearing shoes like that." He pointed to Parker's mismatched Converse All-Stars.

"Well, that's their problem."

"Are you trying to make a statement or something? Is that what this is about?"

"*No.*" Now Parker stood up. "Look, this is how I feel, all right? It's who I am. Not everyone looks like Alex Keaton, you know. Why should it matter if I want to express my, I don't know, my *individuality*? You should be happy I'm not some pathetic *conformist*. At least I have a brain. At least I have my own *identity*."

"Okay, okay." His father stood, hands raised in surrender. "You've made your point. Relax." He went to the door but then stopped at the threshold. "Look, let's make a deal. I'm the one who has to listen to your mother, so have a heart. Think of your old man. If you want to dress all new wave or whatever you call it, be my guest. Just keep it from your mom. If you have to carry your clothes out the door and change in the bathroom, so be it. Just let your mother think you're wearing all those clothes she bought you last summer. Deal?"

Parker's eyes welled with gratitude. How he had underestimated the old man! He understood, he really did! All this fall Parker had seen his father as an enemy, as the one person in the world who most wanted him to be other than who he was. Now he realized he knew nothing about his father. The realization elated him. "You got it," he said, and reached out to shake his father's hand.

"Don't get sloppy, though," his father warned, clinching the deal. "First chance I get I'm tossing that stupid army parka in the trash."

From the moment Parker walked into the locker room, his duffel bag hoisted over his shoulder, he sensed that something was awry. Everyone was quiet and reserved. No towel slapping in the bathroom, no touch football with the tape rolls, no miniature, handheld computer football games beeping away the long hour before warm-up. The only sound punctuating the silence was the desolate groan and plop of Mark "the Mooch" painfully relieving himself in the echo chamber of the locker room toilet. Sitting at his locker and arranging his things—helmet, hip pads, new strings for his cleats—Parker repeated to himself over and over again how important it was—as the coach had exhorted them all week —*to concentrate on the game.* Forget about homecoming, don't think about the dance. Get your mind off Suzy (or Tonya, as the case may be) and think about those Bishops, who were out to kick our ass. Parker recalled all this sound advice as he rethreaded the straps on his shoulder pads and taped up his wrist, appreciating all the while how prescient his coach had been. Because—what d'ya know—he *was* thinking about homecoming, about the dance, and about Suzy (or Tonya). He couldn't quit thinking about them. Tonya was coming to the dance. She had said so Thursday afternoon in chemistry, the same day Parker found out about her "date" with Mike Alvezados. Mike, too, was coming, though on his own terms. Mike's plan was to crash the dance, throw eggs at the Breaks, and make a Statement, and Parker wanted to be there for the event. He wanted to join in. He wanted Tonya to be there when he, Parker, joined forces with Mike Alvezados as they stood up against the forces of conformity and the proponents for a homogenized new wave. His first official punk act! But that had to wait, he reminded himself as he arranged his shoulder pads on his shoulders to make sure he had a snug fit. First the game. Then the egg throwing.

Later, on the sidelines, Parker gnawed on his mouthpiece and watched with a confused sense of anguish and excitement as his team struggled ineptly against the ferocious running attack of the Father Ryan Bishops, whose gold helmets gleamed beneath the stadium lights like an unreturned taunt. From the opening kickoff, which the Bishops nearly returned for a touchdown, the Wolverines were tentative and confused. The offensive linemen stormed up and down the sidelines barking at the second team to *get pumped up*, the defensive backfield threw their helmets in frustration at the Gatorade cooler, the coach tore off his headset every third down.

Still and all, for some reason Parker couldn't suppress a delicious feeling of exhilaration at the prospect of the Wolverines actually losing. He had nothing to do with the loss; the seniors and the other underclass starters were in charge, and if they blew this game that meant they were more human than Parker had thought. With each weekly victory, the Wolverines became more ominous and all-powerful, whereas a loss freed him from responsibility, gave him a leg up on all those who stood over him. He felt like a spurned lover watching his rival get slammed. Plus a close game like this one, a close game in which community bragging rights hung in the balance, guaranteed beyond any contingency his not having to play. Which left him free to think about Tonya Treakle.

"I THOUGHT YOU GUYS were supposed to be unbeatable," Alison said to him the moment he walked in the gym. The place was already packed when he got there, most of his classmates dolled up in variations on suburban new wave—checkerboard shirts, blue blazers and skinny ties, spiked hair, Wayfarer sunglasses. A large percentage had simply pierced the Polo icon on their button-down shirts with a safety pin or two. From the cast-iron rafters overhead hung a basket weave of black and white crepe paper. Near the back, underneath the home-team basket, the Breaks were churning out a fairly decent rendition of a Cheap Trick hit from last spring, the drums echoing through the gym like gunshots on a battlefield.

"We won," Parker pointed out.

"Yes, but barely."

"You caught us on a bad night. You should have seen us last week."

"Oh, that should pretty much do it for me. One game a year is enough, I should think. Though actually I kind of liked it, seeing everyone dressed up on Friday night. My first genuine High School Experience. And here I am gearing up for Experience Number Two. What did you do, by the way?"

Parker stopped scanning the room long enough to ask, "When?"

"Tonight. On the team. I kept looking for you out there but everyone had on these big plastic helmets so I couldn't see who was whom. I don't even know your number."

He could lie, of course. He could tell her he made a few tackles, and she'd never know the difference. On the other hand, he could simply tell her he rode the bench and she'd probably think nothing of it. Instead he said, "I was worthless. You look nice, by the way."

And she did! In defiance of the evening's official theme, Alison was wearing a body-hugging burgundy cocktail dress. Along her smooth thin arms stretched a pair of matching elbow gloves. Her hair she had done up in an elaborate bun from which a delicate tendril had escaped so as to frame her heavily made-up face. It wasn't punk, it was something else. He wasn't sure what it was, exactly, but he liked it.

"So do you." She stroked his tie between her gloved fingers and let it drop.

"Have you seen anyone else?"

"You mean Sid? Yeah, he's here. I saw him outside with a bunch of guys from his study hall. Boy is he dressed to kill."

And suddenly he appeared before them. Flanked by a crew of four or five giggling camp followers, Mike Alvezados marched past them dressed in a plaid Scottish kilt, a chain-mail tank top, and a pair of bulky military boots. Like Tonya Treakle on that momentous night of her surprise appearance chez Hayes, he also wore around his neck a spiked dog collar.

"Mike!" Parker called through the noise.

Alvezados stopped dead in his tracks. He was wearing makeup! Thick black eyeliner and black lipstick, to be exact. Through the chain-mail tank top Parker could see the articulate outline of Mike's muscular frame. He suddenly felt stupid in his skinny tie and parachute pants. What distinguished him from the other playactors here tonight? Nothing. He looked, he suddenly realized, like one more preppy suburbanite in bad costume. Mike was still scanning the room when Parker raised his hand and waved. In response, Mike jerked his head in greeting and kept on walking, his disciples following in his wake.

After a brief pause, Alison broke the silence. "He blew me off, too. I think he's drunk."

"Maybe he didn't see us."

"Could be," Alison said helpfully. "When I went up to him out in the parking lot he basically snubbed me. That girl, Tonya Treakle, was hanging all over him. It was disgusting. Wait till you see her, by the way. That's a sight you won't forget."

In this, too, Alison was right. When he did finally catch up with Tonya Treakle—after a good twenty minutes of mad searching—his eyes nearly shot from his head. She was apparently dressed in the exact same outfit she had worn to his house that night several weeks ago, right down to the fingerless gloves. What his father had not pointed out, and he now understood why, was the placement of the holes in said dress, the most prominent of which opened right at the center of her bosom, thereby revealing to all who cared to look the inner crease between her breasts. With shaking fingers he tapped her on the shoulder.

"Parker!" she cried, a cigarette cocked between her fingers, and before he had a chance to respond she raised her arms and draped them over his shoulders, pulling him into an embrace he had no idea how to return. "You're finally here! I've been looking *all over* for you, but everyone kept talking about the fucking *game,* the *game,* so I figured you were never going to show, the way they were talking you'd think the world had ended tonight, they said none of the football players were coming on account of the stupid fucking score, like the coach was going to make you all practice all night, I mean, please, but I kept thinking, hey, they won, what's the prob. And oh, look, I have a treat."

Her breath smelled of cigarette smoke and something Parker tentatively identified as whiskey. He pulled away from her and looked down at her open palm, in which lay a cluster of little green pills. His blood jumped.

"What are those?" he shouted. They were standing next to one of the amps. The Breaks were performing a tune from the Cars' latest album.

"They're your ticket to fun!" she shouted back, and tugged him off to the side. "Now hurry up and go get one of those overpriced Cokes over there while there's no line and we'll just gobble these right up."

"Aw, Tonya—"

"Trust me, Parker, I know what I'm talking about. They're perfectly safe, I can guarantee you that, my brother gave them to me and he wouldn't steer me wrong. I'm his dear old sis, after all. I've been *sailing* all night, you have no idea. And get this, I walked up to Mr. Behn and started talking to him about chemistry and he had *no* idea, no clue on earth, what I was getting at, he just kept nodding his head and saying, 'Yes, well, that's a rare compound indeed but I suppose it's possible,' all the while staring at my tits, I'm not kidding you. It was a riot, you should have been there. Now hurry with those Cokes, I don't want anyone to see me holding these things."

"I don't know, Tonya, I just—"

"Look. I'm telling you they're safe. Live a little, Parker, break out of the Middlesburg rut. You going to be a good boy all your life?"

"Actually," he said, stepping back as if in defiance, "I'm looking for Mike Alvezados. You seen him?" But of course she had. His gut went woozy as he realized the whole night was falling apart.

"Oh, he's totally blitzed," she yelled. "With my help, of course. Go get the Cokes and I'll track him down." Before letting him go, however, she grabbed his wrist and pulled him to her level. Into his ear, she whispered, "Tonight's the night I finally corrupt you."

Mike suddenly appeared from out of nowhere and seized Parker by the other wrist. Parker was trapped, a wishbone waiting to be torn.

"Where've you *been!*" Mike yelled, a maniacal grin on his made-up face. Both Mike and Tonya seemed possessed by joy, the two of them gripped by a happiness that made

Parker quake in his Converse All-Stars. "I've been looking all over for you, man, everywhere, I almost said, 'Fuck it, he's not coming,' and went on without you."

"I called to you back there," Parker explained, withdrawing his wrists from both of his captors.

"He had to wait around and get yelled at by his coach," Tonya announced, and fell into a helpless fit of laughter. "He had to get lambasted by that stupid fucking jerk who teaches auto shop, can you believe that!"

"Whatever," Mike said, and grabbed Parker forcibly by the arm. "You're here now, so hurry up. They're about to take a break."

"Hurry where?" Parker called, but before he could receive an answer Mike dragged him through the throng of pogoing teenagers and deposited him smack dab at the front of the makeshift stage, inches away from the Breaks, who were bouncing through a Police tune from several years back.

Mike was right about one thing: the Breaks *were* middle-aged geeks. The bass player had bleached white hair and a black mustache, the lead guitarist wore a prim beard, and the lead singer had a full head of feathered bangs. They all wore matching black shirts and stark white ties. They looked like REO Speedwagon.

"Here," Mike shouted. Turning his back to the stage, he fished something out of a wadded-up paper bag he had apparently been carrying under his arm. Parker knew what Mike had in that bag: a dozen Grade A eggs. Mike popped open the paper carton and elbowed Parker in the side. "Load your weapons."

With more trepidation than he had felt all night, Parker removed three of the gleaming white eggs from their snug little cardboard nests. Impatiently, Mike turned the carton over and collected the remaining eggs against his chest. "Okay," he yelled, "on three, turn around and open fire. One, two—"

Someone rammed into Parker from behind, throwing him against the stage. Then someone else crashed into his right arm. With the eggs still held precariously in his two hands he struggled to stay upright amid the moiling mob of teenagers crashing this way and that. A loud clang echoed through the gym, and it took a few moments for Parker to realize the Breaks had stopped playing: only the bass player continued to run through the Police number, his solo instrument—"a bass movement," perhaps—providing an eerie bottom to the chaos exploding all around, like the sound track in a pornographic film.

"Hey!" Parker yelled. Because his hips were still pressed against the stage, he couldn't turn around to see what had caused all the ruckus. What he did see was the hailstorm of eggs raining down on the stage, first one and then another egg splattering on the astonished faces of the Breaks, who stood all in a line with their instruments held before them like shields. The eggs kept coming, one after another, and through the shouting Parker could hear Mike's ringing war cry: "Die, you lame motherfuckers! *Die!*"

Valiantly, Parker shoved himself from the lip of the stage and into the mob, the eggs held aloft over his head as if they were detonated hand grenades. And that's when he figured out what had happened. Just to his right he caught a glimpse of Mark "the Mooch" Munster, Adam "Alice" Cooper, and a swarm of other first-stringers deep in a full-scale rumble with a vicious mob of Father Ryan Bishops, who had apparently crashed the dance. Parker gingerly threaded his way through this crowd seeking escape. Behind him, Alvezados shouted, "Throw 'em, Hayes! Hurry up!" while to his right "Alice" Cooper broke away from his current victim and yelled, "Hayes, over here! We need reinforcements!" But Parker kept moving. He felt against his back a pressure he couldn't withstand, an urgent command to escape all this, to rush outside and head straight home to his bedroom, where he could take solace beneath the consoling thunder of his stereo headphones.

He almost made it, too. But just as he saw daylight someone grabbed his arm, thereby forcing him to juggle his eggs, the trio of which fell with a dull crunch on his own head.

"Oh my God!" Tonya cried, laughing hysterically. "What's that on your face!"

Rather than respond, he broke free and ran across the gym, against the flood of traffic heading the other way. He dashed past the principal, the physics teacher, and his very own football coach, all of whom were racing against him in the name of Order and Decency. He kept running and did not stop until he burst out the door and into the parking lot, which opened before him like a lake under moonlight. No one out here knew what was going on inside. Outside, everything was calm.

"Parker?"

He whipped around, expecting who he had no idea. But of course it was only Alison. She was sitting on the steps leading up the gym, nursing a Coke and staring across the parking lot toward the empty football stadium, which lay serene and still beneath its canopy of stadium lights like a pool table in an empty bar. He stopped where he was and let his shoulders sag in defeat. What was one more humiliation?

"What are you doing out here?" he asked.

"Waiting for my mother to come pick me up, if you must know. Oh, the heartbreak of adolescence. Wow, you sure bolted out of there in a hurry."

Disaster simplifies things. With the night's long list of strange triumphs and more punishing defeats still clinging to his skin like a piece of armor, Parker found himself unaccountably grateful for Alison Hartsfield, his study partner, his phone friend, the last girl on campus he thought he'd want to see right now. Torn between a desire to go to her and an equally strong need to wave good night and walk home alone, where he could wash off the egg yolk in private and begin the long, and perhaps endless, process of trying to forget this night had ever happened, he chose the former. The choice was astonishingly simple.

"There was a lot to bolt from," he said as he sat down beside her on the steps.

She reared back, took him in. "My God, what is *that?*"

"Egg yolk," he laughed. He patted his shaved head. The yolk felt like liquid soap on a Brillo pad.

"This should be good." She set down the cup and crossed her arms. But she wore a smile on her face, bless her.

"Mike and I were supposed to throw eggs at the band," he explained, his head down, his arms crossed along his knees, "but we were interrupted by a riot between my football team and the Father Ryan Bishops. If you hurry back inside you can catch the last of it."

"You're kidding me."

"Serious as a crush."

Alison stared at him for a moment, then looked back at the empty stadium, where his gaze was directed also. "Someone has to say it."

"Be my guest."

"You got egg on your face."

He nodded his head and smiled. A moment ago he had meant to say "crutch" instead of "crush." Now it was too late to correct the mistake.

"Seriously, though. I'm sorry you struck out."

"With whom?" He emphasized that last word, for her benefit. "Lot of people qualify for that honor."

"With Tonya. Who'd you think I meant?"

He turned to her, but she was still staring off at the stadium.

Behind them, through the open door to the gym, a bank of lights came to life, flooding the parking lot. Apparently the party was over. "How'd you know about Tonya?"

"I have my ways." She dropped her head to her left arm and met his gaze. "If it's any consolation, I struck out, too."

She meant Alvezados. He could have told her as much beforehand, could have saved her the humiliation she was so ineffably bound to suffer. But no sooner did he make this observation than he realized, with a chill in his veins, that she could have done the same thing for him.

Back in the gym some authoritative voice had commandeered the microphone. The voice was barking out orders.

Alison said, "You know what we should do?"

"Transfer?"

"I just meant we should get some breakfast."

"I thought your mother was coming."

"I lied. My mom's on a date tonight. On my honor as a Boy Scout, I was sitting out here waiting for someone to walk me home."

"I can do that," Parker found himself saying, and without thinking he stood up and offered her his hand. She eyed him for a moment, her lips pursed in contemplation, then slid her gloved fingers into his palm. The feeling he got when he hoisted her up—and she gracefully acquiesced—was like kissing a locomotive head-on.

5. GRUB WORM

February is the cruelest month. The lilacs won't breed, the snow won't forget. It is less a month than a lethargy that passeth understanding.

My day begins at or around eight-thirty, to the shrill and dire pronouncements of National Public Radio. The first thing that hits me—the very first thing—is Joyce's absence. It is an emptiness so agonizing and sad that it has acquired shape, mass, density: I can literally feel it pressing down on me, my chest straining at the weight. The radio plays on, the seesaw music churns and churns, and I resume, without missing a beat, the one-sided conversation with which I had kept myself awake the night before.

Listen, Joyce, I imagine myself saying—and I always imagine I begin with these two words: just pretending she's in the room with me when I say them aloud raises my cholesterol level two hundred points—"*I* do *understand how you feel, but it's imperative that* you *understand how* I *feel.* . . ." Generally, this is all it takes and I'm off and running. Under the pretense that I'm talking to a shy and repentant Joyce Askew—her head lowered in shame, her manner pliant and acquiescent, a woman who, through her own astoundingly bad judgment and aching loss, has become only the merest and most vulnerable shell of the sorceress who so thoroughly the month before scythed me at the knees and left me groveling, alone, in this very apartment—I work through my grievances. They are, how shall I say, *inexhaustible.* They go on and on and on. My various perorations —always with Joyce as my silent auditor—change daily, as I rework and refocus what I imagine to be the same basic gripe. I want to be ready if she ever deigns to come talk to me. Oh, I'll be ready, all right. For just about any situation I can work up a self-righteous head of steam so thick and beclouding she'll never get a word in. I can even imagine the inside of my head swirling and billowing like the grill of an overheating car. If she returns affectionately, I can be self-righteously affectionate. If she returns angrily, I can be self-righteously angry. If she returns tentatively, I can be self-righteously tentative. I'm prepared for anything. Absolutely anything.

This is all I do: I script, I imagine, I dwell. Even at work, even on the phone, even out with a friend, I can hear the undercurrent of my resentment gurgling within me like sewage

in a pipe. At a bar I will excuse myself to the bathroom, and
in this five-minute lull I'll construct an entire conversation
with Joyce. At work—by accident, not design, I wait tables
at a fajitas and hamburger joint called Dapper's—I can polish off an absolutely thrilling kiss-off line in the time it takes
me to walk from a customer's booth to the kitchen. I go
miles and miles out of my way for the most rudimentary
errands—the grocery store, the dry cleaners—just so I can
imagine she's in the car with me as I grip the steering wheel
and talk and talk and talk.

Thus does my day begin. After about a half hour of this—
NPR has given way to the morning classical DJ—I push my
cat, Rikki, off the bed, pull myself out of my mildewed mattress, pad barefoot to the kitchen, stand at the refrigerator
and talk to Joyce some more, swill a Diet Pepsi, and get
dressed. Rikki, still groggy from sleep, sits primly in the center of the kitchen floor and watches me dress, yawning pe-
riodically as if to register her boredom. Does she sense my
anguish? Does she wonder what happened to that curva-
ceous girl who used to sleep over sometimes, that sweet-
smelling humanoid with the soft lap and the cooing kitty
voice? How Rikki adored Joyce, curling onto her lap the moment she sat down, purring along her side at night while I
spooned myself from behind. But now the cat seems as content as ever, stuck here alone with sad, old, lugubrious me.
She seems just fine, as happy as can be. The miracle of it.

By nine I am sitting alone in a nearby Waffle House where,

armed with a newspaper and a book (neither of which I am able to give even the merest edge of my attention), I drink coffee, ruminate, and eat pancakes smothered in butter and maple syrup. I stay for as long as my waitress feels inclined to fill my coffee cup, after which I drive around for a while in hopes that some crucial errand will claim some more of my time. By noon or so I'm back home. I tiptoe past Bill Pruitt, my Neanderthal neighbor, a white-haired, mustached unemployable with a belly the size of a Volkswagen Beetle and a bewildering array of interchangeable offspring, all of them with faint mustaches, cutoff Van Halen T-shirts, and padded high-top sneakers. Over the years the Pruitts have completely commandeered the gravel backyard of our shared duplex, into which they have deposited something like seven automobiles representing the full range of possible automotive disrepair, the result being that my backyard is a minefield of carburetors and transmissions and leaded-gas V-8s. Upstairs in my apartment I put on my running clothes, tiptoe past Pruitt again and streak through Forest Park. I have taken to running not because I am worried about my health but because, one, I can resume my one-sided conversations with Joyce, and, two, Joyce's apartment overlooks a small slice of the trail I run daily. I run four, sometimes five miles at a shot, and yet the whole thing is a blur except for the brief exhilarating moment when I turn a corner, jump over some ice, and see, like a mysterious shining city in the mist, Joyce's apartment building. If her car is sitting in front of her apartment, my heart drops: *She's in there! I know where she is right now!* If her car's not there, my heart drops as well: *Oh God, I have absolutely no idea where she is right now!* Both situations are unbearable—and yet I can't keep away. The final half mile of my run disappears in a surge of adrenaline, and sometimes when I finish I consider starting all over, just so I can fly past her apartment again.

Not once have I seen her enter or leave.

And not for lack of trying, either. Everywhere I go I expect her to appear before me, clodding along in that awkward gait of hers, smiling about something (me! she's thinking of me!), hoping, as I do, that we will run into each other. I expect it, yes: I also dread, anticipate, will, hope, invoke, beseech, and avoid it. I am endlessly preparing myself for the thrilling and unimaginable possibility of her sudden apparition: Joyce emerging from her apartment, Joyce shopping in the mall, Joyce leaving the library, Joyce entering a Kroger. But she never shows.

I return from my run, tiptoe past Bill Pruitt for the third time, shower, and get dressed for work. My shift at Dapper's begins at three-thirty, which is way too early, as they very well know, and yet no one seems prepared to say anything, and I am, quite frankly, more than a little grateful for the diversion. Before each shift, one of the restaurant's four managers—all of them overworked, frazzled, and more or less my age—conducts what we in the business call a Dapper's Server Lineup. Lineups are basically pep talks during which we waiters, arrayed spendidly in khakis, bow ties, and jaunty green Dapper's suspenders, lounge about in the back of the restaurant while that evening's floor manager, pacing back and forth like a football coach in front of a kindergarten class, cajoles and inspires us to ever more spectacular feats of customer service and ticket-total upgrades. *Push the appetizers! Sell the specialty drinks! Don't forget dessert!* It is during lineup that I eat my second meal of the day—usually an appetizer—and bullshit and flirt with the other waitresses. This constitutes the first sustained conversation with a live human being I've had all day.

One particular waitress, a heavyset, bucktoothed, custard-filled bowl of a girl named Kelley Mullens, harbors what is nothing less than a tentative crush on me: this fact has been corroborated by several of the other waitresses. So Kelley is my one source of self-confidence. And she's cute, too, sexy in a lush and sloppy sort of way. I can fully imagine the weight of her terrific udders pressing down on my face, the wide warm animal fat of her buttocks in my hands. But I don't press it. Instead I settle for the hollow thrill of bending past her for the ketchup at the server's station, or feeling her gaze on my (supposedly) indifferent cheek, or watching her stammer nervously when I ask her the most rudimentary question. She is a better server than I am, her nightly tips exceeding mine by at least 50 percent. And the customers love her, particularly elderly couples. Christ, do those blue hairs just eat her alive, squinting up at her from their padded Dapper's booths and cackling inanely about their college-aged grand-children. I, on the other hand, manage to charm absolutely no one. My stomach wilts each time a customer sits down at one of my four tables, I can never remember to place the appetizer order independent of the main course, any drink more complicated than a scotch and soda baffles me entirely, and I have never once successfully opened a bottle of wine. Kelley, bless her heart, helps me out—she runs my food, picks up my drinks, clears away my tables—but what dis-tinguishes her from everyone else at the restaurant is the rather salient coincidence that she is a paying member of the same sorority as (you guessed it) Joyce Askew.

"Joyce?" Kelley says, after I have made this remarkable connection. "Brown hair, right? Yeah, I know her. She's a senior, I think."

Yes! Yes! Yes! That's her! Good God, that's her!

"Well, we went out for a while," I tell her. And how thrilling it is to hear that from my own lips! When Kelley sees Joyce at the sorority meeting next week, she will look across the room at my former beloved and think of me. Joyce will be, for her, only a peripheral figure in my life— instead of vice versa. Leaning against the ice machine and wrapping my arms around the little brown tray we Dapper's waiters are required to have on our persons at all times, I ca-sually add, "We broke up about a month ago."

Kelley avoids my gaze. "Actually, I don't know her all that well. She's friends with some girls I totally can't stand."

Kelley, it occurs to me, is more like me than Joyce ever was. If I took her home right now she'd give herself to me entirely—I just know it. She could nurse me back to health, give me renewed confidence, help me forget about whatsername. Instead, I say, "What do you think of her?"

"Who?"

"You know: Joyce."

"Oh, I don't know. Like I say—"

"Because the thing is, I was crazy about that girl"—the past tense verb sliding off my tongue as easily as a politician's lie— "and for a while there I was a real mess. Whew. I'm serious. I was a total and complete nervous wreck. But I haven't talked to her in months."

In response to this astonishing (and unprovoked) confession, Kelley Mullens hesitates, nods her head. "Wow." After some consideration, she adds, "She's all right, I guess. What I know of her, anyway. It's just . . ."

What? What information does this girl possess? What does she know? "Go ahead," I tell her, my heart racing with anticipation, "I can take it. I told you, we've broken up."

"I just think she's kind of . . . I don't know. Obnoxious. Or flashy or something."

But it isn't enough. It doesn't satisfy. I urge her on. "How do you mean?"

"Look," she says, trying to escape (I'm breaking her heart! I'm putting her through hell! And I can't stop!), "she's just this girl in my sorority, I've talked to her three, maybe four times in my life."

"Okay, okay, I'm sorry. It's cool. I just thought—"

"I will say this, though"—and here she reasserts herself, even moves closer to me as if to make me uneasy, which, as it turns out, does the trick—"she doesn't seem your type at all."

After work I am juiced. A wad of ones bulges in my front pocket, a night's worth of sustained flirtation burns in my chest. Although I keep telling myself I need to get a steady schedule going, put some money in my checking account and write up a résumé, each night I find myself unable to go home. Twenty minutes after clocking out I am sitting with the rest of the night shift in an all-night bar in the Central West End, drinking beer after beer with my evening's wages, smoking cigarettes I am convinced I no longer want anymore, and considering, considering, considering my next satisfying encounter with Joyce Askew. This goes on for about two hours, or until I can't stand it any longer. The problem is I can't think while I'm in the bar. There are too many people around, the music is too loud, all of it is interfering with my concentration. So at two in the morning I take my leave (Kelley watching crestfallen as I stumble out), check my phone messages (no call from Joyce), and lie in bed for an hour or two scripting yet another exhausting monologue. Then the morning comes and it starts all over again.

MY FIRST MISTAKE was dating an undergraduate.

Each night when I went to her apartment I would find a loud, uproarious party in full swing, the pot smoke swirling in silvery strands against the ceiling and the couch littered with shouting, shrieking college students, the girls holding half-smoked cigarettes and the boys belching into beer cans. I would try to mingle, but in every case the talk was about people I didn't know and classes I wasn't taking. My only option was to draw tenuous parallels between my years at the university and their current sojourn, short lessons in revisionist history that no one, least of all me, wanted to hear. What *I* wanted to hear was some hint of approval from Joyce, who was usually on these occasions scrunched cozily on the couch between her roommates and a bunch of other jerks in ski caps and long-sleeved T-shirts. There she'd lounge, bong in hand, laughing extravagantly at everyone's witticisms but my own. And I'd pick at the carpet and tell myself, *You're too old for this, you've already got your degree.* Yet for some reason I couldn't let her go.

My second mistake was letting her go.

And my biggest mistake of all was telling her not to call me ever again.

Because she didn't. Not once. I told her not to call me, and she did exactly as I asked. The first two weeks after we broke up I didn't hear a thing. Almost all of January passed and still not a peep. Meanwhile I'd lie in bed till daylight listening to the cars swish by my window. Occasionally someone would pull into my gravel driveway, yank a parking brake, and step out—all of which would sound to my ears exactly like *Joyce* pulling into my gravel driveway, yanking her park-

ing brake, and stepping out. *It's her!* I would suddenly realize, bolting upright in bed like a dog waiting for its master to
come home. *The lonely nights have become too much for
her!* Then I would rush to the window and see, with a sad
pffft of disappointment, Scott (or Jeff or Shawn or Mike)
Pruitt lumbering inside after work.

Then, one sunny day near the end of the month, I walked
into Walgreens and saw her. She was in the checkout line
with some guy I'd never seen before. She was buying a twelve-
pack of beer and a pack of smokes. It seemed inconceivable
to me that this woman, this beguiling creature who had
made herself the source of so much distress, could be found
on so banal an errand as buying cigarettes. I had assumed
that if I ever did chance upon her she would be engaged in
an activity so vile and unforgivable that I could lay to rest all
my anger, pain, and resentment. Perhaps I'd encounter her at
a restaurant with six lascivious men, all of them in tuxedos
and all of them leering and pawing at her as she giggled
drunkenly and spilled her champagne. Or maybe I'd open
my front door and find her pointing at me from the downstairs landing, her new boyfriend standing behind her and
snorting derisively. But no, there she was, buying smokes in
the drugstore. Perfectly harmless. And perfectly, agonizingly
beautiful.

"Oh, hey," she said, waving. Though she was dressed in
jeans and a college sweatshirt, with her hair gathered into
a tortoiseshell comb, she looked to my astonished eyes as

celestially remote as a movie starlet. In some other life, this exquisite creature had granted me all the privileges of intimacy —had granted them and then just as quickly revoked them. Everything about her, even her shoes—crisp white Keds, tied so that the laces hung on either side like stirrups—announced to anyone who cared to notice that she was way too good for me. She broke the spell by looking away and making an elaborate pretense of counting out her change, most of which she dropped. Then she looked up again and smiled. "Wow. You kind of surprised me, ha ha."

Something round and solid entered my throat, which I tried to swallow down. "Surprise, surprise."

She introduced me to the guy behind her—Eric something, I didn't catch the last name—then explained to me that the two of them (!) were in charge of planning and writing a skit for the university's annual spring carnival, held each year in the front parking lot. The beer and cigarettes were for inspiration. I glanced briefly at this Eric character— brown hair, Vail ski cap, T-shirt, jeans—and realized instantly that I knew everything there was to know about him. I knew he lived in that Vail ski cap. I knew he drove a beat-up Volvo littered with empty Copenhagen cans and balled-up McDonald's bags. I knew he wore plaid boxers and shot hoops a lot and drank Jack Daniel's diluted with Coke. Eric acknowledged my gaze by flicking his head back exactly once in that smug frat-boy gesture that, roughly translated, means, "Hey, dude." I turned back to Joyce, smiled, and arched my eyebrows. In response, she cleared her throat and asked me—just as she might ask anyone she hadn't seen or called in two weeks—how I was doing.

"Fine," I said.

"Any new job prospects?"

"Nothing yet, but I'm, you know, I'm working on it."

"Well, that's good. Great. By the way, I keep meaning to come in and see you at—Dapper's, isn't it?"

"Dapper's, right."

"What nights do you work?"

"It varies, you know. From week to week."

"I see."

And that was it. She said good-bye and walked out to her car with Eric, and I stood in the drugstore trying to remember what I had come in there for. I left without making a purchase, walked into my apartment, and fell into a rage that ended with me kicking a volleyball-sized hole through the Sheetrock in my living room. Then I called her.

"We need to talk," I said.

"But you told me—"

"I know what I told you. I just think now we need to talk. I haven't heard from you in two fucking months and when I do you act like I'm just some guy you had in a class or something. I mean, Jesus Christ."

"Do you want me to hang up?"

"Hang up?"

"You keep up this tone and I'll hang up. I don't need to listen to this."

I took several deep breaths, looked around in vain for a

cigarette, and said, "Okay, I'm sorry. I'm under control. I'm relaxed."

"Fine. Do you work tonight?"

"No."

"Wait, I'm busy." Eric Something. All at once I saw him standing in her kitchen, manfully yanking the tab off a can of beer. "How about tomorrow night? Do you work then?"

"Tomorrow I'm free."

"Then I'll come by tomorrow night and we can talk. I have a meeting for this skit at five, then we're all supposed to go out for dinner, and then I'll come right over."

"You're sure?" My mind latched onto that *we're* as if it contained everything I needed to know about Eric Something—which, in a sense, it did.

"Look, if you don't want me to, I can—"

"No, no, I want you to. Come over, that'll be fine."

All that night and the next day I tried to anticipate what she was going to say, and for each proposal I scripted a long and scrupulous reply. If these rebuttals had a common theme it was this: no matter what she said, no matter how earnestly she begged, I would not, could not, get involved with her again. I was still telling myself, *No, Joyce, it simply cannot be,* when, late the following night, I let her in my apartment. She was flushed and nervous, her skin bristling with a radiance that made me think of bubble baths, exercise, sex. Immediately I forgot everything I had told myself. *Say the word, Joyce. Just say the word.*

And what did she say? Pretty much what I'd expected her to say, though I didn't realize that until much later. At the time everything she said seemed original and new. The experience reminded me of high-school football. Each week in practice our coach would make us watch game films of that week's opponent, memorize the names and jersey numbers of star players, play against a prototype of our opponent's offense comprised of the sad and unhappy members of our third string—all so we'd know what was coming. Yet the moment that opening kickoff arched through the air, I was on my own. The offense I had studied so diligently on Thursday night became a mass of hurtling and crunching bodies. After each play I would pick myself up from the ground, stare in amazement at how far the running back had advanced, and think, How had he done it? What form of magic had he employed? And all he'd done was run past me—the truth of which would hit me hard the following Monday as I sulked in the darkened locker room watching the game film. "Well, looky there," my coach would drawl, his tone inviting laughter, "is that Hayes again, all alone in the corner?" With relish he'd rewind the film, my teammates snickering in glee. "Yep, there he is, flat on his face. We went over this, what? Fifty times last week? Now there's your split end, Hayes, *he's* your read. And what do you do? You go straight in and down—bam!—arms out and grass in your teeth: a perfect grub worm tackle. Now where the hell is your head?" "In my ass, sir." "That's right, boy. That's exactly where it is."

Which, apparently, was also where my head was at when Joyce suggested we give it another go.

"Really?"

"Of course," she insisted. "I mean, it was never really my idea to break it off in the first place. Entirely, that is. You were the one who'd insisted on that."

Quickly, I consulted the booze-stained transcript of our breakup conversation. Blah blah blah *needs space,* something something, *didn't feel we should sleep together, needed time to think things through,* yadda yadda, *remain friends, keep in touch, date other people,* so forth and so on. I am, of course, paraphrasing. My response to all this—these lines were relegated to the endnotes, so that's why they weren't as fresh in my mind—was, and I quote, "So you want to break up?"

"All right," I said, "how do you think we should do this?"

"Slowly. Take it one day at a time, just to see how it goes. I don't think we should jump right back into what we had."

Yes, fine, great, you got it.

I asked her if she'd dated anyone.

"Well, I went out with this guy Gary from my complex, but it was a disaster. Never again."

This guy from my complex. I liked the sound of that.

"And, I don't know, I've sorta been seeing this guy who I'm doing the skit with—you saw him, Eric—but it's not anything serious. We just get along."

To which I added what was surely the only intelligent, objective, and reasonably sane thing I said that whole evening: "So why do you want to do this?"

"Because I miss you, Parker. I really do. It was such a shock seeing you yesterday—I was so nervous, couldn't you tell?—that I almost called you as soon as I got home, but then I remembered you didn't want me to call, so I didn't. But I'd been thinking about it for a couple of weeks now."

"Thinking of what?"

"Of calling you. Seeing what you were up to. I want you to be a part of my life, Parker. I'm not sure how big a part, but we can work on that if you're willing. If you can give me some time, then maybe we can work something out. I just don't want to lose you entirely."

Believe it or not, all of this sounded simply wonderful to me. She was asking me to accept the very same arrangement she'd presented two months ago—the *same thing*—and now I was ready to swallow it whole: hook, line, and lead weight. As I nodded and said, "Sure, I think that could work," all I could hear was her saying, "I don't want to lose you." It was, in some ways, precisely the sort of thing I'd been hoping she'd say.

She stayed. She slept with me in my bed, dressed demurely in socks, panties, and one of my blue Oxford shirts—my only good one. I left the room while she changed. Then we hugged and kissed dryly, afraid to talk, unsure what the boundaries were. She smelled different—new perfume?—and her lips felt like someone else's. It was as if I had admitted a strange woman into my bed. After the kissing was over, she sweetly gave me her back and fell into a deep heavy sleep, most of which—all eight hours' worth—I more or less watched. Twice I got out of bed and went into my living room to read. At one point I fixed myself a stiff unchilled scotch. I swallowed three aspirin. But nothing worked. I couldn't sleep a wink. Each time I crawled back in bed I saw her—her!—and yet I knew I was kidding myself if I sincerely thought I had her back. She was in my bed, okay, but only because she had to sleep somewhere. I wasn't even sure she wanted me in there with her. I no longer heard her say, "I don't want to lose you"; all I heard now was, "I don't want to lose you *entirely*," which was a different matter altogether. Was this "not losing me entirely" this functional use of the bed? When she'd said, "I want you to be a part of my life," was that exactly what she'd meant—that I was to occupy nothing more than a "part" of her everyday existence? Had she come over here just to put me back on her payroll? Or maybe just to relieve herself of the slight pang of guilt she felt at dropping me so unaccountably? I was giving her everything she wanted—freedom, me, and whomever else she decided was worthy of her time—and I was getting nothing. I wasn't even getting her, for Chrissakes. I thought of Kelley Mullens, not so much because I wanted her but because I saw that I was more or less in her shoes. I really had no intention of pursuing Kelley Mullens; the only reason I was stringing her along at all was because I enjoyed the adoration. Who wouldn't? And that, I finally realized, was all

Joyce was doing with me. She *was* just keeping me on her payroll. I mean, really now. It was as obvious as the ache in my heart. Was I really going to stand there and let her do this to me? Was I? *Was I?*

How could I not?

When she woke up, fully refreshed, I was in the kitchen brewing coffee. She walked in, still in her socks and shirt, and slipped her arms around my waist. "You're up awfully early."

"I never slept."

She released me and stepped away. "Why not?"

I stared at her, hesitated, then opted for full disclosure. When you're not getting anything, you've pretty much got nothing to lose. "I just couldn't sleep. I kept wondering why you wanted to do this. And I remembered all that business about wanting your space. Then I imagined you going out with someone else, and I—"

"Parker," she said, then grimaced. She looked impatient. "We talked about all this last night. You sounded like you understood."

"I did. I do. I mean, I think I do. It's just that—"

"What? Do I have to spell it out? It's simple. I want to be involved with you. I miss you and still care about you, end of story. We need to go slow because we need to see if it can work—that's all."

"I know, I know. But you'll note that we didn't sleep together last night."

"Were you ready to?"

"No," I said, and I meant it.

"Okay. Then we'll work on it. We'll take it as it comes."

"Till what comes?"

"Till . . ." She shook her head and shrugged. "I don't know, Parker. I'm not quite sure what you're asking me."

"I'm not asking you *anything!*" I whirled away from her and stood shirtless in the middle of the kitchen. I couldn't believe it: as amazing, as unthinkable as it seemed, I was about to do it all over again. I was about to *break up with her,* right after we has just gotten back together! I now understood that line about dogs and vomit. "I'm just saying you don't really know what you want."

"Ex*act*ly," she exclaimed, and moved toward me, her socks sliding across the linoleum. "That's what I'm trying to tell *you,* Parker. I'm just not sure yet. About anything—you, me, my life, whatever. All I need is a little time, that's all."

"Oh, but Joyce—" My voice cracked. Before I could finish what I was about to say I seized both her wrists and brought her hands to my chest. Resistance radiated from her bones. "Joyce, sweetie, don't you get it? Don't you see? I *do* know what I want. I'm absolutely positive. And that's why this can't work."

She paused. As if already sensing her victory, she slowly relaxed into my grip. "Parker," she whispered, "I don't know what else to tell you."

"Tell me you love me." I just said it. I don't know why, really. It was like a grub worm tackle, one of those desperate, face-saving gestures you hope will look better on the game film.

"I can't tell you that."

"Why not?"

"Because you just asked me to."

"So what?"

"Parker," she sighed, and looked me squarely in the eye. "If you have to ask someone, then you already know the answer."

I nodded. Right. Got it. Releasing her, I raised my hands as if to ward off a blow. "I really wish you'd go," I declared. "I just . . . I don't know. I can't be around you right now." Another one for the game film.

Now all bustling energy and indignation, Joyce swiveled away from me and said, "Fine, if that's what you want. Forget I ever showed up, forget I ever even came *back* to this crummy place," and so forth and so on, all these terrific exit lines delivered in one unbroken stream of happiness and exhilaration as she tore off my Oxford shirt, slipped on her pants, gathered her jangling keys and stormed out my back door, which she slammed forcibly behind her like an exclamation point, leaving behind a hollow, empty echo that, even now, more than a month later, has not stopped resonating inside my head for a single minute.

WALKING OUT TO THE PARKING LOT one evening after work I find Kelley Mullens sitting in her car. I had registered her absence all night, it suddenly dawns on me. At least I think I registered it. Little else can quite explain what happens next.

She pokes her head out her window as I walk by and says, "My one night off and here I am. Boy, do I need to get a life."

I consider for a second. I had planned on getting home early. I hadn't fed Rikki, for one thing. For another, I wanted to get an early start tomorrow on a résumé.

Apparently she senses my reluctance because she says, "Just a drink somewhere. Otherwise I'm going to go home and watch TV till 4 A.M."

I smile and grimace. I think of Rikki staring at the door, her tail thumping indignantly.

"C'mon," she says, tilting her head at an elaborate angle. "It's Friday night." Which is true enough.

Ten minutes later we're sitting in a booth at a college hangout on Delmar. The place is so dark you can barely see your hand in front of your face. Blues music meshes with the zings and pings of video games and pinball machines. As it happens, Kelley's "one drink" turns out to be a full pitcher of Killian's Red, and though I keep telling myself I've quit, I am urged to help myself to her cigarettes.

"So this asshole," she's telling me, "who I was ready to marry, if you can believe that, who I was willing to move in with while he twaddled around trying to put together a band—this asshole calls me two months ago and says, 'Kelley, I'm moving' and suddenly, just like that, he's out of my life."

"Oh, man," I say, "same thing happened to me, I swear."
And though it isn't anywhere near the same thing, I launch
into the long and anguished tale of my seven months with
Joyce Askew, drawing as I go along as many parallels as I
can between her situation and mine, just so she'll think I'm
really trying to help her out. She doesn't buy it, I don't think,
but she lets me talk anyway. She listens attentively to everything I say, and gives me encouragement and support at all
the right moments. In the dim light her skin softens, her
scent reaches me through the cigarette smoke, and I harbor
the fantasy of crying on her shoulder. At some point we
finish our first pitcher, and miraculously a second appears
on our table. I pour us two fresh mugs and keep talking. In
no time we polish that one off, too. And I'm nowhere near
finished.

After quite a bit of this sort of thing, she looks at her
watch and says, "Wow, it's late. Look at the time."

And I know I should leave it at that—I know it, I know
it!—but of course I don't. Outside on the sidewalk I take her
hand and insist that she come home with me. "I live right
around the corner," I tell her. "I promise. It's way too late for
you to drive home by yourself anyway. What if something
happened? I'd never forgive myself. And like you said, it *is*
Friday night. You can't just call it quits now. Besides, I insist
you meet my cat."

For some reason this string of perfect nonsense seems to
be working. She wavers, bites her lip—a cute, bucktoothed
cartoon gesture that seizes my stomach.

"I'll be a perfect gentleman," I say. "I just can't bear the thought of going home alone. I've done that too much lately. C'mon, what do you say?"

She agrees.

When we step into my apartment Rikki is precisely where I imagined she'd be—directly in front of the door. She meows once, looks up at Kelley, and pads across the linoleum. Kelley claps her hands together and cries, "*Oh.*" The two converge in the middle of the kitchen, Kelley swooping down and cuddling the cat under her chin, Rikki responding with a purr so loud I can almost hear the rumble of it from the bathroom, where two pitcher's worth of Killian's Red sploshes raucously into my bowl. When I return to the kitchen —site of my last humiliating encounter with Joyce Askew— I pour an overflowing mound of Purina Kitten Chow into Rikki's bowl, and then, in the soft light of the outside street lamp, I peel the cat from Kelley's arms and kiss her full on the mouth. Rikki hits the floor with a thud but keeps on purring. Kelley tastes of cigarettes and patchouli. I am besieged with the smell and feel of her, and my hands, as if of their own accord, begin traveling up her waist.

Grabbing my wrists, she says, "Do you have a shirt?"

"Sure sure sure," I chant, and make a lunge for my closet, readjusting myself as I go. When I return to the kitchen I find Kelley crouched over my cat who, very much as if Joyce Askew never existed, sprawls happily on the floor kneading the air with her front paws and arching her neck against

Kelley's expert hand. The vision gives me a momentary jolt: Rikki has moved on. I'm the only one here still hung up on Whatsername.

"Here," I say, and hand Kelley a blue Oxford button-down. She takes the shirt without comment, gives Rikki one last stroke, and disappears inside the bathroom.

In the interim I ready the bed. I turn on the lamp, fold down the sheet, turn off the lamp, turn it back on again, take off my shirt, turn off the lamp. Part of me wants her to walk in now, while I'm undressing: that way she can direct me, let me know how much to remove. I can hear her mill around in the bathroom. The toilet shudders. I drop my Dapper's khakis, heavy with ones and quarters. I peel off my socks.

When she finally emerges, the seashell whoosh of the bathroom trailing behind her, I am standing cross-armed in the center of my bedroom, in my boxers. She's carrying her clothes, neatly folded and stacked like a pile of newspapers. The tail of my shirt touches the tops of her milky thighs, the collar yawns wide open. When I see her bra on top of the stack of clothes a liquid warmth travels down my throat and settles in my gut.

"We sleep, okay?" she says, as she places her clothes on top of my dresser. I catch a glimpse of her bikini underwear: silk, firetruck red. She had prepared.

"Sure, you got it." I slip into the cool sheets.

No sooner does she join me than her thigh drops heavily over my waist. Then she snuggles close and finds a niche. We burrow deeper into the sheets and rub noses, snuffle collarbones, kiss eyelids. All number of deplorable visions enter my head lightning fast, and squirming from underneath her leg I prepare a some sort of stupid come-on I hope will yield an all-systems-go. But Kelley's thigh stays right where it is, fiercely, to which obdurate message she adds a hand on my bare chest.

"You know," she whispers into my ear, "everybody gets slammed one time or another."

The sentence registers, more or less, but I can't place the context. In fear of losing what I might as well call "momentum," I reply, "No idea what you're talking about," and try to sit up again.

But the thigh stays right where it is. She smiles. I suddenly realize this girl knows her way around a StairMaster.

"I don't think you understand what I'm saying."

"Sure I do." But actually, I don't. I have no idea what she's saying. A complex moment, this. A situation riddled with complications. After a few moments, I turn to her and admit, "Okay, I have no idea what you're saying."

She smiles again. Pats me playfully on the chest. "Exactly," she whispers, and it does not entirely escape my notice that this is the exact same word Joyce used right before I asked her to leave me alone so that I could complete my own psychic undoing. "That's your whole problem."

I lie beside her and stare at the ceiling, my stomach the size of a child's angry fist. I have no idea what I'm supposed to do next. Am I being scolded or seduced? Am I being helped or reprimanded? I'm back in that formless psychic battlefield of singlehood, for which I can only blame Joyce. I then note the ethical dilemma of thinking of her now, at this moment, with Kelley's thigh still firmly pressing on my torso. With each passing moment my momentum diminishes, but I can't decide what to do next, can't figure out how to salvage this situation. I'm torn between a burning desire to start kissing her on the mouth and an equally powerful urge to roll over and give her my back. Which would she prefer? Which would *I*? Soon, Rikki jumps onto the bed with a little ragged catch in her purr, turning three times and coiling herself into the valley between mine and Kelley's legs. Even the purr annoys the fuck out of me. All this time Kelley hasn't moved so much as an inch. Her breathing, slow and deliberate, could mean either sleep or impatience, but before I can decide what to do next I slide helplessly into one of my interior monologues with Joyce. I tell her off once and for all, then ask for her forgiveness, then imagine her tearful apology and her heartfelt request for another try, and when Kelley, finally getting the message I suppose, slowly removes her thigh and rolls away from me I realize, with a feeling I can only grudgingly interpret as shame, that she probably feels as bitter and betrayed as I felt a month ago when Joyce—dressed, it now hits me, in the exact same Oxford shirt—slept in this same bed, on these same unwashed sheets. With the exception that Joyce probably didn't feel like a complete asshole.

FINALLY, IN MAY, I see her for the very last time.

In truth, I am out looking for her—I look for her all the time, of course, though not always so overtly—but this time it works. Holy shit, I see her. It is a Saturday near the end of the school year, and I am wandering drunk and sunburned through the end-of-the-year carnival set up on the university's front parking lot. The carnival has attracted a motley collection of students and inner-city kids, and the two factions don't seem inclined to mingle. Since I belong to neither group, I feel comfortable walking around alone. Rides spin and loom over my head—a black Octopus, a Rockin' Toboggan, a Ferris wheel—and at every corner I encounter food. Nervously I scarf down a conch fritter, a corn dog, then a gyro, in that order. Beer is served in plastic grain cups with a colorful design advertising this year's carnival theme, and I drink three of these in no time flat.

But the rides aren't what interest me. I'm interested in the skits. It is a university tradition that all the fraternities and sororities team up to put on a series of plays. Each fraternity/sorority team builds out of scrap wood a complete playhouse—a "facade" they call it—the front of which is intended to advertise the contents of the play inside. One play this year is about Martians who visit the Oprah Winfrey show, so the facade looks accordingly like an enormous television set, complete with knobs made of automobile tires and a cat-eared antennae fashioned from two tinfoiled hula hoops. Another one looks like the Globe Theatre crossed with a disco: the play inside is a "musical" starring Hamlet, Macbeth, and Cleopatra. But it is Joyce's facade I want to locate. I search all over the carnival looking in vain; astonishingly, I can't remember the name of her sorority. I even pay my dollar and sit in on two or three skits, thinking each time that I'm in the right one. But no Joyce.

Then, just as I am heading to my car, I see her. She is standing off to the side of a facade made to look like a comic book laid open on its spine. The front is decorated with a series of panels, each one containing what looks like a full-scale Lichtenstein. The patrons enter through the lowermost panel. Because she is in costume I almost don't recognize her. It is the costume, not her, that catches my eye: red knee boots, metallic blue hot pants, red shoulderless bodice. A shiny red cape swings around and I find myself looking straight into the eyes of Wonder Woman, gold tiara and all. It is only with concentration that I realize I have finally located Joyce Askew. She sees me, and for a split second I have a vision of her crouching down and taking flight. But then she walks over to the mesh fence and pokes her hand through. I squeeze her fingertips.

"Hey, Hayes." Her dreamy smile tells me that she is stoned.

"You look great," I tell her, and I mean it. My knees tremble.

"Thanks. Have you seen the play?"

"Actually, no. I couldn't remember which sorority you were in, if you can believe that, so I went to all the wrong ones, all of them terrible."

"Well, come and see it now. We've got a performance in about three minutes."

"I'd love to," I say, stepping back, "but I've got work." I point to my watch and shrug.

"Hey—" she calls, and I stop. "Congratulate me. I got into Columbia for grad school. I found out yesterday."

The news sears through me like a blast of winter. "That's great." I smile and nod. What else can I say to her? That I sent some résumés, for no good reason, to Miami, Florida, the farthest possible point south from where she'll be? That her sorority sister Kelley Mullens won't look me in the face anymore? That I've wasted this entire winter doing nothing but getting over her? The gold eagle on her chest glistens in the sun. Her cape lifts in the breeze. "I wish you all the best," I add lamely.

"Maybe we could have dinner some night," she says, but I know better than to grab hold of this. It's just something people say to each other when they no longer have anything in common anymore. Let's do lunch. Call me sometime. God, I've been so busy lately.

"Sure," I tell her. "Just call me whenever."

"I'll do that." She points her thumb to the facade behind her and shrugs. "Show business," she vamps, fluttering her eyelashes. "What can I say?"

To avoid the sight of her walking away from me, all over again, I turn and leave *her* for once. But before I reach my car I look back just in time to see the end of her cape disappear through the stage door. Then the door closes. For a moment the whole facade wobbles, while off in the distance, far beyond the wire-mesh fence, Ferris wheels turn and children shriek and marching-band music pounds the air, a sound so loud that my chest, even from this distance, registers the hollow thump-a-thunk of a brainless bass drum.

6. STIR CRAZY

For a brief period—sometime between college graduation and the rest of my life—I lived next door to two strippers. Which wasn't what they told me at first.

"Cocktail waitresses," said one.

"An unbelievable drag," said the other. "You have no idea."

I was twenty-four years old, two years out of college and totally unencumbered by such things as structure or direction or ambition. Lacking any compelling reason to live anywhere else, I'd moved to Miami to chase away the persistent ghost of Joyce Askew.

"I'm sure it's not so bad," I told them. This all happened outside my apartment about a month after I moved in.

"Trust us," they said in unison, and fell to giggling.

Nikki and Lesley. Cocktail waitresses. If you think about it, they weren't actually lying all that much. Cock. Tail. Tips. The tools of their trade.

"So where is this place?" I asked, being neighborly. "What's it called?"

"Oh, you don't want to come in there," Lesley assured me.

Lesley was the bigger of the two. Much bigger, actually. I admit she unsettled me, towering there in the grass behind my apartment. The sunlight gave her bleached hair a slick, lemony sheen. Easily five nine, five ten, she was an enormous girl, not fat so much as husky, her ample hips and thighs rippling as if an undulating current had been frozen underneath the skin. She possessed a curious masculine appeal—that and an absolutely stupendous set of tits. Truly first rate. In due course, I was to learn she had a little boy named Bruno, who, at age three, was understandably unaware of what a disaster he had for a mommy, though I think he suspected something. Nikki, on the other hand, struck me as both harmless and alluring, in a crisp teenage way. Her hair, in contrast to Lesley's, was naturally blond, cropped at the neck and moussed into a gummy spike at her forehead. She looked like a hot high-school number, cozy and suburban in cutoff jeans, bikini top, and unbuttoned men's shirt. Her fingers were jammed into the pockets of her shorts and she rocked back and forth on her stiff legs. I have no doubt Nikki went through a horse stage; I'm willing to bet her sport in middle school was gymnastics; she was the product of a quarter century's intake of diet soda and peanut butter. She was conventionally pretty, her pleasant face marred only by a slight Germanic underbite.

"No, really," I persisted. "I'd love to go. I'm new in town and I don't know anybody." In fact, I'd been desperate for a reason to get out of my apartment and this seemed as good a way as any.

Nikki smiled at Lesley, as if waiting further instruction. Clearly, old Lez here was the leader.

"Trust me," she said. "It's not your sort of place"—still not naming it—"nothing but creeps and lowlife scum. Them and your basic greaseball jerks. Save yourself the trouble." Lesley had me pegged me already. I was a safe bet.

THE LADY DID HAVE A POINT. Then again, she was a pathological liar. The facts, which I uncovered on my own, went as follows: Tuesday through Saturday, from 9 P.M. to 5 A.M.—like nocturnal secretaries—Nikki and Lesley stripped to their smiles at a place called Stir Crazy, located in southwest Homestead right off the expressway. For the last month I'd passed it almost on a daily basis. Basically, it was a box and a parking lot. It had a lone front door and gratuitous cast-iron bars across its bricked-in windows. A bad place, to be sure, beaming with bad karma. Absurdly, it was sandwiched between a Blockbuster Video and a Wal-Mart shopping plaza, this being Miami, the City That Absorbs Anything —any culture, any language, any crime. The sign out front guaranteed those brave enough to enter an ALL-NUDE RE-

VIEW. As if to underscore the sincerity of such a pledge, three silhouetted nudes performed a Dionysian jig inside a martini glass. In addition, pool and darts were offered as alternative attractions in the event one grew bored (but how?) with the all-nude review. I confess to being stirred the first time I saw Stir Crazy. As I am—sociologically, at least—white, Anglo-Saxon, and Protestant, I experience a WASPish thrill whenever I am confronted with a remnant, however insignificant, of Gomorrah. Those cast-iron bars on the windows haunted my imagination; that sign sent an unsettling warmth to my groin.

And so I was more than a bit surprised when, one night on my way home from work, I espied my two lovely neighbors dashing across the street en route to the forbidden lair. *Wow,* I thought, *what a coincidence! Imagine running into them down here!* They were dressed casually—shorts, T-shirts, sneakers—and under their arms, they carried overnight bags. For all the world, they looked as if they'd just returned from a slumber party. I honked as I sped past, but without so much as glancing my way, Lesley raised her arm and flipped me the bird. Just like that. At first I was nonplussed, then quickly realized that, to her, I was just another honker, simply one of an entire race of automotive rodents. I looked into my rearview mirror and caught a last glimpse of them as they kissed the bouncer by the door and sauntered inside Stir Crazy, bags slinging. Cock and tail. Brick windows. Pool and darts. My mind raced and I put two and two together.

• • •

Two nights after I'd found them out, Nikki and Lesley asked me to help them move a couch into their apartment. It was a Sunday night, hot and muggy in that broad, persistent way of Florida summers. There was beer. We made a party of it.

"How's work?" I asked, not without some satisfaction. I imagined this was how parents felt when confronted with a child's subterfuge.

"Man, I've gotta get out of that place," Nikki said, handing me a Budweiser. "I'm serious."

"Oh, pipe down," Lesley called from the kitchen. "You're not going anywhere, kiddo."

Nikki rolled her eyes.

We were sitting on the new couch, a lush blue sofa sleeper to which the dry, dusty scent of the furniture warehouse still clung. Moments before, Lesley and I had somehow hoisted the thing from the bed of her pickup, dragged it grunting and cursing down the hall and squeezed it through the deceptively narrow front door of their apartment. Throughout Nikki had served as navigator, motivator, and—in my case at least—agitator. It was her pants that did it: soft gray gym shorts, snug around the thighs and creased down the back so as to suggest the blithe absence of underpants. Nikki, Nikki, Nikki. Upon completing the task—the couch had landed with a thud cockeyed in the middle of the room, where, in accordance with Nikki's designerly admonitions, it had stayed —I was ashamed to realize that Lesley had frankly outmuscled me. Twice I'd dropped my end. *Twice.*

"Why do you want to quit?" I asked, delivering the line as if I'd read it somewhere. "Aren't you making enough?"

"Oh, I'm making plenty," she said, curling her leg into her chest. A smooth slope of underthigh widened into a buttock and then disappeared into the couch. "It's not that. It's the people. Weirdos like you wouldn't believe. Just sitting and staring. Get a life, you know? And they don't stare at your— um, at the dancer's face or even at her boobs. They stare somewhere else."

"No kidding?" I asked, sincerely curious. "Where do they stare?"

Nikki looked at me coyly, fluttering her lashes. The gesture seemed to say, *Take a guess* or, perhaps, *Don't press your luck*. I wasn't sure.

"They stare at the pussy," Lesley announced, entering the room with two beers dangling from a six-pack ring. Evidently, they were both for her. She plopped down and fixed her gaze on me. "Innat what you'd look at, Parker Boy? The pussy?"

Silence. Invisibly, the air conditioner hummed. "Maybe," I said.

"Don't you know?" She popped open one of her Buds. "Or is this all too dirty for you?"

"Oh," I said, forcing a smile, "I'm not such a prude."

Coming to my rescue, Nikki stretched a leg across the couch and kicked Lesley playfully. "Jesus, Lez, be cool."

"Oh, I'm just *playing* with him," Lesley quipped, her face aglow. "You know I'm just playing, don't you, Park?"

In fact, I didn't know she was playing. But to let on that I couldn't take a joke was surely to invite more of her invective, so I said, "Hey, man, of course."

"Well," Nikki said, "Okay, then." We all drank our beer.

After a while, Nikki burped demurely. "Anyway," she continued, "what I mean is, what is it with men? No offense, Parker, I don't mean you. I mean, you know, men in general."

Lesley snorted in disdain.

"Pardon me?"

"Wake up, honey. Don't you know by now? Haven't you figured it out? Watch this." Lesley turned to me, stared me straight in the eyes and said, "Hey, Parker, we're lying our asses off. We're not cocktail waitresses. We're dancers. Nude dancers." Without taking her eyes off mine, she reached for her beer.

I was clearly being outcooled here, plain and simple. But to save face, I performed a not very convincing shrug and said, "I'd figured as much."

Lesley sent a current of venom my way. "What's that supposed to mean?"

Changing strategies, I stammered, "I saw you guys Friday night. You were walking into Stir Crazy with your work clothes under your arms." I let this sink in, in full anticipation of their amazement: a conjurer in our midst! But only Nikki evidenced the slightest twitch of surprise. I charged forward: "When you said you cocktail-waitressed at a strip bar I thought, 'Now, why would a strip bar hire cocktail waitresses when they already have strippers?'" Actually, this piece of logic had only just occurred to me.

"Well," Lesley informed me, "sorry to burst your bubble, Sherlock, but there *are* cocktail waitresses at Stir Crazy. Have you ever been to a strip joint?"

"Sure," I said, imagining with satisfaction how nimbly this admission would slip through a lie-detector test. What I mean is, it was true: One night in college, I went to a topless place called Charley's with some buddies. We were doing some male bonding. We'd also, prior to entering, done a fair number of bong hits in a friend's car. I remember a woman on stage in crotch-high cutoffs writhing to a song called "Rock You Like a Hurricane." I also remember throwing up an order of potato skins in one of Charley's gleaming black bathroom stalls.

"So why'd you go?" Nikki asked. Lesley was sitting back and smiling into space.

"It was something to do." Which wasn't too far from the truth.

"But why a strip bar?" Nikki wanted to know. "What's the big deal about seeing naked boobs?"

I gave the question some consideration. I wanted to let them know I was above bourgeois morality, above archaisms like sin and decency. Besides, the question was an interesting one: What *was* the big deal, anyway?

"Well, it's not just the naked chest," I told her. "I mean, let's face it: a boob's a boob. That's not it at all. I think what guys get off on is the fact that they are watching a woman take off all her clothes in a room packed with other men. It's like, I've been in restaurants or whatever and a woman will walk in, and from out of nowhere, this little voice will say, 'I wonder what she looks like naked.' You know the voice I'm talking about? It's the same one that says, 'I wish I had a million dollars' or 'I'd like to punch this guy in the teeth.' So when you're at a strip bar it's like that woman you're looking at hears what you're thinking and says, 'You really want to know? Okay, I'll show you.' Which is pretty mind-boggling, if you think about it."

Neither woman seemed to find any of this particularly mind-boggling, or even insightful, so I kept right on going, digging desperately for profundity. "I mean, this woman you don't even know is going to undress for you. And why? Because you want to know what her body looks like. You and all the other people in the bar. And because you've paid her to take her clothes off, which, of course, is another thing: the money. If it were free, I don't think it would be nearly as interesting."

"Same goes for cocaine," Lesley said, laughing.

Nikki shook her head but didn't say anything. Was she impressed? Did she admire my critical acumen? Was she aroused by my liberal openness?

"Well," Nikki said, "all I know is, women don't do that stuff."

"Oh, yes they do," Lesley disagreed.

"Okay, right, they do. But they're not as bad as men."

"Not as bad as men?" Lesley repeated. "Are you kidding me? Let me tell you something, honey: Women are every bit as bad as men when it comes to sex. And we're better at it, too. Not only can we talk about it more, we can also do it longer. And you know it, bub. You know it and it scares the bejesus out of you."

She let this hang for a second. Only gradually did I realize she was addressing me now. No one argued. "Basically, men are cowards when it comes to sex. Simple as that. If they aren't in charge, they turn into bullies. And if they're too nice to be bullies, they're just plain afraid. Men like to fantasize about women who initiate sex, but honestly I don't think half of them would know what to do if some woman actually did it. So that's why they go to strip clubs. Not to pay money and look at boobs, but to get off on the idea that all these beautiful women just can't wait to take their clothes off and *get down*. Snap your fingers and she's naked: the ultimate harem fantasy. But they don't actually do anything with these women—that would *really* be scary. Instead they walk out the door and return to their pathetic little relationships with their pathetic little wives who wait for hubby to get a hard-on while hubby closes his eyes and pretends he's fucking a stripper."

Here she stopped, her words hovering in the air. No one knew what to say, least of all me. It was probably my place to object, I don't know. Maybe Lesley was just "playing" with me again. Nevertheless, I felt . . . oh, six inches tall. Give or take an inch.

"Hey," she finally said, tapping me lightly on the knee, "I'm just talking. Spouting off bullshit. Surely you have a *little* teensy objection to what I just said." She was smiling now, dissolving the tension, her index finger and thumb pinched together in the universal symbol for *little*. Boy, did this girl know how to command a room. "I mean, this is just a discussion, a debate. Now it's your turn."

"Okay," I said tentatively, looking at Nikki for support (and getting none: she was staring into her beer), "I do have a little objection. First of all, you're assuming that all men go to strip clubs. You're assuming a lot, in fact. I mean," I continued, only now discovering my actual objection, "maybe you've just been hanging out with the wrong men."

Lifting her beer, she said, "Present company excepted, I suppose," and gave us each a hearty wink before downing the entire can in one long, muscular gulp.

BRUNO WAS AN ABSOLUTELY gorgeous child, a perfect little man in miniature Nikes and garish pink-and-black swim trunks (I never saw him dressed in anything else), his round little head near to bursting with energy and suggesting —in the chin, in the flat nose—his mommy. Mommy had let his hair grow long in the back so that it curled at the ends, as delicate and thin as Bible pages. It was weeks before I properly met him, as he spent most of his time with "Aunt

Doddie," a woman who was apparently not Lesley's sister and whose job it was to watch the kid while Lesley earned the keep. When Lesley and Nikki talked about Bruno, they accentuated their encomiums with guttural purrs of maternal affection. *Grrrrr*.

As for Bruno and me, we didn't hit it off all that well.

"Bruno, my man!" I erupted, dropping to my haunches. I swooped on the child and extended my hand. I wanted him to slap me five, but I now see the poor little boy must have thought I was after his cash. Three years old and already the street was asserting its territorial rights. He clutched at one of Mommy's tree-trunk thighs and hid from his attacker.

Slammed. Rejected. Bruno whimpered and I stood to receive my just deserts.

"He's just cranky," Lesley was kind enough to say. She reached behind her and stroked the child's head. "He didn't get enough sleep last night"—turning around to Bruno—"*did* you, pumpkin?"

Bruno whimpered again.

How did Lesley come to be with child? The facts on that were hard to ascertain. Stories varied. During that early period when Nikki and Lesley were still "cocktail waitresses," no mention whatsoever was made of the boy. That night of the big couch move, however, the lady herself, from out of nowhere, inundated me with Bruno snapshots, Bruno toys, Bruno art—an entire compendium of Bruno memorabilia. There was no end to the kid's talents, nor was there any perceivable end to Lesley's affection. In short, she was the model of the proud loving mother. I know this because she told me so herself.

"I don't want to sound conceited," she prefaced, "but I'm a great mom, you guys. I'm serious, you should see me. You know, Nikki. Tell him how good I am with Bruno. She's seen me, Parker. When all my friends come over, they can't believe it, how good we are with one another. They absolutely love him. He's such a lucky little shit, he's got women waiting on him hand and foot all the time. Isn't he lucky? I bet you'd trade places with him, wouldn't you, Park? Surrounded by women like that . . ."

Once Lesley started talking about Bruno, she couldn't stop. In fact, she refused to stop talking that night, period. She told us how long she'd been stripping (two years, ten years: it varied), what she planned to do when she quit ("I'm going to New York, get a leather jacket, and apply for a job on MTV. I want to be around *real* people, you know?"); she told us what a good Mommy she was and how she ended up with Bruno (version 1: she got pregnant via some customer she slept with once and never saw again); she shared with us her religious beliefs (although she wasn't "real religious or anything," she firmly maintained that there was a God who in His wisdom and love watched over her and guided her and would transport her to heaven after she died because there was no way this was all there was); we learned why she hated her parents but adored her sister, whereupon it was also revealed that her sorry upbringing compelled her to this day to be a terrifically loyal friend despite *some people* who seemed unable to approach her plateau of devotion; and we learned, again, how she ended up with Bruno (version 2: Dad was a guy named Hugo who was currently embarking on the second year of a seven-year prison term by way of a heartbreakingly botched cocaine deal he'd gotten himself roped into). Near the end, somewhere in the middle of her second Bruno tale, her voice began to shake. She started rocking back and forth on the couch, hunched over with her arms between her legs, an ankle clasped in each hand. She also began clacking her teeth together, in sync with some internal, stuttering rhythm. When Nikki got up at one point Lesley damn near split her own skull in panic.

"Gah, Lesley, I'm just getting a beer," Nikki said, giving me a God-what-a-space-cadet look.

"*No!*" Lesley shouted—and loudly. The abruptness of the outburst startled even her.

Much later that night, after Lesley had whirled out of the apartment on the arm of yet another Stir Crazy stripper called, alternately, Alex or Star (one name, just take a guess, was her Stir Crazy nom de guerre), Nikki and I did some redecorating in her room, which, to my mind, looked sufficiently lived in as it was, which showed how much I knew.

"I want to put this painting over my bed," Nikki told me, displaying for my visual enjoyment an enormous pastel drawing of a bottle-nosed dolphin emerging from a foam of ocean water. "Think you could hold it up while I see how it looks?"

I had to admit it was quite beautiful—its lush washes of blue and green and the glossy white strip of translucence highlighting the animal's tumid flesh. No question about it, the girl had talent. So, as per my role, I bestowed on her the line for which I had clearly been summoned: "Did you do this?"

"What?" she asked, with a barely concealed smile. "Oh, that? Gah, years ago. Junior, sophomore year or something, I can't even remember now."

"Hold up a second. You went to college?" I tried to swallow back the incredulity in my voice, but it was too late.

She regarded me with scorn. "Yes, *I* went to college. Is that so hard to believe?"

"No, no, no," I insisted. "I just thought you said you . . . I don't know, I must have been thinking of Lesley." Surely, I thought, Lesley didn't go to college.

But Nikki was kind enough to wave my pomposity aside —why, I have no idea. Frankly, I think I should have been raked over the coals. What Nikki did instead was rather astonishing. She completely, and with no prodding on my part, opened up to me. She sat down on the floor where she was standing, picked at the carpet, and began opening. Here's what I learned.

Late in her junior year, while attending an art institute in Connecticut she was offered a job as a dolphin trainer at the

Miami Seaquarium, a position she immediately accepted, owing largely to her still unexplained (though why explain it?) love affair with sea life in general and porpoises in particular. Earning a mere five dollars an hour, she served as a trainer for a year, doing seven to ten shows a day for tourists and old folks and elementary-school children. But eventually she incurred enough debt to elicit serious panic, and since she was too proud to ask her parents for help (especially as they'd disapproved of her leaving school in the first place), she began looking for ways to earn a little extra cash. A month prior to this a friend of hers had left the Seaquarium for similar financial reasons, so Nikki gave the friend a call to see what kind of work she'd found.

"As first, I was totally shocked," Nikki told me. "Tricia—that was her name—was always sort of wild, but I never thought she was the stripper type. But she assured me it was no big deal. And anyway, she was rolling in cash—150 bucks a night, over 200 on weekends. That was like a whole week's pay at the Seaquarium. So I told her I would check it out. What was there to lose?"

One night Nikki went to see Tricia at Stir Crazy.

"The owner was a pretty nice guy, and Tricia told him I was looking for work—which I really *wasn't*, you see, Tricia just *assumed*. But he seemed pretty harmless, and he told me I could try it out for a night, to see if I liked it, and that I could keep the tips I made, and I was thinking, 'Car payment, Visa bill,' all that shit. So I went back the next night and I did it. I was wasted out of my skull—stoned, drunk, you name it—but I did it. The funny thing was, everybody was so cool—the other girls, the customers, the DJ—it just seemed so harmless. So, I don't know, *innocent,* I guess. Besides, I walked out of there with enough money for rent *and* utilities."

But those Stir Crazy nights didn't start until roughly 10 P.M. and they didn't end until early the next morning, so it wasn't long before Nikki began missing days at the Seaquarium. It also wasn't long before she was out of debt—her Visa bill got paid, she began paying off a student loan, she even thought about buying a car—and so all geared to put Stir Crazy and her short but lucrative life as an all-nude stripper behind her, she walked into her boss's office at Seaquarium to apologize for all the days she'd been missing only to be told that she'd been sacked. All of a sudden, it was Stir Crazy or starve.

That was three months ago.

"But I don't mind," she insisted. "Not really, anyway. I know I won't be doing this my whole life. I just act like I'm someone else when I'm up there, which is true, in a way: That's not *me,* Nikki Coleman, dancing in the nude, but Trixxi Park—my stage name—this sexy girl who can fuck the daylights out of a pole. The pole—I'm sorry—there's, like, this pole at the end of the stage and you sort of, I don't know, fuck it, I guess. Guys get off on it. But sometimes I get kind of spooked, you know? Like last Friday night. I was perfectly sober and I was just dancing like usual and from out of nowhere it suddenly occurred to me that I did *not* want to be on that stage. There I was, under the lights, and all I could think was, 'Man, what am I doing here in the nude in front of all these guys?' It wasn't even that crowded —or maybe *that* was the problem, I don't know. The bartender was watching a Braves game on the television and some guys were playing darts and out of the corner of my eye I could see Lesley and Tricia and Alex all on the couch sharing a smoke like nothing was the matter. It was just so weird. And in front of me was this guy who'd been there all night drinking ginger ale, and he hadn't moved once, not even to take a leak. He was just sitting at this table, all alone, nursing a soda and staring at my vagina, like a kid staring at a video game."

What, she thinks that's weird?

"But now that I'm sharing rent with Lesley," she continued, "I can save even more money, maybe enough to buy a car after all. And as soon as I do I'm packing up and moving to Oregon."

Presently, we did a bit of stripping ourselves, and got a little stir crazy to boot. But we didn't have sex. Not really.

"No, Parker," she pleaded in the dark, her pastel dolphin looming above us, "not so quick. I need to get to *know* a person before I . . . well, you know."

Actually, I *did* know. In truth. I wasn't entirely sure I was ready to sleep with her, either. Not that she wasn't arousing.

Boy was she ever. Her hips were a bit squarish and her bottom had a sad, deflated flatness to it, but her skin was luminous and smooth, her legs sturdy and nimble, and her breasts soft and . . . I don't know, perky or whatever. Besides, she came absolutely alive when her clothes came off—a case of "bringing the office home," I suppose, though not really. The thing was, I genuinely liked her. I found her smart, lively, interesting, strong-willed, funny, and terrifically sexy. I was utterly capable of falling for her. And once I realized this, there in the nude in her girlish bedroom, I found I strongly disapproved of how she earned a living.

"You're better than Stir Crazy," I told her, after the "Should we have sex?" question had been sufficiently settled in the negative. "You really should quit."

"I know, I know. I will—I told you I would already, remember? When I say I'm going to do something, I do it."

"Good," I told her. "That makes me feel better."

"By the way," she said, sitting up all of a sudden, "that reminds me. I've been meaning to ask you what you do for a living. You never told me."

I thought about this for a moment and then said, "I'm setting up contacts." I was suddenly afflicted with a full bladder. "Hey, how do I get to your—"

"Wait a second. What's that supposed to mean? How are you paying rent?"

I plopped back down on the pillow, holding my breath. "I

wait tables," I finally admitted. "At a place not far from Stir Crazy. Right off U.S. 1."

She took this in. After a bit, she said, "Didn't you tell me you were in graduate school or something?"

"No," I fibbed. "I said I was *thinking* about graduate school."

We both remained silent for a while. Nikki finally punctured the stillness between us by saying, "Oh," and with that I slipped on my shorts and went back to my own apartment.

For the next two or three weeks, Nikki and I were devoted bed partners. She generally slept at my place, as Lesley was slowly becoming unmanageable. Bruno was living there twenty-four/seven now, Aunt Doddie having told Lesley she was tired of baby-sitting and not getting paid. So the poor child had himself a full-time mommy—and a mommy who couldn't work nights anymore. With no money coming in, Lesley responded as any financially strapped single mother might: she considerably increased her daily intake of cocaine. Boy, was she a mess. Boy, was Bruno a mess. During this dark period, the little guy and I became pretty good buddies: the poor kid just didn't have anyone else. Lesley was nearly always strung out —and if she wasn't, she wanted to be. All of which cast her— and, by innocent extension, Nikki as well—into appalling debt.

Eventually, she found a new baby-sitter; the problem was that the woman—an adorable Hispanic grandmother named Mrs. Monteleagre who lived upstairs—agreed to watch

Bruno during the day only, and so Lesley became one of Stir Crazy's handful of day strippers. As you may have guessed, there isn't much money in day stripping—folks generally like to read the newspaper with breakfast. Most of what she made went directly to Mrs. Monteleagre; the rest went to an enterprising cocaine dealer who also lived upstairs.

Meanwhile, Nikki and I slowly ran out of things to say to each other. Initially we'd drawn comfort from the fact that neither of us liked what we were doing with ourselves; in bed after lovemaking, we'd smoke cigarettes, spin plans, imagine scenarios, work out our finances. But we grew tired of reminding each other that nothing much was happening with our lives. The longer we stayed together, the more pronounced became our relative failures. We reminded each other of how much we hated where we were right now. Hence our conversation increasingly turned toward Lesley's dramatic disintegration—a neutral source of encouragement to us both.

Or at least I thought it was neutral.

"I'm telling you, Nikki, you have *got* to get out of there," I told her one night in my apartment. "She's determined to bring you right down with her."

"I'm fine," Nikki assured me. "It's a bad month for Lesley and she needs a friend. I can't walk out on her—what about Bruno?"

"But you've already poured all your savings into the entire rent, the electric bill, the phone bill. What about your car? What about moving? Her coke problem isn't your problem."

"You want me to move?" she asked. When I didn't answer, I sensed a throb of resentment pulse between us. "Anyway," Nikki continued, "Lesley's under a lot of stress right now. It helps her cope, she says—which is bullshit, I know, but she helped me out when I got fired at the Seaquarium, she took me to work every night—I owe her my support is all."

"Support?" I shouted. "Lesley needs treatment, not support. I can't believe—"

"Hey, just stay out of this, all right?" She sat up and wrapped her arms around her legs. "You don't know anything. You wait tables, you're still mooching off your parents —yes, you are, don't feed me that crap. If your folks quit bailing you out each month, you'd be in worse shape than Lesley is. You have no idea what it means to be on your own, completely self-sufficient, nobody supporting you or putting shirts on your back. Not only does Lesley have herself to worry about, she has Bruno. It's harder than you think."

I didn't say anything at first. I was still taking in the fact that Nikki sounded like a grown-up.

Finally, I said, "She needs help is all I'm saying."

To which Nikki said, "And just what do you think I'm trying to do here?"

A few minutes later, she got dressed and went home.

• • •

I NEVER SAW HER again after that. For starters, one of my "contacts" came through. I was hired as a management trainee for a wholesaler in Miami that specialized in children's toys and restaurant supplies. I quit my table-waiting job and started putting in fifty-five- to sixty-hour workweeks, driving all over Miami in hopes of persuading some toy retailer to start carrying a new Mario Brothers videocassette we were offering that summer. I also wasted hours and hours trying to peddle a table-waiter beeper system no restaurant in its right mind would waste money on. On Friday nights, I went drinking with my old waiter buddies from the summer.

Since I was working days now and Nikki worked nights, it was no major feat not to run into her. As for Lesley, I never saw her, either—or Bruno, for that matter. Each night, as I dragged my tired body past their apartment, I stopped and listened for some sound to drift through their door, but I never heard a peep. I began to wonder if they even lived there anymore.

And then, one night—a Friday, actually—I was getting soused with the gang at my old restaurant when I started spilling my guts about Nikki and my little summer adventure. I had never told anyone—not even my closest friends —and it was so wonderful to get it all out in the open that I literally felt something lift right off my shoulders. Talking about her made me miss her. Granted, I'd been missing her

for months, but this was the first time I'd admitted it, even
to myself. What's more, as I gave her name public utterance,
I also lent her a reality I'd been suppressing all fall. My
new life as a management trainee, my new clothes, my new
acquaintances—all of it seemed suddenly unreal and insub-
stantial. What mattered was Nikki, in my bedroom, squirming
out of those cutoff jeans.

What happened next was something of a blur. One minute
I was at the bar at my former place of employment, the next
minute I was within breathing distance of the Stir Crazy
bouncer I'd seen Nikki and Lesley kiss that day last summer.
I stood there at the door with my ID, waiting for the guy to
recognize me. But then I remembered I'd never been to Stir
Crazy.

We tumbled inside, all five of us. The place was appallingly
small, about as spacious as a medium-sized lecture hall. Every
wall contained a glittering mirror, while all about lay plush
burgundy sofas and chairs. Extending from the bar like an
enormous outstretched tongue was the stage, lined with flashing rows of light and tipped at the end by the pole Nikki had
claimed she was rather adept at "fucking." The moment we
walked in, a woman I vaguely recognized provided a visual
demonstration of this very activity, writhing and undulating
in time to the European synthesizer music pulsating from the
loudspeaker. In one corner, under bright lights, two men
played pool. MTV flickered from the bar TV.

"So, Parker," someone said, "where is she?

"Seriously, dude," someone else joined in. "Let's see the old missus."

But I was having second thoughts. "Aw, let's get out of here." I started maneuvering my way toward the door.

But on my way out, I ran into Alex, a.k.a. Star, who, I was stunned (and not a little flattered) to find, recognized me.

"Nikki," she said to me, as if that were my name. She'd just finished dancing and was heading back to the dressing room, her tiny things—a pair of crotch-splitting shorts and a bikini top—clutched modestly over her chest, thereby leaving the glistening moss of her pubic hair bare as God had made it.

"Right," I said. "Nikki Coleman. We're pals. Is she here?"

"Here?" Alex, a.k.a. Star, said. "God, she quit ages ago. Went to Connecticut or something to go to school."

My heart sank. Now I knew I wanted to go home. Immediately.

"How long ago was this?" I asked.

She hesitated. *You should know all this,* her look seemed to say. Or maybe all she meant was, *Can't you see I'm naked?* "How long? I don't know, a month, two months, something like that. It was after all that shit with Lesley."

"What shit?" I wanted to know. I tried to will myself sober.

"Forget it," Alex, a.k.a. Star, suddenly corrected herself. "Look, it's great seeing you, but I've got to run. Have a good

time." With that, she disappeared behind a curtain, her plump
bum quivering behind her.

I got a Jim Beam at the bar and sat down at a table by myself, trying to piece together this new information. I'm not
sure how long I sat there, but before long, and from out of
nowhere, a high-heeled shoe suddenly smacked down next
to my arm. As I looked up, I felt pressure on my shoulder,
and before I could get my bearings, an enormous woman in
a one-piece minidress had hoisted herself, pumps and all,
onto my table. Whoops and hollers came from the bar.

"You asshole," said a familiar voice. "I knew you'd come
crawling in here eventually."

Looming above me, her face foreshortened above the
stately cliff of her chest, was none other than Lesley Lupus,
back on the night shift. I couldn't think of a single thing
to say.

"Well, a howdy-do would be nice," she sneered, and began grinding away on my table. Her dress—what little there
was of it—clung to her as if she'd been sealed in the thing.
"Some neighbor you are. You live next door and I haven't
heard shit from you in months."

"Same here," I said, which was intended to mean "Hello."

"Whatever," she said into space. By the whoops from the
bar, I surmised that Lesley had been "purchased" for me by
my thoughtful friends. Reading my thoughts, she said quietly, almost tenderly, "She bolted two months ago."

"I didn't know that," I lied.

"And why not?"

It was a good question. A valid question. What was I supposed to say? I clutched the side of the wobbling table, watching as Lesley's spiked heels cha-cha-ed dangerously close to my fingers. I waited for the moment to dissolve. At the bar, my friends grew unsettlingly quiet.

Lesley's heel scraped across the table and came down hard between my thumb and forefinger.

"I can't believe you didn't have the guts to even show your face," she was saying. "Or call. I mean, we were next door. And what gets me is she thought you were this nice guy. 'But, Lesley, he's really this, he's really that.' I said, 'If he's got a prick, he's a prick.' And I was right. You're a prick."

But my drunkenness emboldened me, so I looked up at her face. She wasn't moving anymore; her hands were on her hips and her hair was haloed by the overhead lights. "She never came by to see me, either," I pointed out.

"Because you threw her out!" Lesley snapped. An old codger at the next table looked up for the first time. All this while, he'd been staring at his drink, so as to honor the territorial rights of my purchase, I suppose.

"That's baloney," I said, slowly feeling absolved of responsibility. "She told you that?"

"She didn't tell me anything," Lesley said. "Nothing at all. She helped me pay off some debts and I found her a ride to Connecticut. End of story. She split for school, started living with her parents or something, and I haven't seen her since."

She looked over at the bar and I looked with her. One of my friends was waving an unidentifiable bill. "God, what an asshole," she said.

"No kidding," I agreed. I suddenly experienced the frightening realization that this towering woman still lived next door to me. That realization inspired in me a tentative hard-on. I chanced my first look up Lesley's snug, crotch-high skirt and I saw that she was wearing leopard-skin panties that only partially covered the brittle French cut of her pubic hair. I detected on her the faintly sour smell of urine. Her thighs were glossed with a light layer of sweat.

"Well," she said finally, "nice shooting the shit, neighbor, but I've gotta make a living. My boss is starting to wonder what I'm doing, so here's the deal: this is going to cost you twenty extra bucks. You understand?"

In fact, I did not understand. In my drunken state, I grew suddenly indignant—Nikki or no Nikki.

"Wait a second," I said. "I thought those guys already paid for it."

"They did," Lesley said, grinding in earnest now but still staring at the same vague spot in the middle of the room. "They paid money to see my tits. But remember that little voice you told us about? The one that's been asking you what my body looks like? Naked? In front of the guys? Well, that little voice has to cough up another twenty dollars or no dice." She pulled a shoulder strap down and my friends began to whoop again; the old man looked up, too. "It's the money, remember? That's what makes it interesting. I'm keeping this interesting for you, Parker Boy."

I thought about that for a second. I looked at my friends, I looked at the old man, I looked round the bar. Everyone's attention was focused on our table. Even the petite Asian woman preparing to take the main stage seemed captivated. Clutching a teddy bear (part of her act, I presumed), she waited at the edge of the stage and regarded Lesley with a bemused, admiring gaze.

My head hummed furiously. So did my groin. I had a boner in a strip bar—one of the cardinal no-nos, Nikki had once told me. There was no way I could get up without being detected, but there was also no way I could sit there and let Lesley grind forever, fully clothed. For now, we were the entertainment. The whole bar was depending on us.

The old man at the next table said, "Let's see it, honey— get the lead out."

"You got about five seconds," Lesley hissed, "and then I'm going to poke this heel into that little thing behind your zipper."

Hollering issued from the whole bar now. Pool cues were pounded, "Funky Cold Medina" burped through the sound system, and my hard-on was evidently not going away. *This woman lives next door,* I told myself.

"One . . . ," Lesley said, dropping another shoulder strap. The shouting got louder.

"Two . . . ,"

I shifted in my seat, stretching my leg.

"Three . . . ,"

With what I hoped was insouciant ease, I plucked a twenty out of my wallet and gingerly slid it between the twin towers of Lesley's glossy thighs. Verily, my left hand did not know what my right hand was doing.

Lesley smiled and brought her undulations to a halt. Slowly she crouched, her solid knees nearly bumping my shoulders. Her heady smell—sweat, cigarettes, bourbon— engulfed me.

"Not only are your friends pricks," she said, "but they're also suckers."

She stepped rather gracefully off the table and smoothed her dress. Meanwhile, Miss Teddy Bear was mounting the stage. I held my breath, waiting to see what was going to happen, but Lesley simply reached for my Marlboros on the table and helped herself to a butt.

"Wait a minute," I said, "what are you doing?" I was unable to hide the panic in my voice. Honest to God, I had no idea what this woman was up to.

"I'm leaving," Lesley informed me. She drew the cigarette under her nose and smiled smugly. "Got a date. I only came in to pick up my paycheck."

With that, she fluttered her fingers in farewell and began weaving through the tables toward the front door.

"Hang on a second," I called. She turned around and grinned. I wanted my twenty back, but I didn't dare ask for it. Instead, I stayed right where I was, pegged to my seat by a doggedly persistent hard-on. "You mean to tell me you aren't even working tonight?"

She turned around and shook her head. "You pathetic jerk," she called back, the unlit cigarette dangling between her lips. "I'm *always* working."

7. KARMA WHEEL

Parker wasn't alone. Trina, too, was having one bad mother of a week. Honestly, it was just one thing after another. Actually, Trina was having more or less the same bad week she had been having, over and over again, since she was twenty-one. Boy problems. Happiness problems. Unhappiness and unease and terror and self-loathing, all that sort of thing. Parker, on the other hand, was experiencing lots of little problems all at once, insignificant nagging little glitches in his karma that were beginning to pile up and tip him off balance. Two days ago, for instance, his landlord—a disreputable alcoholic troll named Jarvis (not "Mr. Jarvis," not "Jeb Jarvis," just Jarvis)—called Parker to tell him that the rent check Parker had written last week against a then-empty bank account had, not at all surprisingly, bounced. Also, coasting into the parking garage this morning, Parker's car suddenly, and mysteriously, began emitting a low guttural moan, and died. And last night Donna, his girlfriend of three months—and, not uncoincidentally, his office mate at work—had told him, all of a sudden, from out of nowhere, that she wanted "just to be friends." Or was it "to be *just* friends"? He couldn't remember. Which wasn't to suggest he hadn't been through this sort of thing before. In fact, his last three girlfriends—or was it four?— had wanted *just* to be *just* friends, so this was not exactly unfamiliar territory. Still, what with the car and the rent and all, it was really getting to him.

"I hear you, man," Trina said to him that morning at work. "I'm with you 100 percent."

Like Donna, Trina was an ex-girlfriend. And an office mate. You'd think Parker would have learned his lesson the first time around. You'd at least think Parker would have thought some such thing. But Parker didn't really think about such things—not overtly, anyway. Not so he could admit it out loud. Parker and that sort of thinking were on glancing, shaky terms. They encountered each other on the street, acknowledged each other with cold civility, and kept on walking.

"Oh hell, Donna's the least of my problems right now," he told her, sitting down at his cubicle. But he looked around for Donna anyway.

"She's in a meeting," Trina informed him. A silence fell over them both. Whereas Donna attended meetings, Parker and Trina, both former temps who had stayed on for the benefits and the security, remained at their adjoining cubicles all day, every day. To be sure, this wasn't exactly the sort of life Parker imagined for himself two years ago when he moved to Atlanta from Miami with the bold idea of starting over and jump-starting his adult life, but then again who ever said the imagination was a reliable source of information about adulthood?

After a pause, he said, "The car is the main thing. If it's the transmission, you know, I'm totally screwed. You have no idea. Skeee-roood."

"You should get another car, Parker, you really should. That thing is more trouble than it's worth."

She was right, of course: he should, and it was—a green 1982 Chevy Impala that his father had driven, with smug middle-class aplomb, all through the Reagan administration. But he resented hearing this from Trina: if Trina wanted a new car, she simply dipped into her trust fund and bought one.

"Yeah, " he said, "well, when I complete my leveraged buyout of this place I'll buy a whole effing fleet of new Chevy Impalas, one for everyone at the office."

"Boy, you *are* down. Listen to you." A supervisor walked by. Trina and Parker swiveled away from each other and began tapping randomly at their keyboards. When the coast was clear, she removed her hands, swiveled back, and said, "If it makes you feel any better, Jack and I are officially kaput."

"Really? How many times is that?"

"The last time, that's how many. Trust me. Trinkets flew, lamp shades fell, things were said. Lots of things. I'll tell you all about it if you go out with me tonight. I want to get totally *rocked*. We'll commiserate."

"Oooh, Trina, I don't know."

"C'mon, it'll be fun."

"I'm sure it will. I'm just so broke. And anyway, I—"

"We won't spend any money. *Please,* Parker, I really need to tie one on tonight. You can come over and give me all the gory details, my treat. I'll rent something."

Parker nodded, though he had misgivings. Secretly he wanted to leave the evening open. Maybe for Donna. Maybe because he wanted to sit at home and brood. He'd cancel later.

By EIGHT THAT EVENING, Parker was sitting on Trina's new Pier 1 couch sipping beer, smoking pot, and pouring his heart out. His thoughts rushed at him as if along sleek looping Hot Wheels tracks. He couldn't stopped talking. First, he told her all about the Donna business. Then he told her of his harrowing drive, after work, to the garage, his car poking along in the service lane at a breezy twelve-mile-an-hour clip, in the hot rush-hour sun, with no power steering and no air-conditioning (and no radio). Next he told her how he had run across the street to the bank after dropping off his car at the shop and how he had withdrawn $500 in cash—$475 for Jarvis, and $25 for himself, his weekend's entertainment budget—thereby leaving him a remaining balance of $46.78, which he calculated as just enough to float him until payday next Friday. And he told her about trudging home on foot amid the late afternoon crunch and stopping off at Jarvis's office to settle his debt in person.

But just as he was arriving at the part of the story where he took the wrong bus to Trina's apartment, he realized her eyes had glossed over and her attention had turned inward. He was narfing. "Narfing" was what you did sometimes when you were stoned. You begin telling a simple story but then you get sidetracked and start sniffing after every tangential thought that appears on the horizon, the same way a dog on a walk will catch a scent and veer off unexpectedly to the left or to the right or behind you or whatever, tangling the leash around your legs and generally pissing you off. That's narfing.

"Oh God," he said, "please shut me up."

As if roused from hypnosis, Trina blinked and looked up. "Oh no, go on, this is interesting."

"No it isn't." He waited for her to contradict him, and when she didn't he laughed it off. "You're just being nice."

"No, it sounds awful. I mean, it's interesting because it's so awful. Or something. It's like with me, like all the bad shit that always happens to me. How come? Why do so many bad things happen to me? And all at once, too, that's the thing. Why is that?"

"Weren't we going to watch a movie?"

"In a minute, yeah. Hey, are you okay? Are you hungry or anything?"

"No, I'm fine. I'm just kind of . . . Wow."

"I know. It's wicked weed, isn't?"

Parker nodded, grinned, sipped his beer. His teeth felt like plastic, his cheeks ached with smiling. What a strange place to be in right now. *Parker is here,* he told himself. *And I am here also.* He giggled.

"When bad stuff happens to me," Trina was saying from the floor as she fiddled with the VCR, "I get this kind of feeling like, I don't know, like the world is conspiring against me, that cosmic forces are hovering over my head and sending down curses. So then I start reading the horoscopes, because I figure, you know, maybe the same cosmic forces that are making me so miserable can start making me happy again. Why won't this work?"

"Press Play," Parker said blankly. He looked around the room. Trina had stuff everywhere, yet nothing was where it should be. Pots and pans hung on the walls, lamps sat on the floor, plants balanced on top of tables, carpets hung from the ceiling. Weird. He asked, "Why do you have throw rugs on your ceiling?"

She stopped what she was doing and looked up for a minute or ten minutes or an hour—Parker couldn't tell. Crouched there on the floor, with her long, brown hair cascading down her back and lamp light rimming the outline of her neck, she seemed somehow . . . what? Angelic, maybe. As if she were deep in prayer and supplication. The blood in his ears sang a falsetto hymn. Blood sang elsewhere as well.

"No reason," she finally decided, and looked back at him. Taking note, apparently, of the expression on his face, her eyes suddenly grew round. "What?"

"Nothing," he said, and shook her image free from his mind. Shame coursed through his bloodstream. Gotta watch yourself, boy.

No reason, she'd said. *No reason.*

All during the movie, which he'd seen already, he kept turning to look at Trina, who sat perfectly still beside him on the couch, the television images flickering across her face and her cheek glazed by a thin layer of down. Even through the lingering pot smoke he could detect her perfume—Chlöe? Giorgio?—a sharp potpourri of scents that made his blood race some more. In the latter part of their affair Trina had become, all at the same time, hysterical, difficult, and needy, yet for all of that she had never lost for him her peculiar, at times unsettling, sexual allure, an allure he associated primarily with that perfume, whatever it was (Obsession? Chanel?). He thought about that little fact off and on throughout the movie.

When the video finally ended—less funny the second time around but somehow more poignant—he looked around for a clock but couldn't find one. He felt trapped. "What time is it?"

"Beats me."

"It feels late, though, doesn't it?

"Not particularly."

"Really?"

"Really, Parker. You got here at eight. The movie was an hour and a half long. You do the math."

He nodded. "I guess you're right. It just feels kind of late."

In some inscrutable way he felt she was maneuvering her way around him, or perhaps toward him, or maybe even away from him—he wasn't sure. As was usually the case with him and Trina, he wasn't sure about a lot of things. "Good flick," he said, "but actually I'd seen it before."

"Me too," she answered.

He sat still and pondered the implications of this. Then he stood up. *What was going on here?* The thought of work tomorrow sent a chill through his veins, as did the thought of his car, of Donna, and now of Trina. Everything in his life seemed ominous, all of a sudden. His stomach fluttered the way it did when he was late for homeroom. He felt he should be at his apartment right now, at that instant, nurturing the mess he had made of his life. But how was he going to get home? Did the buses run this late? (How late *was* it?) He couldn't afford a cab, that was for sure. Trina could drive him home, of course, but was she capable? Were either of them capable? The floor swayed beneath his feet as he blinked to regain his balance. Christ.

"Well, here's the thing," she said, cupping her hands between her knees and rocking back in the couch, "and don't wig out because I meant to say this to you earlier but I just forgot."

He looked at her, not without interest. Something big was coming, some justification, he felt, for the delicate, unnerving position he felt himself occupying right now. "Do I want to hear this?" he asked.

"Chill out. God. I mean, it's no big deal. It's just that I got my license suspended the other day—traffic tickets, now wait, let me finish—which means I really shouldn't be driving my car, like, at all. So here's what I thought: I thought you could drive my car to your place and pick up a change of clothes for work tomorrow and come back and crash here, no biggy, and then you could drive us both to work in the morning and also back home after work, how's that sound?"

She spoke in one long, unbroken sentence, as if the speech had been rehearsed. He thought for a second and said, "That doesn't make any sense, Trina."

"No, wait, listen. See, tomorrow at lunchtime my mother is coming by at work to take me down to the courthouse so I can square all this away, which means that after tomorrow morning you're basically free and that's all there is to it. This way, see, neither of us will have to take the bus in the morning."

"So tomorrow you were going to take the bus to work?"

"That's what I'm telling you."

"But you drove today, didn't you?"

"Yes, but I shouldn't have, and besides you need a ride *any-way* so this works out for the both of us." She beamed at him.

All at once Parker realized he was in the Trina Vortex. The thought comforted him, somehow, almost gave him a warm shot of nostalgia. He was in familiar territory after all. *The Trina Vortex* was the term he had devised years ago to describe the strange experience of arguing with Trina. The thing about her emotional logic, he recalled from experience, was that it had an uncanny way of achieving a kind of self-referential clarity all its own. You could argue with it, but only according to its own rules. The problem was, the rules kept changing. Hence the Trina Vortex.

"Okay," he said slowly, testing his way, "let me think here for a second. If I'm driving you to work in the morning, then why don't I just drive your car home tonight and pick you up in the morning?"

"Oh, so you don't *want* to stay here?"

"No, Trina, it's not that—"

"I mean, *nothing* is going to happen, don't you worry about that. Jeez. Actually, forget it. Forget I ever said anything."

"Wait, now don't do this."

"Do what?"

"This. Where you turn everything against me and make me . . . I don't know. Decide."

"Decide *what*? I'm not doing anything, *you're* the one making such a big deal about this, I just—"

"You know exactly what I mean. You always put me in this position."

"What position?"

"The one where I have to choose whether or not I'm going to be an asshole or a putz."

"God, are *you* overreacting. Which is nothing new. Ha ha ha. A joke, Parker, a joke. Look, if it makes you feel any better, I have no designs on you whatsoever. No offense or anything, but after all that's happened between me and Jack I just want to get my shit together and that's *all*."

"Then why—"

"Because I thought it would be nice to have someone here tonight, is there anything wrong with that? Is there? We'll watch television and you can sleep in the guest bedroom. Seriously. Look at me, Parker: I'm dead serious."

He obeyed. He looked at her. He had always loved her mouth, that was another the thing about her that had always gotten him. There was something irresistibly, humanly flawed about it, as if her top of row teeth were too wide for her lips, her canines holding up the edges like two pegs stretching taut a volleyball net.

She looked serious enough.

"Okay," he finally decided, "give me the keys."

ON THE DRIVE BACK to his apartment in Trina's Volvo, he took orders from a sensible, matter-of-fact voice lodged somewhere in the deep left-hand corner of his brain, a voice that sounded vaguely like his own and that told him things like "Signal for your turn" or "Now get in the left-hand turn lane." He kept his cool, he thought. Handled himself like a pro. With a little help, of course. Still, when he pulled into his own parking lot he felt a surge of relief, as if he had just coasted all the way home with his lights off. Which, he realized when he turned off the car, was exactly what he had done. Fear gripped him hard.

Inside his apartment he gathered together an outfit for tomorrow, avoided all thought of prophylactics (a depressing realization: he didn't have any), and found himself more than once standing stone-still in the middle of his living room having lost track of what he was doing. Eventually, he gathered everything together (suit, shoes, tie, workout clothes), checked his phone messages (there were none) and walked back toward the Volvo.

The sensible voice wasn't there anymore: he was entirely on his own now. Every car he saw in his rearview mirror he imagined to be surmounted by a siren and blow-horn, but each time the car passed he encountered nothing more terrifying than, say, a bunch of college kids in a Jeep. *Chill out,* he consoled himself. *You're doing a nice thing here. You're helping out a friend, and that's all you're doing.* These thoughts gave him succor as he drifted into the empty space in front of Trina's house, the speedometer reading ten miles per hour and the car, he noticed for the first time, in second gear. He couldn't remember if he had shifted it once the whole drive there.

"What happened?" Trina called as he helped himself in. "I thought you'd gotten lost or something."

"Nope!" he said—cheerfully, he hoped. He bounded up the stairs and into the living room. Trina was sitting on the couch in a pair of sweatpants and a Cure T-shirt. She had poured herself a glass of wine.

"Where are your clothes?" she asked, a dreamy stoned smile on her face.

He thought for a second. "In the car, I think."

She nodded, then patted the couch cushion. Without speaking, he sat down precisely where she had indicated and said nothing more for the next half hour. At one point she got up, went to the bathroom, and returned with a ring of toothpaste on her lips. He held his breath and kept his eyes on the television.

Finally she said, "Well, I'm beat," and stood up and stretched, the T-shirt riding up just far enough to reveal a rim of her midriff.

So when he stepped out of the bathroom after brushing his own teeth, he should not have been at all surprised to find Trina in her bedroom folding down the comforter on her bed, dressed now in what he could only term a "teddy," and a fire-truck red one at that, sheer and basically see-through but for the demure doilies on her breasts and across her pudenda, with leg openings that rode to the top of her hips and thin spaghetti straps along the pale skin of her bony shoulders. But he told himself he was surprised. He stood in the doorway of her bedroom and tried to think of something to say.

"You don't mind if I wear this, do you?" she asked, her voice barely concealing a surface quiver.

"Trina—"

"Look, it seems pretty clear to me what's going on here."

"It does?"

"Oh, c'mon, Parker, what did you think this was all about?"

"I don't know, I . . . I mean, you told me we were just going to watch television and that, you know, with you and Jack and all . . ."

She sat down on the bed but did not take her eyes off him. Her gaze froze him in his tracks, a frog hypnotized by a flashlight. Then she looked away and smiled sardonically. "God, am I such a fool."

"No, wait, Trina. Hold on a second. I just think, I don't know, it just seems like it would be a very bad idea, in general, you know? I mean, in theory, is what I'm saying. We just shouldn't is all."

"Then why did you come back here?"

He thought for a moment. He had an answer for her but he could not bring himself to utter it. Perhaps because he had been unable, or unwilling, to utter this selfsame answer to himself all night.

"I don't know," he finally said. "Because you asked me to."

She took this in. Kind of swished it around in her mouth, like a sip of wine. Then she looked away. "Oh, Parker," she sighed, "when are you ever going to stop doing what everyone tells you to do?"

THE NEXT MORNING, when he went outside to fetch his clothes from Trina's car, he discovered that her passenger-side window had been smashed. He couldn't remember if he had noticed it the night before. When he inserted the key into the car door his heart dropped again, for he suddenly realized he had left the car unlocked all night. Of course his clothes were missing—the suit, the shoes, the tie—as were all the cassette tapes Trina had left lying about. What got him most, however, was the loss of a red Prince carry-all bag he had had since high school, a bag that had gotten him all the way through college and which had been his trusty companion at every Grateful Dead show he had ever attended, each one of which he remembered fondly.

"Someone broke into your car last night," he told Trina as she emerged from her bedroom, dressed in boxer shorts and that old Cure T-shirt from last night. "They broke the passenger-side window."

"Fuck," she said absently, and shuffled into the bathroom, scratching her bottom. Then she slammed the door and turned on the shower.

At noon he asked his boss if he could leave—he said he wasn't feeling well, which was true enough—and was stung by how readily his boss let him go. A wave of the hand and that was it. The guy didn't even look up. If Donna ever asked to leave early, he thought, the whole place would crumble.

He took the bus home, walked into his apartment, tore off his tie and played his sole answering-machine message.

It was the bank: his landlord had redeposited the check, thereby adding another overdraft charge to Parker's account. Which wouldn't have happened, he reflected grimly, had he not withdrawn that $475.

Actually, he had been hoping the rent business would just take care of itself. He really had hoped for that. The way he saw it, everything hinged on his random position on the karma wheel. He was afraid that taking action would somehow influence adversely the wheel's inscrutable rotation. A great many things in Parker's life got dealt with in this manner. Maybe too many things. For though he tried to avoid it, he couldn't help thinking that his life lately had become a strange form of anticipation—days and days and days of blind hope for the welcome yawning silence of no news whatsoever.

"PARKER? HI, IT'S ME, Trina, listen, I—wait, hold on . . . Okay, listen, I've got to hang up but don't go anywhere because I'm going to call you right back, all right?"

Parker stood in the middle of his smoldering living room and clutched the phone. It was Wednesday. Since his Friday afternoon debacle with Jarvis, Parker had borrowed money from his parents, picked up his car from the mechanic's, taken it back for more repairs, picked it up again, talked to Donna twice, Jarvis not at all, and Trina, he suddenly realized, not since Friday morning. *What now?* he thought to himself, staring up at the ceiling, his tie undone and his apartment as musty and humid as a log cabin in the Mississippi Delta. The phone beeped in his hand and he pushed Talk.

"Are you there?" she whispered. "Parker? Listen, now you've got to promise me you're listening. Parker?"

"Christ, all right," he said, sitting down, "I'm listening, I'm listening."

"Do you have your car?"

"Trina, are you okay?"

"Yes, I'm fine, just answer my question."

"My car. Yes, I have my car."

"Great. Now what I need you to do—are you listening? —is drive over here to my house *right now,* like at this very moment, because I have a little package for you. But before I give it to you you've gotta promise me two things. Parker? Are you there?"

Parker dropped his head back along the back of his couch. He could almost feel his grip slipping, his feet sliding, as he fell with a roller-coaster drop of the stomach into the Trina Vortex. "Yes," he groaned, "I'm here."

"Two things. First, you've got to promise me you'll take the package, no questions asked. Second, you must swear to me—and this is, like, major important—you absolutely *have* to promise me you won't look in the package until I tell you to."

"Please, Trina, just tell me what this is all about."

"No can do. But it's kind of fun, isn't it? Ooops, gotta run. See you soon."

When he arrived at her house she was waiting for him out on the sidewalk, dressed primly in a pair of black linen slacks, silk blouse and pearls. She rarely dressed this nice, even for work. Slowing down he saw that in her arms she held a box, which, contrary to what he had been imagining on the drive over, was not wrapped and tied with a bow but was rather bare except for the faint evidence of stripped packing tape. He felt cheated. Before he could come to a complete stop, Trina had dashed across the street and opened the passenger door of his moving car. She dropped into the seat like a bourgeois hobo jumping a freight train. Then she shouted "*Go!*" and shut the door, the package on her lap clanking heavily.

"Go where?" Parker asked.

She looked behind her, then at the passenger-side mirror, then past Parker's window. This seemed to calm her. Tilting her head coquettishly she whispered, "I *really* appreciate this, Parker, you have no idea."

"Trina, where am I going?"

"Oh," she said lightly, waving her hand, "anywhere, I guess."

He reentered traffic. They passed a Krispy Kreme, a Churches, a Krystal, a Circle K, a Winn Dixie, a Dairy Queen. No one said anything. This went on for five or six minutes. At the interstate junction he stopped and said, "Where now?"

"Left," she commanded.

He turned left. She reached for the package at her feet and set it on her lap. Then she turned to him.

"I'm in major shit," she declared calmly.

SLOWLY, SHE BEGAN TO EXPLAIN. Things between her and Jack had gotten a little weird lately, she said, maybe a little out of hand, or maybe *very* much out of hand, she didn't know. Maybe things had gotten too weird, but she didn't think so. Not really. She had broken some things, okay, and Saturday night there was that thing at the Shoney's—it was a long story, she didn't want to go into it, suffice it to say she would never be welcome at a Shoney's restaurant ever again for the rest of her natural life—and of course Parker knew all about her own broken car window and all like that. So anyway, what happened, basically, was . . . Well, on Wednesday, Trina had done a seriously stupid and crazy thing—and oh, by the way, *fuck* that doctor *and* his fucking Prozac—anyway, Jack had refused to talk to her and she was kind of losing it, fair enough, but honestly all she had wanted to do was apologize to him for the Shoney's thing, and he goes and changes his number, if you can believe that—Can you change it that quick? Seriously?—so, well, okay, what she did was, she called the cops and *kind* of suggested that maybe she knew who broke into her car—

"You did *what?*"

She glanced at him, startled. "I told them Jack did it," she said.

After a moment—during which his heart slowed down from a gallop to a trot—he said, "Oh, right. Okay."

Which he didn't, of course, Trina continued, but she was *so* mad at him, you have no idea, and besides all she wanted to do was talk to him, to apologize . . .

Parker had begun to tune her out. He'd heard these stories before. More than that, he had *lived* them. But he let her rattle on, for he recognized that their telling was for Trina their primary raison d'être, for only in the telling could she both face up to her own irrational desperation and at the same time exonerate herself. Usually the facing-up portion came somewhere near the middle, surrounded by a mantra of "So okays" and "I admits," only to be swept aside by a twenty-minute conclusion during which she enacted the spin that, Parker thought, gave her the strength to go on. He worried sometimes that he should call her on her behavior more than he did—in Trina's own well-learned therapy-speak, he was increasingly becoming her "enabler"—but he rationalized his passivity by recalling the team of therapists her wealthy widowed mother had sicced on her over the years. She needed him in this capacity, he figured, and it cost him nothing.

". . . and so I went by this morning," she was saying, "and gathered up every one of them and, well, here they are."

He now had no idea what she was talking about. *Every*

one of them. Went by this morning. During his reverie, her story had taken a few unexpected turns. Embarrassed, he said, "Gathered up what?"

She shot him a venomous look. "Weren't you listening?" She dropped back in her seat and clenched her fists and closed her eyes. "His *guns,* Parker. I took Jack's guns. I went by his house yesterday morning and took them all."

"You took his guns?"

"That's what I'm telling you."

"Trina—"

"So now I don't know if—"

"Wait, wait, wait." He hesitated a moment, trying to process what he had just heard, to line it up so that it made some sense. But line it up how? What sense? "You're telling me you stole his guns?"

She stared at him fiercely. "You weren't even listening."

"As in plural gun*s*? As in, like, more than one gun?"

"As in more than one gun, yes."

"So Jack is something of a gun collector is what you're saying."

"Basically."

"And you stole it. His collection, I mean."

"Stop it, Parker. Just stop it. Listen, I'm trying to tell you—"

"Rifles? Shotguns? What exactly are we talking about here? Pistols? What?"

"He wants to have me committed!"

"Who?"

"Forget it, Parker. Just forget it. Please, take me home."

"Wait, Trina, hold on. *Who* wants to have you committed?"

"Jack, you fucking retard! This is what I've been telling you—"

"But what do you mean, committed?"

"You *are* familiar with the term, aren't you?"

"You mean to a hospital?"

"To Charter, yes."

He nodded. Flatly, he said, "Was this before or after you took the guns?"

"Before."

"So you heard he wanted to have you committed, and in retaliation you took his guns."

"Exactly."

"And you hid them where, exactly?"

"Nowhere. They're right here."

"Where?"

"In this box."

He glanced at her feet. He recalled the heavy clanking sound the box had made when she jumped in. "And that's the box you want me to take away from you."

"Now you're getting it," she said, smiling.

Parker got off the interstate and turned around.

SOME OF THE OTHER little details about this incident, details that she had "forgotten" to tell him at first but that she parceled out, piecemeal, on the drive back to her house, included the little detail about Jack calling her mother that morning, the little detail about her mother calling her immediately afterward, and the big detail about Jack and her mother's scheduling a visit to her house to fetch her, either of her own accord or by force, to Atlanta's primary psychiatric facility.

"So they'll be there when we get back?" he asked her. Without her asking or protesting, he was taking her home.

"Probably."

"And you want me to go in with you?"

"Oh, Parker, please, please do this for me, pretty please, I swear to you I will be forever in your debt, seriously, I—"

"But what am I supposed to do, Trina? What can I say to them?"

"You can vouch for me."

To which—try though he did to think of something, anything, to say—he had no response.

Jack was sitting on the couch when they returned, a powerful broad-shouldered lawyer with moussed hair and suspenders and a pudgy face that matched the slight paunch swelling over his black pleated pants. He stood up, smiled, and forcefully shook Parker's hand as if the two of them were about to sit down and hash out a business deal. No one talked for the next moment or so. Then Trina's mother walked in. Parker stood up to shake her hand, but she ignored him. It was as if he weren't even there. Trina's mother, though easily sixty-plus, was an imperiously forbidding woman of considerable elegance, with a long torso and a narrow, smooth-complexioned face sitting proudly atop a gnarled turkey's neck. A faint tinsel layer of gray permeated an otherwise sumptuous wreath of brown hair, her chief genetic gift to her daughter. Otherwise Parker couldn't trace the resemblance. Apparently, Trina took after her father, a dissipated Southern mogul who died in an alcoholic stupor three days after Trina's fourteenth birthday.

"So," the mother said, "I think we can begin."

"I hate you," Trina told her, apropos of nothing.

"I suppose you do," she responded icily.

Jack sat forward and began speaking in a slow, businesslike voice. Basically, he said, Trina had two choices. Either she could check herself into Charter Hospital willingly, in which case her stay would be covered by her current healthcare provider, or she could resist and thereby submit to forceful incarceration at Grady General, which visit would *not* be covered by her insurance. If she chose the second option, she could expect state authorities to arrive at her house—or wherever she decided to run off to—first thing in the morning. If she chose the first option, she could check in that very evening and be processed before she went to sleep that night. Now, it was important that she understood—

"Fuck that," she snapped, and stood up. "You can't make me do this, you sonofabitch, there is no way, no *fucking* way, you can make me do this. I won't go, I absolutely won't—"

"Now Trina, listen, I don't think you realize—"

"Listen to him, Mother! Do you hear this guy? Are you listening to this bastard? *This* is what I've been dealing with for the last six months, don't you see?"

"I have listened to him," Trina's mother said in a level tone. "I've been listening to him for about a week now. And after that stunt you pulled yesterday with the police—"

"Oh, please! You're going to get all worked up about *that?* Tell them Parker, tell them what really happened."

Everyone turned to stare at Parker. Spotlight, silence, a hush of expectation. And Parker didn't even know his lines. "I don't know," he said, his mind racing. "I guess I left the door unlocked."

No one spoke. Before anyone had a chance to pursue this new twist, she turned back to her boyfriend and her mother and revved her engines for another go.

He sat there for the next hour, listening but contributing nothing. The most agonizing moments included Trina's repeated charges of hatred for both Jack and her mother, her accusation that her mother had been largely responsible for her father's miserable wreck of a life, and her sacred vow to do everything in her power to disgrace the family name, such as it was. For her mother's part, she let it be known that Trina had been little more than a profound disappointment from the moment she was born, and that this particular scene was pretty much the sort of thing she had anticipated since Trina was a little girl. Every now and then, Jack supplied a legal gloss.

All the while Parker tried to sort out how he felt about all of this. That Trina needed help seemed to him more than obvious: he had determined this fact early on in their relationship, sometime after her first hysterical outburst in his apartment, during which she had taken a broom to his bookshelf. But he didn't like the semitragic Scott-and-Zelda quality of the whole thing. And he liked Jack's dispassionate legalese even less. She should go to Charter—she should have gone there a long time ago, probably — but she shouldn't be *forced* to go. No one should be forced to do anything.

Still working through this disjointed chain of thought, he suddenly found himself seized by the arm.

"Let's go," Trina was saying to him. "We're getting the hell out of here."

"Don't do this," Jack told her. "Please, Trina, you don't know what you're getting yourself into."

She ignored him. Tugging Parker to his feet, she stormed past her mother and across the room to the stairs that led down into the duplex's foyer and hence out to the street. Parker followed along blindly, happy to be thus discharged.

But at the door she stopped. Parker stopped, too. The two people back in the living room gazed back at them implacably. A stillness reigned, as if all the electricity had just been shut off at a raucous party. Trina ran her hands through her hair and down her face.

"Come back in here, honey," her mother said.

Trina shook her head vigorously. For the first time that evening she started to cry. Then she looked at Parker.

In a small trembling voice she said, "Parker, help me."

He shrugged. At Trina, specifically, and at everything generally. "How?"

"Tell me what to do."

Time tiptoed. He could have stood there forever, never saying a word, never moving a muscle, the air about him held perfectly still in a delicate matrix that, the moment he opened his mouth, he would irretrievably dismantle. He breathed deeply and thought hard. But he had nothing to tell her.

"Should I go or not?" she asked. "Just tell me that."

He raised his hands in a helpless gesture. "Hell, Trina, aren't you going, either way?"

"You think I should check myself in," she said flatly.

"I think you should do the smart thing. And I think the smart thing in this case is to decide to do something for yourself, to . . ." He lingered here, searching for the right word. But there didn't seem to be a right word.

"I have no choice here, Parker."

"Then what the hell do you want me to say?"

"Honestly, I have no idea." She turned to the others. Silence. Then, turning back, she said in a tiny voice, "I'll call you in a few days."

Released, Parker walked slowly down the steps, out to the sidewalk, and over to his car. Before climbing inside, however, he turned back for one more look at Trina's house, at her window upstairs, through which, against the late summer evening glare, he could see what appeared to be two people embracing. A man and a woman. Though one of the people was clearly Jack, who was the woman? Trina? Trina's mother? He couldn't tell. Which combination made the most sense? Neither, he decided.

Then he turned to his left and noted, for the first time that night, an ambulance parked in the street directly behind his own car, a white and red ambulance from Charter Hospital, to be specific, its roof a chaos of blowhorns and sirens, its side emblazoned with warnings and red crosses. Leaning against it was a black guy about Parker's age. He was reading a newspaper and sipping a Biggie drink from Wendy's. While Parker was still staring at this unexpected sight the driver glanced up and caught Parker's eye. Rather than look away, Parker stared right back.

"Say, Holmes," the driver said, his voice even and sure of itself and laced at the edge with menace, "you got a problem?"

"Probably," Parker answered.

Taken aback by the response, the driver blinked dramatically and smiled. He set the paper down on the sloping hood of the ambulance and stood up. "For real?"

"For real," Parker said.

The driver looked closely at Parker and . . . what? Sort of marveled, actually. Like he couldn't believe it. Like he couldn't believe what was happening. Parker waited for fear to seize him, for adrenaline to flood through his veins, but all he felt was a vast emptiness so urgent it ached. "Seriously," he whispered, "I really do have a problem."

The driver looked him squarely in the eye. Parker returned his stare.

After a frozen moment or two, the driver looked up at Trina's building, looked back and Parker, and all at once relaxed. He had put two and two together, Parker realized. And he didn't know the half of it.

"Shit, man," the driver finally said. "Honestly, I didn't realize . . ."

Parker waved the remark away and smiled weakly. But he didn't move.

"Seriously," the driver was saying, his shoulders bunched in apology, "I'm like *real* sorry and everything, but, you know, I'm just the driver."

Parker understood. Really he did. Smiling—sincerely now —he bestowed on this kind, wise driver a wave of gratitude and climbed inside his own car, situated himself behind the wheel, and inserted the key. He started the car. Then he put the car in gear and drifted smoothly into traffic. From his rearview mirror he watched the ambulance driver take up his Wendy's Biggie and resume reading. Trina's house receded from view. At a Texaco he swung a sharp right as the box of guns sitting beside him slid against the far door and clanked and rattled like an old dying automobile engine.

8. VENUS/MARS

My best friend's girlfriend—or I should say his fiancée—taught me what I consider to be a remarkably effective method of picking up women, and I don't care what your feelings are on the matter, I'm here to tell you the lady knew what she was talking about: she told me what to do, I did it, and it worked.

"The thing you have to remember," Pamela told me, "the key thing, is that women aren't trying to impress men. Not really, anyway. What they're really doing is competing against one another."

Duncan was out of town. That I was suffered to spend evenings in his apartment, with his fiancée, in his absence, surely testifies to the amount of trust he invested in me. I admit this freely. His and Pamela's apartment was an opulent affair, with a living room as big as an airport hangar and an assortment of leather furnishings so plush they threatened to swallow you whole in their slick aromatic embrace.

"Explain," I said.

"It's simple. When a woman walks into a bar, what's the first thing she looks at?"

"The guys," I answered, though even then I knew I was just her straight man.

"Wrong. The first thing she looks at is the other women. She walks in and scopes out the prettiest women there. That's how she knows what the competition is—by looking at the women first."

"I thought the men did that."

"Exactly. The women are the center. Don't you get it? Both men and women look at women. Think of *Vogue*, think of *Cosmo*, all of that. Think of Botticelli. The whole culture's obsessed with female beauty."

"So where do the men come in?"

"Men," Pamela said, leaning forward, "are just the spoils."

"Do you talk to Duncan this way?"

"Of course not. Now listen closely, because I'm about to tell you something not many men know. But let me ask you a question first: How do you make yourself more attractive to a woman?"

I arched my eyebrows, did a basset-hound drop of my head, and said, "Be thenthitive."

"Cute. But you're dead wrong. If you want to make yourself attractive to other women, just make sure you're seen with another beautiful woman."

I should point out here that I met Pamela before Duncan did. I should also point out that I introduced Pamela to Duncan. Our lives, it seems to me, are punctuated by bad decisions, little coordinate points onto which we map our fate. Introducing Pamela to Duncan, I realized sometime later, was one of those bad decisions, one of those coordinate points.

What did Pamela look like? She looked like Greta Garbo on a health kick. She looked like a picture of your best friend's mother, back in 1962, say, when she was a busty college coed. Pamela's brown hair, the bangs held at bay by the white arch of a headband and the ends hooked behind her ears, gleamed luxuriantly beneath the track lighting with which Duncan illuminated his living room. She also wore thin tortoiseshell-framed glasses, a slight and tasteful brush of eye makeup, and hooped earrings. Her smile, with its accompanying dimples, was like sunlight streaming through a cloud.

I said, "If you're with a beautiful woman, Pam, you aren't necessarily in the running."

"Precisely. That's part of the appeal. You're not going to hit on all these women—therefore, your stock shoots way up."

"So what's the other part?"

"The other part is competition. Women need validation—they need to know that they can compete with other beautiful women. And so any guy who's with a beautiful girl must have something—money, intelligence, prowess quote unquote—simply because he's with *her*. The other women think, 'Well, if I can hook up with this guy, then I can compete with that bimbo.' Voilà! The guy with the beautiful girl becomes the target for the rest."

To which I said, "Very interesting, but what's your point? Surely you didn't ask me over here just to give me a lesson in feminine wiles."

"It's like this," Pamela said, and placed a warm palm on my forearm. "I want to be your beautiful woman."

I waited a few seconds for the cobwebs in my throat to dissolve, and then, after a cough, I said, "Come again?"

"We're friends aren't we?"

I shrugged. Then added, "Sure."

"Oh, Parker," she said, letting go of my arm. Then she stood up. "I get so bored, you know. I mean, not always—not very often, actually—but still. Duncan works these long hours—I don't blame him, you know, but still—and then of course there's this new thing about drinking." I gave her a wave of my hand, as if to brush the subject aside. Last summer Duncan had sworn off alcohol, and rest assured I've heard enough about it to last a lifetime. About his job and his salary I've heard enough to last *two* lifetimes.

"Okay," she said, "right. More wine?"

"I'm set." I thought about my apartment, about all the reading I had to do for class the next day—after six years of dithering about I had finally entered graduate school—then banished all that unpleasantness from my mind.

"Take me out," she said.

My heart skipped and bobbed. Inanely, I asked, "Where?"

"Anywhere." She sat back down and gripped my arm again. "Take me out dancing, pretend I'm your date, pretend I'm not your date, whatever. Just take me out—out of this apartment, out of this living room. I sit here every night with Duncan while he unwinds, and when he's gone he expects me to stay home and read a book. I can't stand it. I want to go out tonight and pretend I'm single again. I want to flirt and dance and drink. I want to go out, and I want you to take me."

My first reaction was to say *No way* and walk out the door. In retrospect, that's precisely what I should have done. But I hedged my bets and said, "Have you told Duncan all this?"

"Sure. I mean, we've talked about it and all, but . . . Look, if you don't want to do this, just say so."

I hesitated, and when I did she released my arm—again!—and got up to leave the room. The effect was instantaneous: I felt as if I had been set adrift in outer space. Before she could get as far as the kitchen I said, "We'll tell Duncan, all right?"

"Oh, forget it, Parker," she called, and disappeared. When

I found her she was standing at the counter, pouring herself the last of the wine.

I said, "Then you don't want him to know?" When she didn't answer, I grabbed her arm and forced her to look at me. "But why? Why don't you want him to know?"

Placing her palm flat against my chest, she said, calmly, "Because I'm twenty-six years old, that's why. I don't have to clear *everything* with him, you know."

And that was all I needed to hear.

"Okay, then," I said. "Let's get a move on."

SINCE PAMELA HAD BEEN out of commission for several years, she left it to me to choose a night spot, an office I performed perfunctorily while listening to her change in the bedroom: hangers rattling, zips zipping, compacts snapping. A former girlfriend of mine once described Pamela as a "Laura Ashley nightmare," and I guess I can understand what she meant: Pamela was born to be married, to run a house with an anteroom and a verandah, to head committees and exploit her civic zeal. And it did not escape my notice that the first two things Pamela did after accepting Duncan's marriage proposal were, one, quit her job, and two, subscribe to *Town and Country*. But she also kept up with all the latest alternative bands, read Margaret Atwood, and followed the NBA with all the passion of a seventeen-year-old male. Her car even sported an Atlanta Hawks bumper sticker. Still, I was surprised by what she was wearing when she stepped out of the bedroom; for her evening on the town she had affected what was then considered a form of Euro-casual chic: faded 501's, thick black belt, white T-shirt and blazer.

Smiling, she took my arm and said, "After you."

She drove. This suited me fine, as my own heap smelled of cigarettes and fried fast food. Hers, on the other hand—hardly a heap: she drove a new Jetta—smelled of nothing so much as comfort and ease. The air conditioner hummed, the dashboard glowed. For some reason, being in Pamela's car made this untoward scenario seem much less sinister than it actually was.

"And you know," Pamela was saying, expanding on her theme, "this will be perfect for you too, Park. The perfect setup. We're about to put a theory of mine into practice, and I'm about to see if I know what I'm talking about. If I'm right, and this works, then not only will you be forever in my debt, but you'll also qualify for royalties from the book I plan to write. It'll be the flip side of that Venus and Mars thing. I'll call it *Women from Mars*."

"But this isn't for me," I said. "It's for you."

"Well, yes and no. I mean, yes it's for me, but not exclusively. You're not just along for the ride is what I mean. You know how you keep telling Duncan and me how hard it is out there, how impossible it is to meet women and all that? Well, this will give you a leg up—no pun intended."

Shamefully, this was true. My whining tales about the perils and vagaries of woman stalking constituted a depressingly large portion of my casual discourse with Pamela and Duncan. Why this was I'm not altogether sure. In truth, they were the only people to whom I even raised the subject. And when I did, when I really got myself worked up to an unseemly steam, I could hear—and feel—something vaguely disingenuous in my tone. That I was perhaps only preening had indeed crossed my mind; for whom I was doing the preening was another question entirely.

"Well," I said, not altogether sure how I meant it, "thanks a lot."

I had decided on Rollo's, a polished-wood-and-brass affair nestled in the heart of Buckhead, Atlanta's yuppie hub. In the abstract it seemed like a harmless enough place for Pamela to reenter, however tentatively, the arena of the Desperate and Drunk. The place was neither hopping nor hopeless—just another weeknight in the big city—and yet, as I entered, I found myself viewing this ponderous commingling of lonely bodies with new eyes—that is, with *Pamela's* eyes. I saw myself as perhaps others—newcomers to Rollo's, say—might see me. Surveillance cameras in convenience stores offer an illustrative metaphor: if you look directly into the camera you can't see your face in the monitor behind the cash register, and if you look at the monitor you can only see the back of your head—what other people see when you're ignoring them. So, standing in the foyer of Rollo's with my best friend's fiancée, I saw myself, as it were, in the monitor.

All of which was very strange if you consider the fact (and

I'll just confess it now) that I generally go out drinking five nights a week. Sad but true. Each night when I return from class I find that I am still hungover from the night before, a condition that disposes me, for a while at any rate, to settle in for a quiet evening of assigned reading. I unwrap my dinner from its tinfoil and Styrofoam, watch two consecutive episodes of *Family Ties,* and dive into the pile of books on my card table—big Victorian novels, arcane works of eighteenth-century mysticism, literary fucking theory. Or I start writing a letter on my computer. Or I call a friend. But inevitably, each of these activities only manages to open wider that canyon inside myself into which echo the voices of all the people in my life who have moved on and up. And soon a mangy mutt who lives in my stomach gets up from the hearth fire of my tenuous contentment and begins whining to be let outside. I ignore the whining for as long as I can, but by ten or so I've given up: the dog is howling by now, while the sickening sprawl of my studio flat—unmade mattress, coffee cups and cigarette butts, cookie crumbs and half-read books—has become unbearable. Just like that I'm out the door, happy and hopeful, the previous night's failures obliterated in a rush of guileless optimism. "Tomorrow," I promise myself. Tomorrow and tomorrow and tomorrow.

I went to the bar and brandished a ten-dollar bill, to no immediate avail. Perhaps nowhere else in life does one feel as insignificant as one does at a crowded bar. One bartender glanced at me and just as quickly glanced away. This went on. It soon became apparent that I should say something to Pamela, and yet my mind was drawing a total blank. I had a vague conviction that once I scored us a pitcher I'd have something to say, but until then—

"There she is," Pamela yelled.

"Who?"

"Over there, the girl in red."

To my astonishment, the girl in question was an olive-skinned Mediterranean beauty whom I had been eyeing all fall. She appeared, like an apparition, nearly everywhere I went—and this is a pretty big town—and in nearly every particular she was an exact replica of Nicole Liarkos, the first girl to teach me how little I understood about women. Not surprisingly, I had advanced no further in my wooing of this girl than to send longing glances her way before slipping out the front exit and winding my solitary way home. Tonight her hair was done back in a ponytail, and her ears were adorned with glistening sterling silver crescent moons. For about the millionth time I noticed her teeth were perfect.

"What about her?"

"She's been scoping you out," Pamela said. "From the moment we walked in here she's been taking your number. I swear to you. She glances over here every five seconds, like she—wait, did you see it? She just looked again. See what I mean? Am I right or am I right?"

She *was* right. My Mediterranean beauty had glanced our

way. That is, she had glanced at *me*. What's more, her face conveyed an unconvincing look of ennui and nonchalance.

"Here," Pamela said, plucking the money from my fingers, "you go to the bathroom and I'll buy the drinks. Ten to one she's walking into the ladies' room when you walk out. Ten to one."

"Let's call it a round of drinks," I said, taking my ten back. "You pay if she stays where she is, I'll pay if she moves."

As I moved toward the john, I distinctly heard Pamela sidle up to the bar and—just like that!—order two scotch and sodas. Then I drifted past the Girl in Red (who, unless I'm prone to delusions of grandeur, blushed cutely), walked down a lurid yellow hallway, and stationed myself, to no real purpose, at a free urinal. Beside me a mustached bodybuilder vigorously and loudly emptied his bladder; I stared at the wall. I was too nervous was the thing. What if she *did* appear? What would I do then? Not only would it mean Pamela was right, it would also mean I would finally, irrefutably, unavoidably *have to talk to her*. But I couldn't hide forever, so after a while I buttoned up, made a pretense of washing my hands, and pushed open the door.

There she was.

Like magic, like the fulfillment of a shaman's spell, like the blithely expected result of a tried-and-true laboratory experiment, *there she was*, tottering my way through the element of yellow light, dressed in black cowboy boots, faded jeans, and a shimmering red body shirt. Since she was fiddling with an earring I was unable to catch her eye, but when she got to the women's bathroom she turned around, put her back to the door, and looked directly into my stunned and disbelieving eyes.

"Hi," she smiled, her brilliant teeth flashing like newly minted money.

Then she stepped back, pushed the door open, and disappeared into the throng of women within.

"I'll get this round," I told Pamela when I returned.

"I saw," she smiled, sipping her drink. "Just like clockwork."

HER NAME—the Girl in Red—was Thella. "It means 'I want' in Greek," she explained.

How did I finally approach her? Easy: I didn't. Twenty minutes after she emerged from the bathroom Thella made her sumptuous way to the bar and stood, five-dollar bill in hand, right next to me. As is usually my way, I acted as if she were nowhere in sight, a strategy that might have delivered me of all social contact with her entirely had I not been elbowed in the ribs.

There she is, Pamela mouthed, raising her eyebrows and elbowing me again.

I scowled at her, as if to say, *Let me handle this,* and gave her my back.

But Pamela didn't let up; before I could even read the Rollo's logo emblazoned on the mirror behind the bar, I felt myself being pushed, and not gently, into Thella—who, upon encountering my person, stepped back, grabbed my shoulder and said, "Whoops."

"Geez, I'm sorry, I must have—"

"No problem," whereupon—miracle of miracles!—she shook the liquor off her fingers, extended her hand and introduced herself.

And that was all it took. The acquaintance was made, names were exchanged and questions got asked. Talking to a strange woman in a bar is like trying to sustain a Ping-Pong ball in midair by leaning your head back and blowing; if you stop to breathe, the ball falls. Similarly, I had to come up with a two-sided discussion topic that would stay alive via its own renewable energy. What's more, I had to think of some way to explain Pamela's presence—if indeed her presence was the chief factor determining Thella's sudden interest. I fumbled around a bit, said some stupid things, and then, like a gift from above, it came to me.

"So, Thella," I began, after we had said everything there was to say about each other's names, "corroborate something for me, a theory I guess you could call it. My friend here"—with a flourish of my hand I indicated Pamela, who was already deep in conversation with the bodybuilder I had encountered in the bathroom—"she claims that women, when they walk into a bar, don't necessarily check out the men first. According to her—and I'm not saying one way or another, this is her theory—but according to her, women look at the other women first. In other words, women in bars are competing against one another. Now, based on your own experience, would you say that's true? I'd really be interested to know, it seems extraordinary to me. What do you think? Yes or no?"

"Hmmm," Thella said, "let me think about that for a second."

This led to a two-hour conversation on men and women, dating and intimacy, empathy versus solution seeking—the whole shebang. And it ended with Thella offering to drive me home.

When I appraised Pamela of this fact, she acted as if she didn't hear me. Instead, she turned from the bar, took my chin firmly in her hand, and squeezed. "Come here," she said, pulling me toward her.

"Did you hear me? I said I'm—"

"Hold on a second, you've got—" She squeezed harder so that my lips made an O, and then she scraped between my front tooth and my right incisor with her pinky nail. "There, got it."

"Got what?"

"A popcorn kernel. You had a kernel stuck in your teeth."

"Oh." I waited half a heartbeat for my toes to uncurl. "Anyway, like I said, Thella's going to drive me home, so . . . you know." I tried to make this sound "prodigious," but I'm not sure I succeeded.

Pamela gave Thella a long, hard look, as if she were casting the girl for a bit part in a movie, and said, "Okay, I approve. You owe me."

"For what?"

"You'll see." And adjusting the collar on my shirt, she spun me around and sent me on my way.

"Who was that girl?" Thella asked as we got into her car.

"Nobody," I lied. And then added, "My best friend's fiancée, actually."

As if that explained everything.

THE NEXT DAY PAMELA called right after lunch. "Well?"

"She stole my watch," I told her.

Which, insofar as I could tell, was true. Here's what happened. Thella did in fact drive me home, and we did in fact fall into an unseemly tangle on my unmade bed. There were problems with the condom—there are *always* problems with the condom—and I don't remember enjoying myself all that much. In fact, I felt as if I were watching the whole thing take place on that convenient store monitor again. But we nevertheless managed to make happen what everyone who goes out drinking on a weeknight hopes will happen. And though I remember wondering, just before I drifted off to a troubled and tenuous sleep, why I had been trying so arduously to succeed in doing what I had just succeeded in doing, I still went to class the next day woefully unprepared but also happy and secure in the knowledge that I had been pursued, that I had been desired. For in the end, this is actually all we want; the messy dance itself is nothing more, really, than Tantalus's untouchable fruit. If only we could remember all this *beforehand!* I should point out, moreover, that my morning's sunny disposition was quite possibly inspired by the fact that, somewhere before the first light of dawn, Thella nudged me awake to tell me that she had to get home and feed her cat. She was fully dressed—earrings and all—and her mascara speckled her eyelashes in little clots. Disturbingly, she had brushed her teeth.

"You're sure?" I said, reaching out groggily though shamefully pleased that she was leaving.

"It was fun," she smiled, and pecked me on the cheek. "I'm sure I'll see you around."

And when I awoke two hours later, still naked but in any case alone, I turned to my bedside table to discover that my watch—a three-hundred-dollar Seiko with three displays and an alarm—was gone.

"That's wild," Pamela said, her voice quiet, as if she were very far away. Then she brightened up and said, "So tell, tell, tell. How *was* it? Did you get her number? What?"

"I told you. It was okay. Just a hookup. And I lost my watch." *Just a hookup.* Like I did this every night. "And no, I didn't get her number. Nor did she bother to leave hers."

"You slut." She laughed. "Anyway, Cassanova, don't worry about me—I'm sure that was your next question—I shook that bodybuilder and found my own way home, thank you."

"Sorry," I said, and I suppose I meant it on several accounts.

"Don't be. I had fun, I feel great and I think we should do it again. Duncan goes to New York next Tuesday and he'll be gone for three days. Let's make it a date."

"Pamela, what if he calls?" I was starting to sound like a nervous adulterer.

"He didn't last night, did he? Listen, Park, don't freak over this. I checked my messages two or three times. I can handle it, this isn't your problem. We're not *doing* anything."

"So why all the secrecy? Why not tell him you and I go out when he's gone? I'm his best friend—he'll trust me." My teeth clacked together, as if to force back the words.

"I said let me handle this. If I tell him, it's not the same thing. It would defeat the whole purpose."

"What purpose?" My voice was rising. Around me my apartment sprawled in lazy disarray—unread books on the floor, cigarette butts at the bottoms of empty fast-food cups, CDs and LPs scattered across the coffee table. I had another class in an hour, for which, once again, I had not done the reading. "Are you *looking* to hook up? I mean, if you are, why don't you—"

"If I were," she said evenly, "I wouldn't ask you to come along. Get a clue, Parker. If you're ever going to learn about women, you're going to have to pay attention to *detail*."

AND SO, ON IT WENT. That following Tuesday Pamela and I went to O'Grady's, an Irish pub two doors down from Rollo's, and there, within forty-five minutes of our arrival, the two of us had hooked me up with a sleek, smooth-skinned Asian named Lee. By Pamela's own admission, Lee was an even better catch than Thella. "You're moving up," she whispered wetly in my ear. "Watch out or I might get jealous." Again, I asked Lee if she looked at the women first, and again we talked about the gender gap—only this time I had Thella to offer up as a test case: "Interesting. A friend of mine named Thella says women generally . . ." All systems were go: the only problem was, we had both come with friends.

"I'd ask my roommate to take us home," Lee said sheepishly, "but that would be so . . . I mean, like—"

"I'll take care of it," I said.

Needless to say, Pamela was more than happy to help.

So as to put me behind the wheel and Lee in the passenger seat, Pamela sat in the backseat of her own car, a gesture that at first seemed thoughtful and generous but soon revealed itself to be otherwise. The whole way back to my apartment Pamela leaned forward and pelted Lee with a steady barrage of innocuous questions—"Where do you live? What sorority were you in? Do you know such-and-such?"—and all the while her left hand, lodged snugly between driver's side door and my seat, performed a Dance of the Seven Veils along my electrified rib cage. I squirmed, I giggled, I slammed on the brakes. And the moment we arrived at my place, she stopped. Incredible. Holding the seat forward so she could climb out, I tried to meet her gaze, but she innocently continued her conversation with Lee, climbed back into her car, and roared away without telling me good-bye. The omission stayed with me long after she left, the way one's cheek still tingles hours after receiving a slap. Though I told myself it was nothing— "She just forgot, that's all"—I couldn't shake the notion that I had done something wrong. Or maybe I had done something right. Who knew? I brooded over the matter all night, both before and after Lee's friend swung by and took her home, but by morning I had approached no closer to the truth than when I began. I started to wonder if I'd ever figure Pamela out.

And a week later I did. More or less, anyway. We were back at Rollo's, and I was on the edge of making my third score in nearly as many weeks, when I felt her grab my arm. "Don't," she said.

The woman in question was named Shama, a lavish blue-skinned Indian so extraordinarily beautiful my mouth went dry the moment she introduced herself. Her eyes were as black and glassy as marble, and the slightest hint of down grazed her upper lip. By my own admission, Shama shamed them all—Thella, Lee, maybe even Pamela herself.

"Don't what?" I said. Shama had excused herself to the bathroom, and I was fishing for my apartment keys.

"Just don't," Pamela whispered. For the first time in my experience with her, she seemed uncertain. "Don't leave with that girl."

"Why not?"

"Because, Parker. I just wish you wouldn't."

And here it was, precisely what I'd been waiting for for nine years. I had a sudden vision of me and Duncan sitting in his kitchen with a six-pack of beer delineating the various levels of my betrayal. Then I thought quickly about the year Duncan and I shared that third-floor suite and about that time he loaned me his Porsche for an entire week. Grabbing Pamela's arm, I said, "But why? Just tell me why."

"I don't *know* why. I just . . ."

"Pamela, listen to me. If you don't want me to, I won't, all right? I swear to you I won't—but only if you don't want me to."

She was looking at me now, but either because of the darkness of the bar or because of something undecided within her, I was unable to read her expression. We stared at each other for the length of a verse and chorus of whatever piece-of-shit music was playing over the sound system, and then something caught her eye. When I turned I saw Shama winding her way back.

"Look," Pamela said, jerking her arm loose, "forget it, okay? Just forget I said anything. You do whatever the hell you want. Don't let me stop you, God forbid." And with that she turned and left.

I didn't leave with Shama. Suffice it to say I made an excuse and she readily consented. The next morning in class I was a wreck: twice I dialed Pamela's number from the student center pay phone and twice I hung up before the first ring. Nothing got done. I frittered away the day in useless anticipation and unseemly projection. I began thinking about a new graduate program, law school, condominium living— I was ready to make any sacrifice, any change. In fact, I was a little *disturbed* by how ready I was.

Finally, at one-thirty, Pamela called.

"Did you score?" It was the first thing she said.

"No, Pam. I went home alone."

"Too bad—she was gorgeous. So anyway, I'm calling because I just got off the phone with Duncan and he says he'd love it if you came over tonight for dinner. He says it's been a month since he's seen you—is that true? I can't remember."

The reason she didn't remember, I reflected grimly, was because she was seeing more of me than he was.

"Tonight's bad," I lied. My brain, despite frantic efforts to the contrary, failed to divulge a believable excuse.

"It's Tuesday night, Parker. What could you possibly have to do on a Tuesday night? Just come over—he says he misses you."

"Then why docsn't *he* call me?"

"Because he asked me to. Look, if you'd rather not, I'll just tell him—"

"No, no, I'll come. Jesus. Tell him I'll be there about seven." I waited for her to add something, but when she didn't I said, "We need to talk, you know."

After a pause she said, "I know."

"So I guess I'll see you tonight."

"And Duncan, too," she said. "Don't forget about him."

Oh, I thought, *I haven't forgotten about him. Don't you worry about that.*

DESCRIBING DUNCAN IS EASY. Picture the best-looking WASP you've ever seen and then imagine someone else better looking. He had thick, glossy blond hair with vigorous streaks of light brown woven in, ice-blue eyes, a long, rectangular face, sharply drawn cheekbones, and the faintest possible eyebrows, so light they blended invisibly into his skin, thereby making his forehead look a bit overlong: his only facial flaw. His smile always evoked for me the approach of a brand-new Jaguar XJ6, the front grille so cool and elegant you want to take a rock and smash it before it speeds by. When he greeted me at the door he was dressed in casual gear—jeans, sweatshirt, Top-Siders—and yet he seemed uncomfortable, as if his body had forgotten how to submit to such ease. The sweatshirt was too clean, the sleeves were pushed up a bit too primly, the jeans betrayed a crease along the shin. This, I realized, was how adults dressed—that is, for occasions. Everything in the adult world, once you entered it, was an occasion.

"Tonight," he said, patting my shoulder and leading me inside, "I might even drink a cold one with you."

"Someone alert the media." I fished around for something else to say but my mind drew a blank, much like it did in the bar that first night with Pamela. Just to fill the void, I said,

"Listen, I'm really sorry about being so scarce, Duncan. It's been a crazy couple of weeks, what with—"

"Oh, I know all about your last couple of weeks." He looked at me for a frigid, unfathomable second, and then cracked a sinewy Jaguar smile. "Relax, buddy. Pamela's told me everything."

Only then did I realize he was leading me into the kitchen, where Pamela, wrapped domestically in an apron, stood at the sink washing lettuce. "Oh," she said as we entered, "that's what *you* think." Offering me her cheek—something she only did, it suddenly occurred to me, when Duncan was around—she added, "I didn't tell him *everything*."

"Then I'll let him fill me in on the rest," Duncan said.

"You'll have to beat it out of him, I'm sure."

"Baby, didn't you know that guys tell their friends every-thing?"

"Of course I do, sweetie. And women tell their friends everything they *don't* tell their boyfriends."

"Beer?"

This last was from me. During the entire exchange, Duncan and Pamela had smiled and clowned as if I weren't even in the room, a case of wishful thinking if I ever heard one. All of which begged the question, What exactly had Pamela told him?

Handing me a beer, Duncan said, "So far Pammy says you've scored a Greek, an Asian, and an Indian."

"Not true," I mumbled, trying to smile. "The Indian got away."

Pamela shook her hands dry, turned off the faucet and said, "Duncan thinks I'm voyeuristic—the way I drill you about your personal life."

"No, no, I didn't say that. I said you were *nostalgic* for the single life. There's a big difference."

"Nostalgic, voyeuristic—it's pretty much the same thing, if you think about it."

"True," Duncan assented, ushering us all into the living room.

I kept trying to catch Pamela's eye while Duncan wasn't watching, but she was keeping her cool. As far as I could tell, he had only mentioned her phone calls; Duncan must have presumed that this was how she'd ascertained her detailed play by play of my personal life.

"I just like it that you two are so close," Duncan continued, dropping into his leather recliner. "I've seen too many of my friends get married and then disappear—the wife and the buddies don't get along or the husband and her friends don't get along. You know, all that shit. Am I right, Park?"

"Sure," I said.

"I mean, things are so different now—we're getting older, our careers are taking off, blah blah blah—and I just think it's important that we all stay together and keep everything open." I made a motion to say something but Duncan cut me short. "No wait, Parker, let me say this. Just let me talk. I know I've been pretty invisible this last year or so, traveling and staying in on weekends. Pamela and I talked about this today—I came home early from work, did she tell you? We talked about how much attention I'm paying her, and she's right. I haven't been paying her enough attention. And she also told me how you guys talk and all, which really got me, buddy. I mean, it hit me hard." He struck his chest to demonstrate just how hard. Then he leaned forward. "I really wanted to see you tonight, Parker. I know I haven't been around for you as much as I could. I know that, and it bugs the hell out of me. And so I want to say—wait, let me say it—I want to say I'm sorry. I'm sorry for being such a vicious yuppie fuck." He laughed uncomfortably. "There, I said it. I'm a vicious yuppie fuck."

Kissing him on the ear, Pamela said, "But we love you anyway, sweetie. Don't we, Parker?"

"Absolutely," I said. "You bet."

As if liberated by his predinner apology, Duncan proceeded to get disastrously drunk on beer and red wine, so much so that Pamela and I had to steer him down the hallway and help him into bed. All through dinner he had rhapsodized about old times—that is to say, college—an endless and unseemly procession of drinking stories marching before us in inexhaustible number. I smiled unconvincingly through it all, not only because I had heard these stories before—or I should say *had lived them,* for the principle subject of most of these tales was none other than yours truly—but because I realized how sad the whole performance was. Were these stories the most interesting thing Duncan could say about me? Was someone else's cavalier decadence really so enthralling to the likes of Duncan Boyle?

"What a night," Pamela said, after Duncan had finally consented to being tucked into bed—whereupon, like a five-year-old, he had immediately fallen asleep.

"Maybe I should go," I said.

She was curled on the couch, comfy and casual in gray stretch pants and a pinstriped shirt unbuttoned so low I could see the front clasp of her bra. Her fingers caressed a heart-shaped locket hanging from a chain around her neck.

"No, Parker, stay." She patted the couch as one might for a dog. "We need to talk."

She gave me a look that brooked no dissent, so I sat down.

"Okay," I said. "I'll ask the first question. What exactly did you tell him? I've been sitting here all night wondering if Duncan wants to kill me or give me the Congressional Medal of Honor."

"He likes you, Park, he really does. And he misses you. Work is wiping him out, you have no idea. You should have heard him before you came over—he was almost in tears. The pressure, you know, it's starting to get to him. So it was great of you to come over, I think it's just what he needed."

She was talking as if Duncan were her fiancé and I were just his friend—which, for some reason, bothered me immensely.

"No charge. But you didn't answer my question."

"I told him about calling you at work—surely you figured that out."

"And that's it?"

"Of course that's it. What do you think I said? How stupid do you think I am?"

"But why did you say anything at all? I mean, I thought secrecy was the A-1 priority here."

"I don't know. I just did. It seemed right. He was talking about work, and about how glad he was that you were coming over, and so I told him. I said I called you at work and asked you about your nights, that type of thing. And he understood, he really did. He started blaming himself and . . ." She turned and looked longingly down the hall. "I don't know what got into him, but he was so sweet tonight, didn't you think so?"

I couldn't stand it. I wanted to throttle Duncan awake and tell him what his loving fiancée had said to me last night. I wanted to force him to confront the problem I had become and then step aside. I also wanted, at that very moment, to hear Pamela say again what she'd said to me at Rollo's. She was so close my eyes tingled from her scent, and each time she shifted on the couch her knee warmly brushed my thigh —a casual gesture, to be sure, though I had my doubts. I wanted her to bend toward me and kiss me on the lips, a desire so visceral and real I could already taste her on my mouth.

But instead, I said, "Look, forget all that. We've got to decide what we're going to do."

"About what?"

"About us, that's what. About what happened last night. Are you or are you not going to tell Duncan about that?"

"But nothing happened last night."

"Of course nothing happened, but something *almost* happened. Or did I just imagine it?"

For a long time she sat silently and stared at the floor. Then she reached over, took my hand and placed it in her lap. "Look," she said, "you're one of my closest, dearest friends —maybe the closest guy friend I have. You should know that. I care about you so much, Parker. Sometimes I wonder what might have happened if, you know, I had never met Duncan. I really do." She laughed, but when I failed to respond she assumed a different tone. "The thing is, I *did* meet Duncan, right? And I really think he needs me right now. I have to *be* there for him, don't you see? I mean, yes, I said some things last night, some things I probably shouldn't have said—"

"You're taking it all back?"

"Yes. I mean no. God, I don't know . . . Look, I meant what I said—I think—but that doesn't mean I'm ready to throw away my relationship with Duncan just because I felt a pang of . . . what? Jealousy, I guess. Or something. Jesus, I don't know. I'm sorry Parker. You'll have to forgive me, I—"

"Why is everybody asking me to forgive them? For God's sake, Pamela, don't you get it? Don't you see?"

"See what, Parker?" She gazed at me intently and pulled my hand deeper into her lap, her fingers interlocking with mine. "What am I supposed to see?"

"I mean, haven't you figured it out yet? I . . ." My voice trailed off. The tingling in my hand increased. My leg muscles tensed, as if in preparation for flight.

She moved closer. "Just say it, Parker. What are you trying to tell me?"

And so I told her. In the white rush of this unexpected situation, I blurted out the three words. The Big Three. By Jove, I said them, right there on Duncan's leather couch. My mouth opened and out they came. For years I'd been harboring this secret. For years I'd felt the words rise to my mouth like an air bubble, only to pop before they could escape. I had swept my piece onto Duncan's side of the chessboard and had forced his queen into action. I could feel a whole new destiny opening inside me like a flower in bloom. My hand shook.

Finally, she blinked slowly, sat back and smiled. "Parker, sweetie, don't you think I know that?"

I took my hand back. "What's that supposed to mean?"

"I've known you for five years. I've seen the way you look at me, the way you act when I'm around. Women can always tell these things."

"So you've known?" My voice, I realized, was much louder than it should have been. Just how drunk *was* Duncan? "You asked me to take you out, to come over here and all that—you've been sitting next to me for five years and all the while you've known?"

"Please, quiet down. I wish none of this had ever come up, I really do. Now everything's different, now you're going to feel weird around me—"

"I'm leaving," I said, and stood up abruptly.

"No you're not. You sit back down, we need to talk about this."

"What's there to talk about? I just laid myself wide open and all you can say is *you've known*. Now I guess you're going to tell me how women figure these things out, how men are so this and that and don't even know it—"

"Oh, here you go. Every time you get hurt you get caustic, did you know that? You're so afraid of your feelings that you build these barricades—"

"Tell Duncan I had a great time," I said, opening the front door. Pamela didn't move. "Frankly, I don't know if I'll ever be able to face him again."

"Parker," Pamela said evenly, meeting my gaze, "grow up."

But since I didn't have anything to say to that, I stepped out into the hallway and closed the door.

I WENT STRAIGHT to Rollo's, proceeded to drink three scotch whiskeys in rapid succession, and was motioning for my fourth when I heard someone say, "Parker?"

I turned. Standing next to me, dressed in black bicycle

pants and a Georgia Tech sweatshirt, was none other than Thella. She was smiling, which I took as one of the evening's few good omens.

"Thella," I said, extending my hand. "How are you?"

"Great, just, you know. Fine. And you?"

Figuring I had nothing to lose, I turned fully around in my bar stool and said, "Not too well, actually. I think I just lost my best friend tonight, among other things."

She looked perplexed, or perhaps overwhelmed, but she managed another smile and said, "Sorry to hear that."

And then something came over me. I don't know what it was. Call it the Imp of the Perverse. Call it exhaustion. Call it base cruelty. Whatever it was, I found myself, before I could do anything about it, saying, "By the way, you stole my fucking watch."

She flashed me a look of genuine, heart-stopping virulence and then, blinking rapidly, said, "Excuse me?"

"My watch. I woke up that morning and my watch was gone."

"From where?"

"From my bedside table."

"You didn't put your watch on your bedside table. The band broke on the way home. You put it in your blazer pocket." And suddenly, I remembered everything! In the car. Giggles and gear shifts. Fishing underneath the seat.

"This jacket?" I said, plucking my lapel. But of course it was this jacket. I didn't own another jacket.

She nodded. Then, with astonishing self-possession, Thella

looked me in the eye, reached into the front pocket of my sports coat and withdrew my missing $300 Seiko.

"Here," she said, dropping it into my lap. "You asshole." And without another word, she turned and walked away.

And what did I do? Well, first, I dropped my watch back in my pocket. Then I paid my tab. And then, just before I walked out, I turned to the mirror, looked at my face between the letters of the Rollo's logo, and thought, *Tomorrow. And tomorrow. And tomorrow.*

9. BETWEEN THINGS

In between things, Parker slept with Rachel. He kept telling himself he wouldn't do it, even insisted, sometimes out loud, that the mere thought of doing it was completely out of the question. Yet for one reason or another, reasons he did not always care to examine, he just kept doing it. Over and over again. Even after he'd said he wouldn't. And he said it all the time. He said it when she called, he said it while he was saying yes, it would be all right if she came over, and he said it—sometimes out loud—as he waited for her to come over. At least part of him said it. One part of him said he shouldn't do it, and the other part went ahead and did it anyway.

Even while he did it he said he shouldn't do it, so clearly there were two Parkers at work here: the one who said and the one who did. The word and the deed. But in this battle between pen and sword, the sword was mightier by a pretty large margin.

He referred to this state of affairs as the Rachel Situation. The reference was mostly private, since not many of his friends even knew there was a Rachel Situation, though most of them knew Rachel. They knew Rachel and they knew Parker used to date Rachel and they knew that Parker no longer dated Rachel: they just didn't know there was a Rachel Situation. For the Rachel Situation was further complicated by the fact that she, Rachel, was one of the "things" he was "in between." He was in between all his ex-girlfriends and someone else who hadn't shown up yet, some spectacular woman who would represent, in full, the last person on earth he would ever desire. More than the girl of his dreams, she was the future incarnate. In a sense, she was *his* future. He knew that when he found her, when she finally arrived in his life in all her perfection, he'd be a whole person at last, fully integrated, all problems solved. And in the meantime, he was sustaining intimate, sexually charged breakup proceedings with his past.

When he wasn't busy with the Rachel Situation, Parker pursued his new life—not really his future so much as the interim existence he began when he first inaugurated breakup proceedings proper. This new life, in which he sold telephone services to small businesses, took place in the real world. The real world was that vast frightening expanse of metropolitan Atlanta that stretched with teeming busyness and activity beyond the walls of the graduate school where he and Rachel were once mutually enrolled. Back then, Parker and his graduate student colleagues liked to theorize about the real world. Many of them wrote papers about the real world. Some of them taught entry-level freshman courses that prepared young people to flourish in the real world. A few of his more flippant colleagues taught their students to interpret advertisements and television talk shows in the manner of literary works, all in order to demonstrate the relative importance of the real world over that of the purely textual and idealistic. Still and all, few of these people had ever actually *gone* to the real world. Some had visited, some had fled, but no one in Parker's immediate set had ever really lived there, in the real world itself. It was just this abstract place *out there,* this throbbing, clashing, quaking world of the ineluctably real. And now Parker lived there himself, in the real world. Nowadays, as he fought his way through rush hour traffic, say, or picked up his dry cleaning, or stood in line at the supermarket in his suit and tie with a little tote basket piled high with frozen pasta entrées, he would say to himself, *I'm finally here, I'm finally a* real person.

Rachel, on the other hand, was still in graduate school. A petite, elfish sprite of a girl, with enormous clear green eyes and a tangle of ginger-colored hair usually bundled into a roll at the back of her head, Rachel eschewed Parker's real world for the world of the mind, for the world of student loans and poor health insurance, for the world of identity politics and bad haircuts and perpetual unemployment. Although nearly a year had passed since she filed her dissertation, "Clitoral Envy and Masculine Anxiety in the Works of John Webster," she was still trying desperately to locate that most elusive treasure in all of modern academia—a job. In the meantime, she picked up section after section of freshman composition. On those mornings when Parker slept over at her place, he would lie back on her mattress and watch her as she bustled about the apartment before class, her tube socks sliding along the hardwood floors and her cat, a mangy stray named Margerey Kempe, scuttling underfoot. By way of class preparation, she would often jump onto the bed and march around in her underwear intoning her lecture to the bedroom walls, a coffee cup in one hand and a rhetoric and comp reader flapping in the other, while Parker, still in the bed, avoided her marching feet ("Jesus, Rache, the *coffee*"). At eight-fifteen, he would gather his things and walk out the door, Rachel running out behind him with a sheaf of freshman essays fluttering under her arm and a bagel clamped between her teeth, and he would continue watching her as she climbed into her old Volkswagen Rabbit and peeled out of her gravel driveway to meet her morning section of freshman comp. Some days she wore billowy peasant dresses. Other days she left the house in low-slung boys' corduroys, thrift-store bowling shirts, and untied Keds sneakers. A dedicated and passionate teacher, she always included her home phone number on her course syllabi, and on rainy evenings when Parker was staying over at her place, her male students, perhaps responding to the melancholy weather, would often call for help. Parker relished answering these phone calls. "Um, gosh, I'm sorry," the students would say upon hearing his voice, "I thought, I, um . . . Listen, is Professor Moore there?" Handing her the phone, Parker would say, "One of your students, Professor, looking for an *extension*," drawing out that last word as Rachel scrunched her nose and took the receiver. "Oh, *hi* Josh"—turning her back to Parker and making her voice soft and consoling—"is there a problem, is everything okay?"

Despite the fact that they were not officially dating—they were, rather, officially *broken up*—Parker spent lots of time at her apartment. He preferred her place, actually, to his own. A spacious, musty-smelling ground-floor duplex, Rachel's pad was a funhouse of clutter and chaos, with miles of hardwood floors, a kitchen full of dilapidated makeshift computer equipment, tapestries on the walls, chenille-covered couches and chairs, an antique wooden dining table buried in mail and shopping bags, three lava lamps and five beanbag chairs, a completely outfitted and mint-condition Barbie Dream House, and, in the cavernous, echoing bathroom, an aboveground lion-clawed bathtub surrounded by mounds and mounds of thick waterlogged fashion magazines and literary quarterlies. After lovemaking, as Rachel cleaned up in this selfsame bathroom, Parker would thumb through her books, most of which fell under the general rubric of contemporary gender theory. The book jackets featured bawdy woodcut illustrations from the Middle Ages and elegantly written critical hosannas, while inside lay the densest, most impenetrable prose he had ever read in his life, all of it formatted in sleek Minion font and printed on sturdy, acid-free paper by some craft-conscious university press in the Midwest. It wasn't the prose he was after, though. What he wanted were Rachel's annotations. They spoke to him somehow. They seemed to possess for him a strange, almost cabalistic significance. Opening the volume on the bedside table, for instance, he might encounter the following passage, the whole of which would be underlined in Rachel's neat, scholarly hand, and in the margin of which Parker could detect a mysterious *P* followed by a question mark:

Although the phe-no(mono)logical "Self," which is, undoubtedly, a Cartesian, i.e., patriarchal, fiction, can only be (re)constituted in relation to an equally fictional "Other," this unstable relation of *différance* is always already thwarted by a de(sire)ing of the totalized Ego, site of masculine "certainty," of longed-for stability. For Ego itself is inevitably "predator of the Other," and hence we see that the fantasy of masculine hegemony exists in a vacuum defined wholly by, and inscribed entirely within, its relationship to this Other, which is itself not only unstable, necessarily and unavoidably unstable, but also, by a similar species of (male) hegemonic logic, undermined by the very same metaphysical "*un*-cert(aint)y" posited by

In a panic he would snap the book shut and put it back where he found it, his hands shaking with paranoia and dread.

Back in bed, Rachel would then narrate for him the most recent grad bash. Having once been a graduate student himself in the same Department—which word all graduate students secretly capitalized, the same way they told their students to capitalize the "White House" or the "National Security Council"—Parker more or less knew all the principle characters.

"First of all," Rachel would begin, supine in bed beside him with her leg hoisted into the candlelight so as to cast a lurid shadow on the wall opposite her bureau, "Carey brought his new flame, a forty-eight year-old Hispanic woman who works for Morgan Stanley, worth several mil, easy. She was a trip, man, Esmerelda was her name, very touchy-feely. Anyway, and then Ethan corners me for like an hour to tell me all about his latest crisis, which basically boils down to, Should he come out before or after his oral exams? Honestly, he was reduced to framing the question in precisely those terms. Christ. Oh, and I forgot to tell you, guess which faculty member was getting stoned in Jennifer's bedroom . . . ?"

These accounts would course through him like an Alka-Seltzer. What was he *doing*? What had he been doing for the last fifteen (twenty? twenty-five?) minutes? What was he doing with his *life*?

"Sounds positively dreadful," he'd say.

"*You'd* think so."

No, they were not going out—not anymore, anyway. Their breakup had been final, way back when. And they certainly weren't seeing each other. Rather, they were seeing other people. That was the important thing: to see other people. And they both planned to start seeing other people, absolutely, just as soon as they quit not seeing each other. Nevertheless, there had been sightings. He and Rachel took in a movie one night, for instance—a Friday night movie, actually; neither of them had plans, and it was so nice out and everything—and they were sighted. They were sighted one night at a taco joint. There were the occasional street sightings: a lot of their arguments took place out of doors. But, so far, they had avoided being the subject of a rumor. So they were okay. They were just two lonely people trying to sustain an intimate breakup. And sustain it indefinitely.

ABOUT TWO MONTHS into the Rachel Situation, Parker and Rachel began devising a set of rules.

Rule Number One. *Each partner is free to date without consulting the other.* This was the most important rule, the single rule they recalled to each other most frequently. So far, Parker had yet to invoke this rule, though he really planned to do so, any day now. More to the point, Rachel, so far as he knew, had not invoked this rule, either, though he had no way of knowing this for sure, did he, since the rule, by its very wording, thereby ruled out all possible knowledge of its being invoked, which was the whole point of the rule in the first place, as Parker very well knew.

Rule Number Two. *Neither partner is allowed to feel guilty.* Rachel, not Parker, devised this rule, astounding as that may sound. She devised it *for* Parker, in fact, though she also claimed it on her own. How this rule was supposed to work out in practice Parker never figured out. Of all the rules they had devised, this was the most difficult one of all. For Parker, anyway.

Rule Number Three. *A partner can spend the night at another partner's apartment but* only *when said partner is too intoxicated to drive.* They both broke this one pretty freely. Not the DUI law, of course: the rule. They broke this *rule* all the time.

Rule Number Four. *Neither partner is permitted to leave a trace of his/her presence at the other partner's apartment.* By way of minor exceptions to this rule, Rachel left two changes of underwear, her Wellesley sweatshirt, her warm-up pants, her hair dryer, her toothbrush, her Hilary Clinton coffee mug, and a box of tampons at Parker's apartment; Parker left a pair of army fatigues, several pairs of boxers, his toothbrush, and his electric razor at Rachel's apartment.

Rule Number Five. *If either partner sleeps with anyone else, all contact ceases immediately.* Both were adamant about this one. *Immediately,* they liked to remind each other. *No exceptions.* It was implicitly understood, moreover, that this rule, Rule Number Five, canceled out Rule Number One, while Rule Number One did not in any way cancel out Rule Number Five. In other words, Rule Number One prevailed insofar as all activity remained within the purview of said rule, yet the moment Rule Number One turned into Rule Number Five, the earlier rule was to be instantly revoked in favor of the newer, more inclusive and urgent rule. Paper covers rock, rock covers scissors, scissors cut paper. Those are the rules.

IN THE WAKE of particularly larky bouts of sex, Rachel would sometimes declare, "You think this isn't a re-lationship, but it is."

"This? A relationship?"

"Yes: this."

"Was our other relationship this good?"

"Sometimes. A lot more often than you're ready to admit."

"I admit plenty, Rachel. I know it was good. If I didn't think we had a good thing, would I be here right now?"

"Oooh, you really don't want to go there, sweetie."

She was right, of course—"there" being why he contin-ued sleeping with her long after he had gone through the hassle of breaking up with her—unexpectedly and without much warning, Rachel was always quick to add. Why had he done that? she wanted to know. And why did he continue doing this?

Parker had his reasons. For breaking up, he liked to cite the fact that he was not then, and was not yet, prepared for that most terrifying plunge of all, the Long-Term Commitment. Rachel, on the other hand, had wanted one, had wanted an LTC, which was a perfectly laudable thing for her to want, he was always quick to tell her. But since he didn't want one, what other choice did they have but to break up?

"Um," Rachel would say, her index finger fully extended, "let's see: for one thing, we could have—"

And anyway, there was also the matter of condomless sex. That was a real selling point. It just was. Two weeks after they first started going out, he and Rachel got tested for HIV, and the day they returned home with their negative test results was also the first day they permitted themselves the luxury of condomless sex. Rachel was on the pill, neither partner was diseased in any way, monogamy seemed the next step, so why not? Now, nearly two years after that fateful day, both Parker and Rachel were operating under the exact same conditions. Since their breakup neither partner had slept with anyone new. "No reason to feel flattered," Rachel always added. "No flattery taken," he would reply. So each time they swore off each other, each time they insisted they were going to leave each other alone, each time they agreed it would be best if they didn't do this kind of thing anymore, they always did so under the remarkable dispensation of a monogamous HIV-negative couple.

"Fair enough. I'll give you that one. What else?"

Well, and there was the whole exciting process of giving in to each other, over and over again. That might have been the biggest selling point of all. Parker's wise and knowing friends, none of whom would have approved of the Rachel Situation had they known it existed, simply weren't around when she stopped at the front door of his downstairs apartment and looked down at her feet, hovering between resolution and surrender, while he waited only three feet away and told himself that tonight he would let her walk away and end it for good. They weren't there to see the look on her face as she took her hand from the doorknob and met his eyes. They weren't there during that unbearably thrilling moment when he locked his fingers behind his neck and she shook her head and said, "Shit." And they were nowhere in sight when he and Rachel removed the sword between them and rolled ravenously into all that glorious, forbidden space.

"Oh God"—dropping back onto the pillow, her hands in her hair—"now we sound like Cheever characters."

What he didn't explain to Rachel was how much he loved the way things stood between them right now. He loved the delicate balance they were sustaining, this tension-filled battleground between full commitment and wide-open singlehood, between past and future. It was, in a way, the best of both worlds. After lovemaking, they would lie in bed and talk about themselves, she doling out select details of her daily existence, and he returning the same. On those languid evenings her life appeared to him like a winding hallway lined with a bewildering procession of closed doors she led him past on her way to the porch out back. Similarly, his life he handed to her in little incomplete bundles. Like many of their old lovers' spats, these furtive, guarded bull sessions sometimes seemed to him as if they could sustain themselves indefinitely. They were just enough, and not too much. These postcoital colloquies kept the two of them together, and sustained their distance, all at the same time. Drifting off to sleep with the first twinge of regret tickling his stomach, he would nevertheless say to himself that his life right now was just about perfect, a golden mean between two alternatives he found too frightening, for some reason, to contemplate. He was like Goldilocks in the baby bear's bed: not too hard, not too soft, but somewhere comfortably, safely, in between.

THREE MONTHS AND two weeks into the Rachel Situation, Parker finally invoked Rule Number One.

Her name was Kimberly Willis, from Marketing. She wasn't really the girl of the future; she was more like Miss Right Now. All sharp angles and protruding elbows, with a pointed chin and a thick sheath of permed hair that looked kind of like dried Ramen noodles, she was attractive enough in her own way, yet even he realized she was less a source of desire than a cause of paranoia. Though they were in different departments, he ran into her every day in the break room, and every time he saw her she was hunkered down in the corner with a girlfriend or two, the whole group of them whispering, conspiring, giggling, and after a month or two he discerned that Kimberly Willis was the leader of the pack.

He soon grew convinced she was giggling about him. And that's why he asked her out in the first place: to assuage his fear. And the minute she tilted her head and said, "Um, sure, why not," he realized he'd made a serious mistake.

"Oh my God," she gushed at dinner that night, "you've seriously never heard the story about her and him? I totally can't believe it: I thought *everyone* knew this story."

"I guess I'm out of the loop."

"*Totally*. Okay, now you have to promise you won't tell anyone I told you this."

"I thought everyone already knew it."

"Well, everyone but her. Promise? Do you solemnly swear? Good. Now, to understand this story, you have to know about Jeff. You *do* know about Jeff, don't you?"

He smiled. "Am I supposed to know about him?"

"Oh my *God!* You are totally going to flip out when I tell you this. Okay, so Jeff, who used to date this other girl who isn't there anymore—whole *nother* story right there—well, he asked this *unnamed person* to join him in Chicago. Follow me?"

He followed her. Before he quit graduate school, he used to complain to Rachel that the only people they ever saw were the other people from the Department. "Real people don't live this way," he complained. "Real people go to work and come home and *then* live their lives. We never leave work. We see the same people all day, every night, every weekend. Work follows us everywhere we go. And that's why everyone we know is so neurotic and screwed up." Now that Parker was officially in the real world, he was surprised to learn that real people in the real world never left work either. In real life, real people went to work and came home and then went back out to spend more time with the other real people from work. Where, apparently, they talked about people from work.

"Really?" he said, in response to a dramatic pause in Kimberly's story. "Isn't that something. So what happened next?"

Which was right about the time he spotted Rachel. She was sitting in a booth on the other side of the restaurant, scribbling into a spiral notebook and nursing a beer. Uncharacteristically, she had her hair down, and through the drapery of her bangs he could detect the wiry glint of her glasses, which, as far as he knew, she rarely wore in public. She was also wearing the denim vest he had given to her on her birthday several years ago, as well as the peach, ankle-length skirt he always loved, the one that outlined so perfectly the articulate slope of her hips. This was how she looked when he wasn't around, it suddenly dawned on him. Then he realized that if he didn't already know her, if he hadn't already dated her, if he hadn't already broken up with her, he would have wanted to meet her. He could even imagine himself not speaking to her tonight—he was, after all, on a date —and then spending the rest of the week mooning about his apartment in a lovesick fugue, excoriating himself for not mustering up the courage to approach her out of the blue and ask her out on a date. So at least he was spared all that.

"... and so when Jeff comes to work on Monday, this person who will go nameless goes up to him and she's like ..."

Earlier in the day Rachel had called him at work to ask him if he was coming over that night, and when he told her no, he was not coming over, she said nothing for what seemed like a very long time. Then she coughed and told him, Fine, and hung up.

" ... so then Jeff was all like—"

"Could you hold that thought for a minute?"

Kimberly Willis jerked her head once, as if she had just been slapped. Her eyelashes beat away like bumblebee wings. "Gosh, I'm sorry. I didn't mean to—"

"No, no," Parker assured her, "it's not ... It's just that I have to—" With what he hoped was an embarrassed look on his face—not too difficult to conjure, actually, given the situation—he jerked his thumb over his shoulder and arched his eyebrows.

"Oh, *right*." Kimberly gave him a sage nod, then leaned forward and scowled. "I think it's called a *bathroom*."

As he approached Rachel's table, he kept his eyes on her cheek, a sliver of which poked through the cascade of her bangs. From past experience he knew that she was one of the world's most inept liars, a woman so ill-equipped for subterfuge she once broke down in tears and confessed that she had secretly told all of her friends to comment favorably on a stupendously bad haircut that he had gotten, for about six dollars, at a Woolworth's downtown, a haircut, it is worth adding, that Parker himself freely declared, with more resignation than wounded vanity, totally beyond redemption. So if Rachel had seen him earlier, her cheek would betray her.

It did.

"You shouldn't write in the dark like that," he said when he got to her table. "You'll ruin your eyes."

For a confused moment or two, she acted surprised to see him. Then she sat back and sighed. The spiral notebook lay open on the table. The right-hand page was smooth and flat while the left-hand page bowed slightly, the underside tinted blue with aggressive penmanship. Beside the spiral lay a greeting card, also face down. She stroked her pen. "For the last ten minutes I've been sitting here trying to figure out how to leave."

"You could try the door."

"Right, but you and that girl are sitting beside it."

Parker looked for himself. His and Kimberly's table leaned flush against the front window, two tables away from the front entrance. His seat, which was empty at the moment, faced the entrance, while Kimberly's seat, which was not empty, faced the passageway leading into the restaurant's bar area. Kimberly stared at him from her occupied seat. Without altering her expression by the merest twitch, she waved. Inanely, he waved back.

"So," Rachel was saying, "I just thought I'd sit here and doodle in my notebook and then leave when you two finished your meal, if that's okay with you."

"Rachel, listen—"

"That *is* a homemade perm I'm seeing, isn't it?"

"When you called at work today, I—"

"She must be an old student of yours. Or a *young* student, I should say."

"She's not a student. She's in Marketing. Look, if you want us to—"

"Marketing? Isn't that where they create all these false expectations and phony desires to make people want things they don't really need? Or am I getting that confused with pornography?"

"Tell you what," Parker said evenly, "we'll leave. How's that sound? We haven't even ordered yet, so no one should mind."

"Oh no you don't." Rachel seized a big burlap backpack off her seat and began shoveling in her wallet, her spiral notebook, her glasses, muttering, "You just stay here and eat your little dinner and discuss your little marketing strategies, all right? Because I have *tons* of reading to do, excuse me, shelves and shelves of reading, so actually this is *just* the break I've been waiting for, all I needed was an excuse to get *out* that front door and home to my cozy little bed and my cozy kitty cat and my, my, *shit*, where is that waitress, I need to pay for this thing." She was standing beside him now, her full backpack slung across one shoulder and the check fluttering between her fingers. Her scent cut through the smoke and steam of the restaurant and tickled the back of his throat.

"I think you pay up front."

"Don't we always." Waving the check in his face, she turned on her boot heels and stepped away.

"Rachel, wait."

Her shoulders dropped. The backpack swung once along the curve of her spine, and his stomach swung with it. He knew he had to say something here; he just couldn't decide what it should be. There was no rule for where they were now. There was the rule about dating, there was the rule about guilt, there was the rule about sleeping with someone else. Rule Numbers One, Two, and Five, respectively. But there was no rule for this.

"I'm waiting," she said, without turning around.

"This is awkward, that's all. We didn't anticipate this."

"*Who* didn't anticipate it?" Now she faced him. "What is it we didn't anticipate, Parker?"

"This," he gestured. "Bumping into each other. Seeing the other person. What*ever.*"

"Fine," she said, and patted him lightly on the chest. "Then here's a new addendum to Rule Number One. Each partner must warn the other where *not* to go when said partner is out on a date. How's that?"

"Rachel, please, this is stupid."

"What part of the addendum did you not understand?"

"No, I got it, that sounds fine. It's a good addendum."

"So you're square on this?"

"Yes, I'm square. I—"

"Good. Then tomorrow night you are forbidden to go anywhere *near* the Rusty Spoon. Do we understand each other? Excellent. Now, if you'll excuse me, I'm going to pay my bill."

She marched off, her skirt swaying one way and her backpack swaying the other, a perfectly balanced pendulum his stomach couldn't match. Before she exited earshot, he asked, "Can I call you tonight?"

And Rachel, still moving toward the cash register, waved the bill in the air and replied, "Parker, go Five yourself."

THE NEXT EVENING he sat crouched and uncomfortable behind a mound of bushes bordering Rachel's duplex apartment. He was staring at a car. For the last hour and a half he had been hiding here in silence and apprehension watching car after car drift mysteriously along Rachel's quaint, deeply wooded street, only to pass her place and penetrate deeper into the humid night. But now a car had finally stopped. He stood up and squinted. Accord? Acura? Something fairly nondescript, in any case, flat and squat with rounded edges and a low-lying hood.

Presently the passenger door opened. A foot, female from the looks of it, emerged from the open door, followed by a small, feminine form dressed in a dark charcoal skirt and white blouse. She clutched a spiral notebook to her chest. Before turning around, she bent over and said something to the driver and then laughed, a tiny sound that barely penetrated the roaring in Parker's head. Then she shoved the door closed with her hip and, with a wave to the retreating car, treaded slowly up the walkway, the notebook still cradled against her chest.

"Hey," he whispered from the bushes.

She stopped where she was and stared blankly into the night. Rachel.

He stood up to his full height and cleared his throat. In accidental imitation of last evening, he waved.

"There are laws against that, you know."

"I'll risk it," he replied, and stepped away from his hiding place.

Very much as if this sort of thing were perfectly normal, she proceeded down the walkway, Parker following along behind, and then she sat down on the porch steps, facing the street. He sat down next to her, his arms crossed along his knees.

"You're barefoot," she pointed out.

"I guess I left in a hurry." He wiggled his toes. "It was a boring night anyway. A shoeless kind of night, you might say. How about you? How was your night?"

"Life altering."

As he could detect no irony here, he supplied some of his

own. "Interesting you should say that, because I was sitting at home tonight thinking about altering my life, as well."

"Parker, look: I'm tired, I'm cranky, and I really need to—"

"Wait, hear me out, Rachel. Just listen to me for a second. This is important. I was sitting at home tonight cleaning my toilet, right? And I'm crawling around there on my hands and knees, scrubbing the porcelain and drinking beer, and I'm thinking to myself, 'What's wrong with this picture'? Have I been keeping myself free so I can stay home on Friday night and clean my toilet? Because that's basically what I do on nights I'm not with you. I clean my toilet, I rearrange my CDs, I, you know, I surf the Net or whatever."

"So it's me or the toilet is what you're telling me here."

"I'm not finished. So there I am, on my hands and knees, like I said, and I'm also thinking to myself, 'You hate this. You hate the thought of her being out with someone else. Admit it, Parker'—and I really did address myself in the third person like that—I said, 'Parker, you're jealous.' No getting around it, no way to rationalize it out of existence. It was just like you last night, Rachel, when you saw me and Kimberly—"

"Wrong. It was *nothing* like you and Kimberly."

"No, I didn't mean that. Wait—"

"Just say what you're trying to tell me, Parker. Tell me what you're trying say and make it quick because I've got things to do."

"Look, all I'm saying is, I can't stand it any longer. This

whole thing is stupid, is what I'm trying to tell you. I'm talking about the whole setup, this in-between thing we're sustaining right now. It's gotta stop. You know what I mean?"

"Yep." The answer came so fast it sounded as if she'd dropped the *e*. Yp.

"Well, okay, then; we agree. So I was thinking—"

"It's over."

"No, no, that's not it. Rachel, listen. I just think we've got to go one way or the other. No more sitting on the fence."

"And which way do you think we should go, Parker?" She leaned back against the porch column, softening her presence somehow. A raindrop hit his face, followed by another.

"I'm not sure." He hugged his knees. "I just know I want things to change."

More rain fell. Already the patio emitted a light, humid scent of damp wood. "Actually," she whispered, "I've got a confession to make."

His heart lurched against his chest. A new twist. He had no idea if this was good news or bad news, if it would elate him or crush him. In either case, he was being saved from making a decision one way or another, and from that he took some bleak comfort. More specifically, Rachel was saving him. As usual. "Yes?"

"Well, for starters, I didn't have a date tonight."

He let a moment pass before he said, "I see."

"No, I'm pretty sure you don't, Parker. I don't think you see at all. I'm telling you I had dinner with my dissertation adviser."

He nodded, though the news meant nothing to him. Not at first, anyway. Slowly, however, a possibility dawned on him. "Is your dissertation adviser male or female?"

"Male, but that's not the point. Parker, look at me." He obeyed. Tears rimmed her eyes, those big, brilliant green eyes. *Surrender,* said a voice in his head. *Let go.* "I got a job offer this week."

Not the twist he had in mind. Not even the *bend* he had in mind. "A job?"

"Yes, a job. A real job. As in, you know, a paycheck and all that."

"Oh, but Rachel," he smiled, and reached out to take her hand, "that's terrific news. I mean, *isn't* it? Isn't this what you've been working for?"

"More or less." She jerked her hand away.

"More or less? What kind of job is it?"

"A teaching job. Small state college with a good reputation. Manageable course load. Private office."

He laughed. "Sounds great."

"One-year contract, but they tell me it turns into a tenure-track next year."

He raised his hands as if speechless with admiration. "Even better."

"It's in Massachusetts, Parker." She was looking at him again. Her expression, which she now presented for examination, offered no clue as to what she might be thinking. No clue at all.

"That's quite a hike."

"And here's the best part." She turned away. "They have a couple of extra sections I can take on this summer if I want them."

The rain now dripped off the roof and sprayed the tops of his bare feet. "And do you?"

"My adviser says it'd be a good idea. He says it could help me a lot next year when they decide whether or not to keep me on for the duration. I think the term for it is 'departmental service,' which is just an academic euphemism for kissing ass."

He listened to the soft spring rain, to the sound it made as it pattered across the leaves and rattled the gutters. "Wow," he whispered.

"How's that for a confession? Didn't see that one coming, did you?"

"Yeah, that's pretty left field." He felt her slump away from him. Cars passed by slowly, their tires licking the road. "So I guess you're gonna take it."

"More than likely."

"And when do you leave?"

"In a couple of weeks. Early June." She faced him now. "Actually, I'm lying."

He felt himself blink once, very slowly. "About what, exactly?"

"The date. New faculty orientation starts this Monday. That means I'm leaving tomorrow." Now she watched his face for a reaction, though in fact Parker had no idea what she was seeing. He could not altogether judge what kind of expression he was exhibiting for the simple reason that he had no idea what he was thinking. Both Parkers were at work now, the one Rachel was looking at and the one wondering what Rachel was looking at. At this very moment one of them was undergoing a very intense set of emotions, while the other was wondering what those emotions could possibly be. So which was which? That really was the question, wasn't it? In a weird sort of way, it had *always* been the question. "So," she sighed, "finish telling me how you were going to alter your life."

He rallied enough to answer, "You just did it for me."

"Hoo, don't I wish." She exhaled dramatically, then shook her head. "Wouldn't that have been something, though? Me altering your life?"

"You did alter it, Rachel. You know that."

"Oh, Parker. I was a very small part of your life." Lifting her pinched fingers to her squinting right eye, she said, "A teensy little part. The, I don't know, the sex part or something. Hah, that's exactly what I was: a sex part. It's almost like being a sex partner, but not *quite*."

"You were much more than that."

"I was?"

"Yes, you were."

"Why are you using the past tense?"

"I didn't realize I was."

"Well, you are." She lowered her finger and, with a dramatic sigh, stretched her legs out into the rain and leaned back onto her hands. "Do you know when I decided to take this job?"

"No." At some point his hands had begun shaking. He had no idea which part of him was responsible for this. He just knew that this was an important event, whatever it meant. He knew he was living through one of those moments the memory of which would stay with him for a very long time.

"About two seconds ago."

For want of a better answer, he answered, "You're lying."

"Isn't it pretty to think so?" She looked down at his feet and laughed, then stood up. When he turned to her at last he found himself staring at her skirt, then at her hip. He had to look way up to locate her face, but it lay in shadows, her hair hanging down like a lamp shade. She towered over him with her notepad, huge and terrifying, and mysteriously no longer his. She was already receding. She was already gone.

From her lofty perch she opened the spiral. When her knee grazed his back he was so startled he looked away, embarrassed, and only gradually did he register that a square pink envelope, stiff and heavy, had dropped into his lap. "You might as well have that," she said. "For what it's worth." He then heard her shuffle across her porch and rattle, perhaps more aggressively than usual, her monstrous clump of keys. The deadbolt sounded with a distant hollow thump; Margerey Kempe squeaked a worried hello. One final creak of the door and she really was gone. He held his breath: the moment hung, and for a thrilling unbearable moment it seemed as if she was going to come back. But then the creak came, followed quickly by the rattle of the door and the sad slide and drop of the deadbolt.

The envelope lay like a hatchet blade between his thighs. He took it gingerly between his trembling fingers and ran his thumb along the seal. But the flap was free: she hadn't sealed the envelope yet. Nor, he noticed when he turned it around, had she addressed it. He tugged loose a thick, glossy greeting card. The front featured a print reproduction of some famous painting or other: Rachel was an art history major in college. Monet? Degas? No, the Don McLean one: *Starry Starry Night*. Van Gogh, then. He opened the card. Yesterday's date was written, in Rachel's careful hand, along the upper right-hand corner. Since there was no commercial inscription (greeting cards weren't her style), the card was mostly blank, save for the following inscription, also in Rachel's hand

Parker,
  By the time you read this I will have

Nothing more. That was all she had written. He stared and he stared at this sentence for a good two, maybe three minutes. He thought of that sequence in the Beatles' *Yellow Submarine* movie where, in the middle of "When I'm 64," the animators count off the sixty seconds of a single minute, each successive number a psychedelic surprise. A minute is a long time, the movie reminds us. *Let us demonstrate.* A thick raindrop fell from overhead and splattered on the card, causing the word *read* to spider outward and sink deeper into the thick paper, so that it looked like a small aquatic creature sealed in a microscope slide. Another drop fell, then another. He did not move until the entire sentence, salutation and all, was completely illegible, the ink running like cheap mascara into all that clean, unsullied white space, and when he was sure the waterlogged card was no longer legible he dropped it onto the porch step and stood up. The girl of the past had become the girl of the future—perfect, unattainable, celestially remote—and now he was a single Parker at least, lonely and clear-eyed and hopelessly, helplessly in love.

10. SPANISH OMENS

Rachel, Parker's wife of thirty-two hours, wanted insurance. The Avis salesclerk behind the sloping white counter—a plump mustached Spanish gentleman of unflagging good cheer—kept misunderstanding her to mean *a*ssurance, vaguely defined. Yeah, sure, is fine *señora,* no problem. But Rachel was adamant: she wanted *in*surance, as in *car* insurance, of the legally binding sort, with riders and underwriters and clearly outlined policy provisions.

"He doesn't understand what I'm asking," she murmured.

Parker nodded vaguely and returned his attention to the fascinating world unfolding all around him. As in any airport anywhere on the planet, the Madrid Barajas International Airport featured wide, incandescently lit walkways with illuminated signs overhead indicating in pictograms the location of ticket booths and luggage-claim depots and his/her toilets.

A mechanized voice—lilting, feminine, smoothed to incomprehensibility by several layers of soft echo—poured down from above, directing travelers to this gate or that and warning patrons to watch their bags. Weird bells went off in the distance. The difference was that this airport was *in Spain*. He had been lifted from Eastern standard time and transported to a disembodied place where everything happened six hours later in an exotic language. Not only did the air smell different—indoor cigarette smoke, mostly, which scent had all but disappeared in the States, plus fried food and coffee and something a bit more elusive, a sour earthy smell Parker tentatively identified as body odor—but also the product packaging seemed brighter and more ingenious, the ads on the wall burst forth with more innocence and energy, the entire atmosphere of the place struck him as somehow more exciting, more *European*. He watched the lovely Spanish girls in their huge clunky-heeled shoes and their trim, tight black flares. He gawked at the handsome Spanish businessmen with their cell phones and their casually held cigarettes and their unbuttoned double-breasted suit jackets. The world around him was familiar yet slightly awry, like a strange cover version of some beloved old tune. Jet lag gave everything he saw a halo of celestial gleam.

"*Parker*," Rachel hissed, and yanked his sleeve. "I could use some *help*, you know."

So he tore his gaze from the bewitching world around him. He and Rachel were trying to secure a rental car for a week-

long excursion through Andalusia, a journey into the un-
known that would constitute their honeymoon. The trip had
been Parker's idea. For years—or at least since his bittersweet, heartbroken year in sunny Miami, Florida—he had
nursed a mild obsession with Latino culture. He owned one or
two Rubén Blades records, read the occasional Latin American novel in translation, and harbored a private and perfectly
chaste and thoroughly embarrassing crush on Gloria Estefan,
whose music he nevertheless found tepid and uninteresting.
Hence, he had always wanted to see Spain, the primal origin
of Latino culture, a country he imagined as the dark over-
looked jewel of Europe. He had friends who'd lived in Madrid
for a year or two and all of them—the women in particular
—returned to the States transformed. They dressed better,
and they all affected pack-a-day cigarette habits. Something
miraculous happened to these people in Madrid, something
strange and decisive. Parker wanted to see if he was suscep-
tible to this same brand of Spanish sorcery.

"Fine," he sighed. "What do you want me to do?"

Rachel glowered at him with her bright green eyes, her
valentine lips puckered into a scowl. At the wedding she had
looked as radiant and crisp as Doris Day in high-resolution
digital color; now, after eight hours of transatlantic travel,
she gave off a softer and more Technicolor aura, with an
analog fuzziness about her only partially due to jet lag. With
her ginger-colored hair pulled back into a knot and the
sleeves of her button-down shirt hiked up past her elbows,

she seemed ready for battle. But it was too early in their marriage for a fight. "Here, maybe I can do something."

She raised her left eyebrow and, like a game-show merchandise model, made a display tray of her hands.

"*Habla inglés*, yes?" Parker began.

The Avis clerk shrugged. "*Un poco.*"

"Terrific." Enunciating each word clearly and, for some reason, loudly, Parker said, "We, my wife and I"—he gestured at Rachel— "need to make sure, yes?, that we are oh kay if we get in a *wreck, sí?*" He brought the knuckles of his two fists together in a pictogram for "wreck."

"Oh Christ." Rachel shoved him aside and gripped the countertop. "Look," she told the clerk, "just hand me the agreement and show me where it indicates insurance and we'll work from there." Parker noticed she spoke normally, as if she were addressing a native English speaker.

The Avis clerk took a drag from a cigarette and, squinting into the cloud of smoke billowing before his eyes, ripped with a loud zip the thick agreement from the rolling pins of an electric typewriter.

"Right here, *señora,* where it says '*seguro,*' that is what means assurance."

"*In*surance," Rachel corrected him.

"Yes, insurance, of course. What you say." He smiled, the cigarette clamped in his yellow teeth.

"And does this cover theft and accident?"

He shrugged again. "*Sí,* sure, no problem." As if to elaborate further, he thumped the rental agreement several times at the space marked *"seguro."*

Rachel turned to Parker, a worried expression tugging at her face. He understood why. She had wanted to go to the Bahamas, to Cancún, to Hawaii, some plush beachy resort where uniformed waiters brought you pink piña coladas frosting away in umbrella-topped glasses and where the bathrooms were cavernous and white and tiled floor-to-ceiling in cool, antiseptic porcelain. A trip to Spain, she told Parker, would be *work*. Hard, arduous work. She also seemed to understand ahead of time that, being the couple's primary organizer, she would be doing most of that work. Parker had promised her he would pick up the slack, and he had meant it. He just didn't want the Avis clerk not to like him.

"It sounds good to me," he told her.

"You think so."

Trying to be Spanish, Parker shrugged.

"Fine, then." Without another word, she picked up the rental agreement and the accompanying pen and held them out to him.

After all the breakups and reconciliations and in-between things he'd put them through, Parker knew he was lucky to have Rachel. More than that, he knew she *was* his good luck, prettily and provocatively personified. An optimist by nature and an innocent by design, he relied on her to alert him to the world's dangers. She seemed to be alerting him to some such danger right now. Yet the presence of the smiling

Spanish man, this happy and pleasant native, exerted a palpable pressure on his sense of resolve, a pressure to give in, to say "I'm in Spain now, just let it roll," to trust the country and its curious institutions. As the Avis clerk had said, *No problem*. Taking a deep breath, Parker took the pen from her, pressed the tip to the multipaged agreement, and, just before signing his name, said, "Relax, Rachel. Everything'll turn out fine."

PARKER LIKED TO REGARD his life as a suspenseful and well-crafted story. He saw major life events as turning points in a narrative governed by symbols and carefully orchestrated leitmotifs. He placed his friends and acquaintances into elusive categories of "main" or "secondary" characters. And he felt any bad thing in his life had to be buttressed by some good thing of equal weight, as if his entire existence were governed by some sort of aesthetic dialectic of right and wrong. Everything had to balance out.

An illustrative instance: Just before he and Rachel left for their honeymoon, a very bad thing happened to them. In the dead of night, a mere four days before their wedding ceremony, a passing tornado lifted and summarily shoved into the roof of their rental home two massive oak trees. Yet this bad thing was immediately preceded by a somewhat good thing, for two days prior to the tornado, Rachel, responding to an elusive and free-floating gut anxiety about leaving their house unattended while they were in Spain, signed them up for renter's insurance. *Two days.* Parker couldn't decide how to interpret this clumsy piece of plotting. Was signing up for insurance an omen for their marriage, or was the tornado the omen? Did they cancel each other out? Was there perhaps any residual karma, good or bad, that no one had accounted for yet? He was stumped.

According to the stopped clock beside his bed, the tornado struck at 2:43 A.M. What first woke him up was an immense, rattling roar. At the time he thought it was hail, when in fact it was the sound of rocks and tree limbs pelting his windows. "What was that?" Rachel mumbled, her voice gummy from sleep. Next, two thundering explosions shook the house to its very foundations. Parker bolted up. The wind grew louder, the trees whistled, the roof shook: he would later identify this as the moment when the giant dragon's tail of the twister made its final sweep overhead before moving across the street and proceeding through the rest of the neighborhood, wreaking havoc all the way. Abruptly, the wind stopped. The air was now filled with an orchestra of car alarms, dozens of them buzzing and bleating their distressful music all up and down the street. Wide awake now, he raced to the bedroom window and cranked up the plastic blind: beyond and even up against his window lay a Brazilian rain forest of tree trunks and leaves. "Holy shit," he whispered.

"What, what?" But by now Rachel was out of bed, too. When they opened the bedroom door he was assaulted by the pungent smell of wood and dirt and sap. Because the electricity was out, he couldn't figure out what he was smelling. Then he registered water on his bare feet. Next he heard drizzling rain. It took a couple of heartbeats for him to realize the rain was falling overhead—*inside his house.* Directly above him, spread laterally across the hallway roof like a prehistoric crossbeam, stretched the fat, enormously heavy trunk of a giant oak tree, the same tree that had once stood with such serene majesty in his rented backyard. With his eyes he followed the tree trunk all the way down the hall to the bathroom, which no longer existed in any real way, the toilet and bathtub both smashed by the fallen tree which, while forging its monstrous path through the house, had split open the back wall as neatly as an ax cutting a wedding cake.

"We've been hit," he whispered.

"And we have *insurance!*" Rachel called through the darkness, and let out a cry of joy.

And why not? Why not be joyful? After all, she had taken on Mother Nature, and she had *won.* Everything the tornado destroyed was insured—including her beautiful Acura Legend which, they would learn in the next ten minutes, sat flattened in the garage beneath yet another fallen tree, this one a five-foot diameter oak from next door. Mother Nature had crashed through their home and declared with a decisive double boom and a sulfuric aftersmell of dirt and oak her final indifference to human events. Yet Rachel had taken precautions—and looked to come out ahead in the bargain!

Why, Parker calculated, that car alone—which they had recently determined they didn't need anyway—would fetch a
good fifteen thousand dollars *at least*.

"In a way," he told Rachel, "this is a blessing in disguise."

She cupped her hands beneath her chin and cuddled closer.
Above and to their left they could see in the mounting morning light an empty path of tree growth, a direct transcript of
the tornado's indifferent path. The car lay smashed before
them.

"I'd hate to see what a curse looks like."

"I know it looks bad, but I'm serious. Do you realize that
instead of paying rent while we're in Spain, we can just put
this stuff in storage and forget about it? I mean, it's really the
best thing that could have happened to us. It's like we *willed*
it to hit us the minute we signed up at State Farm."

"*I* signed us up," she clarified. "And we didn't *will* anything. It's a natural occurrence, Parker, an act of God or
whatever. That's why you get insurance: to protect yourself
against things you can't control."

"That may be," he said. "But good things happen as well.
The way I see it, we're due for a huge residual."

"Residual?" Now she faced him directly. "What on earth
are you talking about?"

"Or the payoff, whatever. We're due for some *good luck*."
His blood surged. Yes, he thought: they've earned it! They
had just bought themselves a *pile* of good luck. Granted,
they had already spent some of that good luck on Rachel's

preternatural foresight in getting renter's insurance, but surely that little piece of prophetic preplanning didn't deplete the entire balance. A tornado versus an insurance policy? No contest. They had *tons* of good luck left over. They were *loaded.* He took Rachel in his arms again and lay his chin on her head. "Just you watch," he assured her. "After this, our trip to Spain is going to be perfect."

THE RENTAL CAR, at any rate, was perfect. Avis had given them a brand-new Ford four-door sedan, the interior saturated with that rubbery new car smell and the tires so factory fresh they licked the road. Zipping down the empty Spanish interstate system, traversing La Mancha and pushing headlong into Andalusia, Parker held his breath and waited for happiness to hit him. On either side stretched miles and miles of rolling hills patchworked all over with olive-tree groves, the broccoli-like tree clumps lined up in neat symmetrical rows. Elderly men in straw hats pumped along the side of the road on old rusted bicycles. Rain clouds materialized in the wide horizon and brought no rain. It was Spain, all right. Most afternoons, he and Rachel had the road almost entirely to themselves, the only other traffic being the occasional self-absorbed native who would tailgate Parker for a kilometer or two and then, with an impatient flick of the steering wheel, zip around him on his left side only to disappear in a flash over the next ridge. No one ever looked back.

"This is the life," he would occasionally remark to Rachel, who spent most of their car time consulting an array of inconsistent maps and a reference section's worth of paperback tour books from the States.

"Uh-huh," she'd say, running her finger down the map she was studying.

Their first two nights out of Madrid they spent in the ramshackle medieval town of Toledo. Majestically situated atop a hill jutting from the arid wastes of New Castile, Toledo still retained not only its ancient Moorish wall but also its old cobblestone streets, which, Parker was more disconcerted than charmed to find, had originally been designed for donkey rather than automobile traffic. The streets were so winding, so narrow and crammed with storefronts and breezily self-assured pedestrians, he feared his side-view mirrors were going to scrape the gilt-edged paint right off the restaurant windows. The city wall joined up at the town's Arabian *al-cázar*, an imposing Moorish castle that sat like a wobbly crown atop the city's apex. There was also a cathedral somewhere and an El Greco museum and a fourteenth-century synagogue and a bunch of other important cultural sites Parker and Rachel never went to see. They spent most of their stay in Toledo holed up in their beautiful hotel room, the shades down and the air conditioner on high as they ate oily olives and made afternoon love—sometimes both at the same time. Rachel had secured their room two months in advance, their only reservation. Parker was so unsettled by his harrowing drive through the town that his hands were frozen into a white-knuckled, three-o'clock steering-wheel grip. Yet the moment he stepped into the hotel's garden foyer, his spine unwound. He was in Hemingway country at last. Picturesque little café tables, each one surrounded by a quartet of bamboo chairs, cooled themselves under a natural umbrella of dense, gently swaying overhead foliage. A marble fountain in the Arabian style made a demure little splash in the garden's center. Beyond the fountain loomed the hotel itself, Spanish to its very bones, with a smooth stone front, manila in color, a sumptuous set of facing staircases that led to a tiled front patio, and an arc-shaped bell steeple on top that perfectly mirrored the shape of the bookend stairs below. An acoustic guitar played somewhere in the distance. It looked like the Alamo. Parker dropped his luggage and opened his arms. "What'd I tell you, huh? What'd I say? Is this *perfect* or what?"

"I just hope the car is safe," Rachel replied, and hoisted her bag onto her shoulder and stomped up the left-hand steps to see about her reservation.

In Parker's vision of their relationship, Rachel filled all his negative space and he, it pleased him to think, filled hers. They fit together as neatly as the pieces of a butcher-block puzzle that, when reassembled, formed a perfect cube. Whereas Parker confronted the world with a guileless optimism and cultivated naïveté about complex adult matters, Rachel scowled at the world with pragmatic suspicion. Parker often wondered about the full scope of that suspicion. At times it seemed to him she granted the outside world an almost bottomless capacity for criminal invention. "Don't leave that credit card slip on the table, honey, some thief could snatch it up and start charging things over the Internet and you'd never know it." "You should always open your bags before you leave the airport, you never know if someone's pulled your suitcase off the carousel and opened it up. It'd be so easy to do, I'm sure it gets done all the time." "Oh puh-lease, those steering-wheel clubs are a joke. Spray a little Freon in the lock mechanism and the whole thing comes apart like a collapsible fishing rod." So vigilant was she in second-guessing and circumventing the tireless efforts of the criminal underworld that she sometimes betrayed a grudging admiration for the art of thievery. More than once Parker had determined that his wife, for better or for worse, possessed a criminal mind.

"I can't get over this countryside" was another thing he sometimes said to her on their daily drives through Andalusia. To which she would look up from her map and squint out the window. By about the third day of driving, Parker began to view the landscapes they drove through as a European take on the American Old West—acres and acres of empty plain, punctuated by little mountain swells and presided over in the distance by spectral mountain ranges streaked in sand and shale. Now he understood why the Spanish colonizers finally made camp in southern Texas and Mexico. One look at El Paso and they knew they were home.

"Yep," he'd agree with himself, "this is some country, all right."

Or sometimes Rachel would look from her map and ask, "Have you seen a gas station lately? I hafta pee."

"I'll keep my eyes open."

"It's totally barren out here, isn't it?"

"Totally wide open. You okay otherwise? You need anything else? Some water, a bite of bread?"

"No, honey, I'm fine."

"You're sure?"

"Um, yeah, Parker. I'm relatively sure."

"Are you bored? Do you want to take the wheel?"

"Not particularly, no."

"Not particularly what? No, you're not particularly bored, or no, you don't particularly want to take the wheel?"

"Both, Parker. I'm not particularly both. I just have to pee."

Late in their stay in Toledo, Parker decided to make his first nonedible Spanish purchase. Specifically, he decided to buy a knife. Toledo was apparently world-famous for the manufacture of knives. Since Parker knew next to nothing about the knife business, he wasn't prepared to argue this point. The problem was, every third shop in Toledo displayed in its window a sinister assortment of knives and swords. Buying a knife in Toledo was a cinch. Deciding which knife was next to impossible.

"How about this one?" he'd ask, pointing.

"Which one? That one there, with the silver border along the side?"

"No, but now that you mention it, I kind of like that one better."

"Oh, I don't. I like that one back there, by the blue pearl one with the dragon on the blade. See which one I'm talking about?"

This sort of thing went on for a day and a half. He just couldn't pick one out. Why this one over, say, that one? Or the other one, there? Or any of the three million other knives the town had on offer? And might this one be cheaper down the road? What's so great about that one? Parker finally bought a pocketknife he didn't even like all that much. He chose it out of exasperation, mainly, and because he thought it was well priced. Also, the salesclerk, a plump matronly Spanish woman in her forties and as ignorant of English as Parker was of Spanish, misunderstood him and retrieved the wrong knife entirely. Parker was too tired to explain the mistake and simply paid for the one she gave him. Why not? It was a knife. A stupid fucking knife.

"You should go *back*," Rachel cried when he joined her in the street and showed her what he bought. "You shouldn't buy it if you don't like it."

"I like it fine, Rache. It's just a knife." He took her elbow to urge her along, but she yanked herself free.

"I can't believe you're walking away with that thing. After all we've been through, after all this walking back and forth. *They* don't care which one you buy, Parker. All they want is your money."

"Well, they've got it."

"Go back and get the one you want. I'm serious. Go now."

"I don't know which one I like, Rachel! That's the whole problem!"

"Give it to me. *I'll* take it back."

But he didn't give it to her. Instead, he stalked away with the loathsome pocketknife snug and heavy in his front pocket, where Rachel, worried about pickpockets, had insisted he also keep his wallet. They walked in silence through the town and did not speak to each other for the rest of the evening—their first fight as a married couple—during which time Parker developed a weird attachment to his knife. Over and over again he ran his finger down the dense, smooth metal that comprised the base casing, clicked the release button so he could feel the solid kick of the blade as it sprang to full length. If nothing else, he told himself, the knife was *his*. At least he was *trying* to get into the Spanish spirit of things. And though the fight was over by the morning, and everything forgiven, he still felt protective of his new purchase. So, while packing the car, he hid it beneath the trunk floorboard and made a mental note to himself to retrieve it when they turned the car back in to Avis.

That was three days ago. In the meantime, they had traversed most of La Mancha—where they each posed as Don Quixote fighting a phalanx of white stone windmills—and scaled the staggeringly beautiful mountains of the Sierra Nevada, which, Rachel remarked aloud, reclaimed for good the overused term *breathtaking*. Parker pulled over at one point to take some pictures, and when he stepped out of the car he realized the air was thinner: they were that high up. Perched atop a state-built lookout post, wind whipping his hair, he looked down and felt vertigo. Miles of sheer rock stretched below him, an almost endless expanse of powerful explosive earth broken only by the winding tread of an insignificant interstate on which little toy cars slowly crept along. It took Parker a few moments to realize he had just traveled along that same road. That's when the vertigo hit.

Then, back in the car, they raced through more empty road, wound their way through sleepy little towns that sprang up out of nowhere, and basically wore themselves out. And each night they confronted the ever-more arduous task of learning, in the space of an hour, the layout of an entirely new city, maneuvering (largely without much success) through said city, and trying, without the benefit of clear and comprehensible communication, to secure a decent hotel room. In the interim, they ate lots of fried food, walked through Arabic military bases, drank lots of sangria, and slept horribly. They learned to spend pesetas. They sat in cafés.

In truth, Spain was boring them to oblivion.

But they were past all that now. The worst was behind them. Tomorrow they were going to the Costa del Sol, where the only two things they absolutely had to do were to lie in the sun and apply more sunscreen. No more long days of car travel, no more crummy beds. They could now settle into their hotel room, dirty up all the towels, get to know the beachside bartenders, use up all the camera film they had brought with them, and basically relax like the honeymooners they were starting to forget they were.

"Just you wait till we get to the Costa del Sol," he assured her, nodding to himself from behind the wheel. "*Then* we can just sit back and relax."

Beside him, Rachel squinted suspiciously at her map.

At three forty-five the next day they arrived at Nerja, a crammed and confusing pile of white stone and tacky tourist traps that Rachel's numerous guidebooks described as both "quaint" and "authentic." It was also, they quickly learned, fully booked. They spent their first two hours in Nerja marching back and forth and around and around looking for a hotel—any hotel—with an available double room, but kept coming up empty-handed. *No, señor. So sorry, señora. Completo esta noche, no habitación.* They didn't know much Spanish, but they knew *this* much. They certainly knew what *"no habitación"* meant. They were getting pretty used to hearing that one. With a sigh, they hoisted up their luggage and marched to the next fully booked hotel on their list.

Finally, they struck pay dirt. Sometime between their hopeful first attempt to secure a room and their almost flippant and punch-drunk fiftieth attempt, a little two-bed *habitación* had suddenly opened up at the very first hotel they had tried.

It was Parker's idea to go back: he kept telling Rachel he had a "gut feeling" about that first hotel, a splendidly modern beachfront establishment shoved into gnarled stone cliffs of the Balcón de Europa.

"Though I warn you," the cheerfully maternal concierge told them, "the room I show you, is very . . . How do you say—?"

"Small?" Rachel asked.

"Plush?" Parker suggested.

"*Muy ruido*, you know? How do you say in English?"

"Loud," Rachel said flatly, and turned to Parker with a smile. "She means it's very loud."

"Loud," the woman repeated triumphantly. "*Sí*, of course, that is what I mean. Is very loud."

On the upside, the hotel provided secured underground parking to its paying guests, which service, Parker pointed out to Rachel as he drove back to the hotel with their things, surely outweighed the noise problem.

"Plus, that's all construction, which won't be going on at night. And tomorrow's Sunday."

"Which means everything will be closed." Rachel stared out the passenger window.

"The restaurants won't be. And anyway, we're here to re-lax, get some sun, knock back a few margaritas."

"The *International Herald Tribune* said rain tomorrow."

"Look"—he slammed the car to a stop as a phalanx of grotesquely loud mopeds flowed around them like rapids displaced by a logjam—"what do you want from me? We've had a few down days, I admit. But I can't solve every little problem that comes up."

"No one said you had to solve anything."

"Well, all you do is complain. Every time I suggest something positive, you return with some bitchy little critique."

"I'm *tired*, Parker. I've just been through a tornado, a full-house move, a wedding, a transatlantic flight, five days of endless car travel through a foreign country, five nights of terrible sleep, and two hours of steady rejection. I *apologize* if I'm not in an Up with People mood!"

"So what are you saying?" He jammed the car back into gear and lurched forward. Already he was getting the hang of Spanish driving. Just push ahead and let everyone else get out of your way.

"I'm saying I'm *exhausted*, Parker. What do you think I'm saying?"

"I don't know," he shrugged, his eyes fixed on the narrow road before him. "Maybe you're saying you wished we hadn't come here."

"Fair enough."

"See? You admit it."

"Admit what? That a honeymoon in Spain was *your* idea? What am I admitting? That's a simple statement of fact."

"Fine. If that's how you feel."

"And how *do* I feel, Parker? Explain it to me, please. Tell me how I feel right now."

"You think this was a mistake."

"What was?"

Her voice, he noticed, had softened somewhat. "This trip," he explained. "The great honeymoon in Spain. What did you think I meant?"

She hesitated. He brought the car to a stop just before the turn that would deposit them back at their new hotel, where they could unpack, pop a *cerveza,* and catch some much needed rays. He stole a glance at her. To his surprise, she was looking directly back at him, her eyes about to spill.

"It wasn't a mistake," she said softly. "I told you, I'm just tired. I'm edgy right now, and I just need to relax, that's all. Let me rest a minute and I'll be fine." She stroked his cheek.

At some point in this conversation, a knot had formed in Parker's throat. He now tried to swallow the knot whole. He almost succeeded. "Actually," he said, "Cancún does seem like a pretty good idea, right now."

As agreed, Parker stayed behind with the car while Rachel dragged the first load of luggage to their new hotel room. Before leaving him, she raised up on her tiptoes and whispered, "Hurry up, sweetie. I might be ready for a little Up with People." Another car was ahead of his in the driveway, so he leaned back against the hood and squinted up into the Spanish sun, waiting. After a few minutes, he closed his tired eyes and thought warmly of Rachel.

He was roused awake by a tiny Spanish man in black trousers and an official-looking blue short-sleeved shirt similar to an American bowling shirt. The man wore a faint mustache and mirrored sunglasses. He was speaking rapidly in Spanish, his arms gesturing toward the parking garage entry door.

"Yes, sorry, I was just—" Parker sat up now and fished in his pocket for the keys. Still groggy but determined to appear in charge and fully present, he scuffled around to the back of the car, dropped the remaining suitcases on the curb, and handed the car keys to the parking attendant who, upon receiving them, nodded enthusiastically. *"Gracias, señor, gracias, gracias."*

All at once, Parker was seized with doubt. "Hold it," he said. "You are the—you know—the parking guy?"

The little man nodded enthusiastically. As if to demonstrate his trustworthiness, he scampered around Parker and began hoisting up the luggage, which, all accumulated, probably weighed more than he did.

Now Parker chuckled, relieved. "No, no, *gracias,* yes, thank you very much, but no, I'll get those, that'll be fine."

The man shrugged and abruptly dropped the bags.

Two minutes later, Parker stopped at the hotel entrance and set the bags down in order to readjust his hold. He registered a nagging little inarticulate worry in his stomach, like a moth buzzing into a lightbulb. What was it? What had he forgotten? He reached in his pockets and panicked when he didn't find the keys there but then recalled that he had just given them to the attendant. He looked back. The car was gone. Not a trace of it anywhere. Only then did he realize the attendant hadn't given him a claim check of any sort.

Oh, relax, he told himself, and rehoisted his luggage. You're starting to think like Rachel.

THE NEXT MORNING Parker woke up with a punishing pain in his side. Actually, the pain had kept him up half the night, but he had naturally assumed the bed was at fault. It was, after all, a standard Spanish twin bed—that is, devoid of box springs. But with daylight came illumination. The fault lay not in the bed, but in him. Without a doubt, he was sick.

"What is it, sweetheart?" Rachel asked, stroking hair from his face.

"Something's in my stomach," he groaned. "I keep burping up that awful paella I had last night at the restaurant. I can still taste it."

"Maybe you're just *remembering* it," she laughed.

"I'm serious, Rache. It's *there*, still inside me. It's like that whole meal is sitting in my stomach, fully intact. I swear there's a bomb down there, and it's about to go off."

"Why don't you make yourself throw up?"

Parker shook his head vigorously. The very suggestion almost made him *want* to throw up. Practical Rachel: he knew instantly that's what she would have done. "I'll be fine, seriously. I just need some fresh air."

But by two in the afternoon, he realized Rachel was right. There was nothing for him to do but detonate that bomb in his stomach. Boom. Just like those trees crashing through his roof. Reluctantly, with Rachel standing watch behind him, he knelt before the tiny commode, stared at the quivering disc of water before him, and shoved his finger down his throat. That was all it took. At once his body was possessed —his chest heaved, his head jerked up and down, his eyes bulged. He felt like one of those star troopers in *Aliens* who finds to his surprise that he's been functioning all along as the incubator for a vicious little life-form that, at some otherwise unexpected narrative climax, suddenly rips through his chest and leaps into view, its head twisting back and forth and its nasty teeth dripping horribly with slime.

"Oh, sweetie," Rachel cried, recoiling from him in terror. "Oh my God, that's . . . You know, I think I'll, um, I'll just wait in the bedroom, how about that?"

The vomiting continued through the afternoon and well into the dinner hour, after which Parker, exhausted and dehydrated, managed to relax a tad. Outside their window a blustery March-like afternoon crashed against the windows, while overhead construction workers whiled away the day by pounding repeatedly on bricks and iron. So much for Sunday.

"I'm so sorry this happened," he croaked before drifting off.

She looked up from her book and smiled. "Well, as you always say: it can only get better from here."

The next morning Parker, feeling somewhat better, looked outside the window, noted storm clouds, and said aloud, "Fuck it." For starters, he wanted out of this room, which still smelled of bile. He wanted out of Nerja, which had proved to be nothing but trouble from beginning to end. And he was about ready to be rid of Spain entirely. A good bed would redeem things, he thought, but only just.

"Let's book," he called.

Rachel was still in bed, splayed out on her back and as motionless as a corpse. The pillow lay mashed over her head and her arms were thrown out on either side, as if she had dropped this way from the ceiling. "Fine," she mumbled through the pillow.

An hour later, they sidled up to the front desk and slid the kind woman from two days ago the key card to their room.

"Everything was fine, no?" she asked, her voice genuinely buoyant.

"No comment," he replied, and laughed. "Our car's in the lot, by the way. Room 406."

"Very good," she said, and swiveled back to peer into their assigned slot on the bank of room boxes behind her. Slot 406 was empty, Parker noted. His heart dropped. She turned back and pursed her lips. "You're sure your car, it is here?"

"Yes, absolutely. I'm totally sure." An urgent quiver had slipped into his voice, which he tried to suppress. The strange talkative man. The stab of panic when he reached into his pocket for the keys. "I brought the car to the entryway like you said and gave the guy my keys and—"

"What's the problem?" Rachel wanted to know.

The woman gazed at Parker with a warm, motherly expression heartbreaking to see. "You have the little card, no?"

"Card? No, he didn't give me a card. He just took the keys and—"

She raised a finger to shush him. Then she picked up the phone and began speaking in rapid-fire Spanish. Parker kept thinking, *He helped with the luggage!* After a few minutes, she placed a hand over the mouthpiece. "What kind of car, *señor?*

"A Ford, a blue Ford. It was a rental. It has an Avis thing hanging from the key, a little plastic job, it says 'Avis' loud and clear. If you want I could go down there and—"

She raised her finger again and shook her head, returning her attention to the person on the other end of the phone. He couldn't bear to look at Rachel who, he feared, was slowly lurching toward the same humiliating conclusion that he had just reached a minute ago. He couldn't bear to confront the enormous stupidity of what he had done. He realized he was not ready for marriage, for husbandhood, for the adult world. His life suddenly appeared to him as a liability he should never have foisted on Rachel. He wanted to warn her, to tell her to run for her life before he became an even bigger problem than he already was.

At long last, the woman replaced the receiver to its cradle, clasped her fingers beneath her chin, and smiled weakly. "I think I got some bad news for you, *señor.*"

THE NEXT DAY, Parker and Rachel were sitting at an outdoor café in Seville, Spain, nursing a pitcher of bittersweet sangria and watching the tourist traffic. To their left rose the town's enormous Gothic cathedral, the largest Gothic building in the world, according to Rachel's Frommer's guide, which Parker had been reading with great attention for the last half hour. The Giralda tower, with its Moorish minaret base and its incongruent church steeple on top, poked through the sky like the nose of a Renaissance rocket designed by da Vinci. To their right loomed the forbidding walls of yet another Moorish palace, another *alcázar*, this one apparently still in use. Spain had a king, Parker was surprised to learn. He hadn't heard much about this king, Juan Carlos by name, a mysterious sort of public figure by Parker's reckoning, with no pop-singing daughters or bulimic wives or taped conversations about tampon envy to keep him in the news. A real king, in other words, aloof and beyond reproach, one who knew how to comport himself and act kinglike, a man who, just like Parker, could vacation in Seville if he wanted to but who, unlike Parker, got to spend the night in a fourteenth-century Mudejar palace built by someone called Pedro the Cruel.

"Spain has a king," he remarked aloud. He looked up from the Frommer's. "Did you know Spain has a king?"

"Juan Carlos," she said without glancing his way. "Everyone knows that."

"Yeah, I guess they do." He returned to the Frommer's.

Yesterday morning, when Parker turned to her at the hotel and began explaining to her what had apparently happened to their car, she shook her head swiftly and whimpered a little bit and stormed out of the lobby and into the street. He raced after her, leaving the luggage where it was, unattended, and followed her through the streets of Nerja for at least forty-five minutes. He stayed about three paces behind her all this time. All at once, and without warning, she whirled around, her face streaked with tears, and cried, "Didn't you even look at his *clothes?*"

"He looked official," Parker tried to explain. "And he helped with the luggage." People bumped into him from behind, from the side. A few pedestrians stopped to look at this dramatic tableau but quickly moved on.

"Of course he helped, you idiot! He was trying to *steal* the luggage!"

"How was I supposed to know that?"

"You just assume it, Parker. You have to assume this stuff." She shook her head in exasperation. Then, as if suddenly gripped by a thought, she blinked once, dramatically. "Where's the luggage now?"

Her jerked his head behind him. "In the lobby, I guess. You took off so fast I—"

She pushed past him, not ungently, and charged back to the hotel. Her new mission: to save the luggage.

After that outburst she channeled all her energy into crisis management, one of her better modes, all things considered. She tracked down the police department, secured a bus schedule, called the Málaga train station and reserved a ticket. All this with their luggage in tow. Finally, this morning they went to Avis to explain why they were unable to return the blue four-door Ford automobile they had rented a week ago in good faith and good standing. For the second time in two weeks, Rachel got to declare, "We have insurance." Parker couldn't help but notice that the joy had kind of gone out of her. And by the time they got settled into their hotel in Seville he realized she had been using the extensive planning and travel arrangements as a cover. Once there was nothing left to plan, her silence became genuine, absolute. A door had closed on him, and he didn't even feel justified in knocking.

He looked up from his Frommer's. "They'll find the car, Rachel. The policeman said they'd—"

"You know what I've been thinking?" She turned to him now and made eye contact, the first such in twenty-four hours.

"I can't imagine," he said.

"I'm sick of learning experiences. My whole life up to now has been a learning experience. Everything I've done, every bad thing that's happened to me, it's all been a learning experience. I'm sick of learning from things. I'm sick of having to endure things I already learned from a long time ago. I want to experience things now, not learn from them."

"Fair enough." Tenderly, Parker pushed aside the Frommer's and locked his fingers together and set them on the table.

"That's all I wanted to say," she concluded. She reached

for the pitcher of sangria and filled her glass. Looked at her watch. Turned away.

"Well, I'm sick of being a tourist," he said He wasn't sure why he said this. He wasn't thinking it, exactly. The words just tumbled out. But they were true enough, he decided. And they were something to say. "I'm sick of waking up each morning and looking at this fucking tour book and figuring out which pile of rocks to go look at today. I'm sick of Spanish beds and Spanish food and sitting in cafés all evening looking at other people like they're inordinately fascinating simply because Spanish is spinning around in their heads instead of English."

Rachel snorted.

"Look"—his voice was booming now, but he didn't care —"I've said I'm sorry about a million times. I don't know what else you want. I'm just trying to make conversation, to make the best of this stupid situation we're in."

"Well, stop."

"Stop what?"

"Stop trying so hard to make it better. You're driving me crazy."

"Well, *you're* driving *me* crazy. This silent treatment, this perpetual scowl. I feel stupid enough as it is."

"So feel stupid, Parker. That's fine. Or don't feel stupid. But quit trying to act like nothing happened, or that this will all turn out fine in the end. I don't want to know all that right now, even if it's true. I'm angry, and I want to feel angry. I have that right, you know."

In frustration, he picked up the Frommer's and slammed it down again. Their tiny round table wobbled once, almost upsetting the sangria. He caught the side of the table and held it steady. Patrons on either side looked up and took a quick read: Americans, being loud, ignore them. Which they all quickly did. With a sigh, he asked, "So what do you want me to do?"

"I want you to let it *pass*," she said passionately. She was smiling now. The smile arrived like the lush swelling of an orchestra. "Don't buck me up, don't convince me everything will turn out better, don't explain to me how all this is a blessing in disguise. Everything that's happened in the last two weeks *just happened*. Some of it was our fault, some of it came from nowhere, but all of it is over and done with. Period."

"We got married in the last two weeks," he remarked.

"Exactly." She sat back in her chair and crossed her arms.

An enormous chasm had opened up between them. Parker stood on his side and, shading his eyes from the sun, tried to discern Rachel's expression. But she was too far away for him to see her face. What had she meant? And why had he pointed out that most obvious of facts? If he had learned anything in the last week *(a learning experience)*, it was the importance of context. In Spain, he had no context. He was loose, unmoored, floating about without a readable map to give him direction. Things that should have gotten better did not. Sights that should have been spectacular failed to excite him. Gazing at the countryside racing past their car windows, he had willed a sense of wonder, and had come up empty-handed. He was a random event within the unreadable narrative that was Spain. And then his reminder to Rachel that they had gotten married last week. Out of the barrage of sensible things she had said, things he needed to hear from her, advice it was entirely her prerogative to dole out, he had plucked from the thin air this random unrelated piece of information that seemed the true subtext of everything that had happened so far and the only thing that mattered in the end. So her almost instantaneous agreement had stung him like a rebuke. Had she transformed what he'd said by sending it back to him so quickly, or had she agreed with him in ways he didn't understand? What had happened here?

And then, from across the street, a face flickered into view and sparked a flame of recognition in his breast. Someone familiar, from some other town. He stood up and removed his sunglasses to get a better look. The street emptied for a moment and—yes, yes, it was *him*, it was exactly who Parker thought it was.

"What are you doing now?" Rachel murmured. "Sit down, you're making a fool—"

"There!" he cried, his arm extended out as if he were a member of the Supremes. "Over there, in the blue shirt, behind that taxicab: it's *him*."

"What are you talking about, Parker?"

"The guy," he insisted, grabbing her wrists and tugging her from her seat, "it's the guy who stole our car!"

She yanked her hands free and plopped back down in her seat. "Enough already. I just told you I've had it with this stupid conviction of yours that—"

But by now he was halfway across the street, dodging through a maze of honking and halting cars. Oh, it was him all right—the little faint mustache, the mirrored sunglasses. As far as Parker could tell, the guy was talking to his girlfriend or a girlfriend hopeful, this slightly overweight dishwater blond woman who, much like Rachel, looked off in the distance while her lover pled his case.

Without waiting for further confirmation, Parker grabbed the little man by the biceps and yanked him to a standing position. "You!" he shouted.

The man reared back with a look of pure terror on his face, and for a brief moment Parker wondered if he did, indeed, have the wrong guy. But then the man's face broke into a broad, toothsome smile. No sooner did Parker let go of the man's arm than he began slapping Parker on the back like they were long lost brothers reunited after a long, arduous battle. From the man's mouth poured a steady stream of excited and thoroughly incomprehensible Spanish nonsense.

Now Parker was really confused. He stood there blinking, waiting for an opening where he could say *Please, please slow down,* but before that happened the little guy seized Parker by the wrist and began tugging him down the sidewalk, talking a blue streak all the while. Everything was happening backward, Parker realized with an almost giddy sense of elation.

The thief was dragging the victim to the police! After tugging Parker a few meters, the man stopped on the sidewalk and, his face still beaming, gestured with open arms toward the street. But it wasn't the street he was displaying. It was Parker and Rachel's rental car, parked neatly on the side of the road with its Avis tag still dangling from the rearview mirror.

"I don't understand" was all Parker could say.

The man didn't hear him, as he was busy fishing in his pocket. With a magician's flourish, he produced the car key complete with its Avis key chain and dangled it temptingly under Parker's nose. *Does he want to grab for it?* Parker wondered. Then the man bustled around to the driver's side, unlocked the door, opened it into the street, and gestured for Parker to join him.

"I'm sorry, I told you I don't—"

"What on earth is going on?" asked Rachel, who had just come up from behind.

He smiled and shrugged, like a true Spaniard. "It's our car," he explained.

"I can see that."

The man was still gesturing, so Parker joined him in the street, climbed into the driver's seat, took the key from the overjoyed thief, and started up the car. The gas gauge jumped to *F.*

"Okay?" the man said in English.

Parker looked up at him and laughed. He couldn't help it.

He just laughed. This wasn't a learning experience, exactly. There was nothing to learn. And it wasn't a clue or an omen to anything tangible or real. It was just a completely weird and bizarre and unexplainable thing that had happened to him and Rachel and which they had survived somehow and which now appeared to be over. He kept laughing.

"Okay," he finally told the man. With that, the thief wiped his hands of the whole affair—no kidding: he literally wiped his hands together—winked once at Rachel, and raced back to his table, where his poor date, again like Rachel, was about to learn they no longer had a ride home.

As for Rachel, she was peering into the car from the passenger-side door, which she had opened at some point. A completely unreadable smile played across her face. "How's it look?"

"Perfect," Parker told her. "The tank is full. The windshield's immaculate. The guy even vacuumed the interior." He looked at his watch. "And, based on our original agreement, we've still got an hour before it's due back at Avis."

Rachel shook her head in wonder. When she looked at him again, she wore a perfectly readable and utterly contextual look of affection and forgiveness. "You are one lucky bastard, you know that?"

"Hey," he shrugged. "I married you."

Hours later, as he and Rachel curled up together on their homebound plane, Parker had a sudden panicky realization: the knife he'd bought in Toledo was still in the car. He had forgotten to get it from its hiding place in the trunk. All that searching, all that trouble—gone! Then he smiled. How stupid. How ridiculously stupid. It was a relief, really. He had no use for the thing. None at all. He didn't even like knives.

With a barely perceptible shrug of his shoulder—he was actually readjusting his position so as not to wake up Rachel —he felt the knife slide right off his back and out of his consciousness. From there it floated into the sky and dropped back into Spain like ballast from a balloon, making Parker feel even lighter than he already felt, so light, in fact, he imagined himself drifting aimlessly through the air, over the sea, across half a dozen time zones and all the way home, where, he remembered before drifting back to sleep, two trees were still sticking out of the roof of their first home.

I have a missing knife st
in my side
— SM